A GATHERING OF VULTURES

Other Books by Donald Michael Platt:

Rocamora
Close to the Sun
House of Rocamora
Bodo the Apostate

A GATHERING OF VULTURES

Donald Michael Platt

PENMORE

www.penmorepress.com

A GATHERING OF VULTURES
by
DONALD MICHAEL PLATT

ISBN-13: 978-1-942756-34-7(Paperback)
ISBN -13:978-1-942756-35-4 (e-book)

BISAC Subject Headings:
FIC015000FICTION / Horror
FIC009070FICTION / Fantasy / Dark Fantasy
FIC031070FICTION / Thrillers / Supernatural
Ist Edition

Cover art: Pam Marin-Kingsley,www.pammarin-kingsley.com
Vulture Alphabet by Peter Szmer, www.peterszmer.com

Address all correspondence to:

Michael James
Penmore Press LLC
920 N Javelina Pl
Tucson AZ 85748
mjames@Penmorepress.com

For Ellen, who always believed

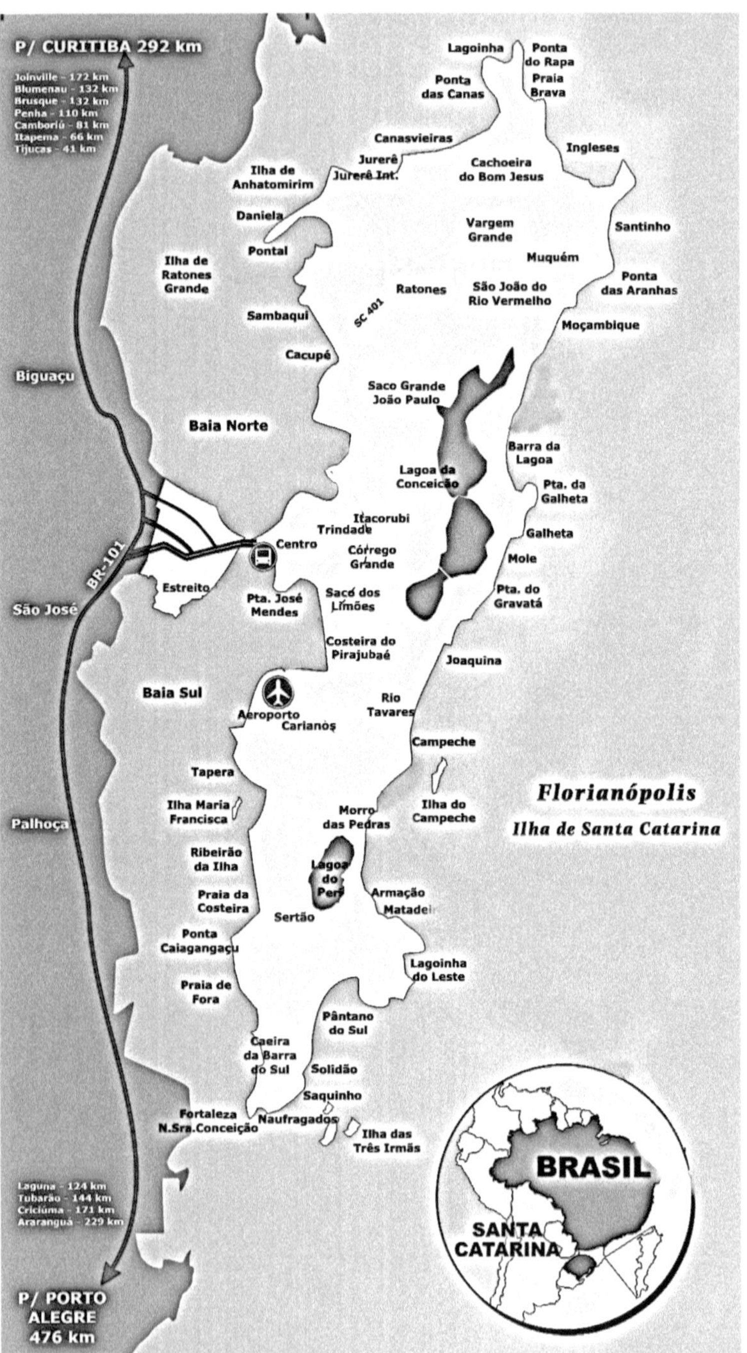

P/ CURITIBA 292 km
Joinville - 172 km
Blumenau - 132 km
Brusque - 132 km
Penha - 110 km
Camboriú - 81 km
Itapema - 66 km
Tijucas - 41 km
Biguaçu
São José
Palhoça
BR-101
Laguna - 124 km
Tubarão - 144 km
Criciúma - 171 km
Araranguá - 229 km
P/ PORTO ALEGRE 476 km
Lagoinha
Ponta do Rapa
Ponta das Canas
Praia Brava
Canasvieiras
Ingleses
Jurerê
Jurerê Int.
Cachoeira do Bom Jesus
Ilha de Anhatomirim
Santinho
Daniela
Vargem Grande
Pontal
Muquém
Ponta das Aranhas
Ilha de Ratones Grande
Ratones
São João do Rio Vermelho
SC 401
Sambaqui
Moçambique
Cacupé
Saco Grande
João Paulo
Baia Norte
Barra da Lagoa
Lagoa da Conceição
Pta. da Galheta
Itacorubi
Trindade
Galheta
Córrego Grande
Mole
Centro
Estreito
Pta. do Gravatá
Pta. José Mendes
Sacó dos Limões
Costeira do Pirajubaé
Joaquina
Baia Sul
Rio Tavares
Aeroporto Carianos
Campeche
Tapera
Florianópolis
Ilha do Campeche
Ilha de Santa Catarina
Ilha Maria Francisca
Morro das Pedras
Ribeirão da Ilha
Lagoa do Peri
Praia da Costeira
Armação
Matadei
Sertão
Ponta Caiagangaçu
Lagoinha do Leste
Praia de Fora
Pântano do Sul
Caeira da Barra do Sul
Solidão
Saquinho
Fortaleza N.Sra.Conceição
Naufragados
Ilha das Três Irmãs
BRASIL
SANTA CATARINA

My destiny was to be linked with the vulture, because in my first memory of my infancy when I was in the cradle, a vulture came to me.

*—Leonardo da Vinci,
from his writings on the flight
of the vulture*

...the archetype
Body of life a beaked carnivorous desire
Self-upheld on storm-broad wings: but the eyes
Were spouts of blood; the eyes were gashed out; dark blood
Ran from the ruinous eye-pits to the hook of the beak
And rained on the waste spaces of empty heaven.

—Robinson Jeffers, Cawdor

ANTIPODAL SEASONS

CHAPTER I.
APRIL IN BRAZIL

t clear dawn, the delegado and two of his detectives from the 7th Distrito Policial approached a narrow strip of beach at Jurerê where golden sands end against steep copper and purple cliffs covered with semi-tropical vegetation. Gentle waves washed over carcasses of fish and penguins and a woman, naked and mutilated: eyes plucked; blood coagulated around pulpy sockets; strips of flesh torn away exposing muscles and tendons; her torso eviscerated.

A quartet of urubús, black vultures indigenous to the island, stood a few feet away from the woman. They ignored the men confident they and not the humans were the true lords of the beach.

After ordering his detectives to place the woman in a body bag, the delegado faced the vultures. They held his gaze. When he blinked first, the urubús spread their wings, soared into the blue, and flew towards the west.

The delegado waited until the last vulture disappeared beyond the cliffs, then gestured towards the body bag. "Dispose of it and write the usual report."

CHAPTER 2.
MAY IN CALIFORNIA

ow, ladies and gentlemen, to begin the individual performances in the International-style Latin Division at the Beach Cities DanceSport Challenge. Here, at the fabulous Airdrome Ballroom, in Westchester, California . . . from Jupiter, Florida, Couple 187. Rick and Terri Hamilton."

To enthusiastic cheering, whoops, and calls from their fans, Rick led Terri onto the glossy maple wood dance floor longer and wider than a basketball court. They separated and affected their mirror-pose, with arched eyebrows and flared nostrils, dramatic exaggerations to give them a scoring edge. They focused only on each other, although their acute peripheral vision enabled them to see everything going on under the glittering chandeliers:

The enthusiastic audience in their seats and elbow-to-elbow in the SRO sections along the far walls of the hangar-sized ballroom—

The PBS TV co-hosts, a former Latin dance champion and an aging B-list actress explaining what was happening for the home viewers—

Men in tuxedos, many in tails—

Women glamorous in gowns covered with rhinestones and sequins, feathers and fringes—

Dozens of formally dressed boys and girls from cotillion classes—

Poker-faced Adjudicators holding marking sheets along the perimeter of the floor—

And inscrutable Scrutineers ready to average the marks and rank the dancers.

Rick thought his wife looked sensational. Terri's abbreviated strapless sparkling black and silver-trim costume defied all laws of gravity. Her long arms and legs had no ugly muscle or bone, and her tapering fingers added graceful extension and completeness to each move. Her coloring, a natural olive complexion intensified by a rich Florida tan, saved her the time and expense of body makeup. The vertical spikes in Terri's blue-black hair created an illusion of more height, adding to her five-six in heels and making them appear more balanced as a couple. Her dark brown eyes blazed with an intense inner fire. Like a ravenous bird of prey on the perch, she was ready to devour the opposition.

Terri adored her sexy, handsome husband. The shirt of Rick's black and silver-trimmed, form-clinging Latin costume opened to his navel giving a tantalizing glimpse of his six-pack abs. His straight metallic white-blond hair, blue eyes, and fair skin dramatically contrasted with her complexion. A natural athlete who had been a swivel-hipped wide receiver on his high school football team, he brought the same coordination, timing, and panache to professional competitive dancing.

The music began. They had chosen the theme from *Somewhere in Time*, a romantic classic from the 1980s. Terri and Rick closed the distance between them, their hips rotating fluidly in Cuban motion, their facial expressions expressing intense passion.. The pace was slower, the moves sweeping and sensual. Terri gyrated against his pelvis, then flirtatiously turned away from him. Rick twisted her around to face him again and moved his hands less than an inch away from her face, body, and legs. He was relieved when his wife's back held up as he led her into an arabesque choreographed to emphasize her remarkable extension worthy of a Plisetskaya, and then twirled her into a sitzspin so smooth they might have been on ice. He raised her to his torso, and they moved across the floor as one to the sensual music. She writhed and coiled around every part of his body, while he caressed her in a dance of desire, first denied then fulfilled. A boisterous ovation cheered their final erotic embrace as they flashed bright smiles at the judges, and sashayed towards the lounge where the other competitors awaited their turns.

Terri hugged and kissed him. "Oh, Cardinho, it was our all time best. Our timing was perfect, and you were so completely in control."

Rick always smiled whenever his wife used the affectionate diminutive Portuguese variation of his name. "You followed perfectly, and you were never sexier. But tell me the truth. How is your back?" From age twelve, Terri had suffered from excruciating back spasms, the cause of which baffled every physician she had seen.

"I'll need a trade-in tomorrow. No matter, though. I know we danced well enough to place in the top three. Maybe, just maybe, we have an outside chance for first."

Rick shared Terri's determination and refusal to believe the DeMarcos were unbeatable, but they would need more than a dancing TKO to dethrone them. Adored by audiences and popular among the judges, the four-time national champions from Houston also had finished second in last year's Ten-dance World Championships.

Terri and Rick stood in front of a 52-inch plasma monitor in the lounge to watch the other couples compete. The worst phase had begun for them. Because they had gone first, they would have to wait five eternities. Tonight they had made the final cuts in the Open International Division for the first time in a major regional competition.

Earlier, they had placed sixth overall in the International Standard Five-Dance program consisting of foxtrot, waltz, quick-step, Viennese waltz, and tango. They also had made the finals in the Latin program dancing the rumba, samba, cha-cha-cha, pasodoble, and jive.

The four-day competition had been brutal for all the contenders—muscles and tendons strained, their blistered feet rubbed raw, toes bleeding. Because their adrenaline continued to surge, they would not feel real pain until tomorrow.

"Cardinho, look. The Canadians are blowing it."

"In spades."

Short and with a low center of gravity, Pierre and Jolie Cadoux from Montreal were personable and energetic in their vivid gold and teal costumes, but their jive had too much stop and flash.

The Yamamotos from San Jose, California, followed the Canadians, and Terri and Rick commented on their costumes. Kokki resembled more an ascetic priest than dancer in his matte black high-collar Latin outfit, and because Mimi's dress glittered chartreuse and silver, all eyes would be on her, a good thing, they agreed. Mimi was the weaker performer of the two.

Less than a minute into the Yamamotos' program, Terri critiqued their performance. "Their samba is technically perfect, but it's over-controlled."

Tourkov and Sosnovskaya stepped onto the floor after the Yamamotos. Now in their late thirties, the former champions were on a downhill slide.

"Terri, will you look at that? It's the quietest pasodoble I've ever seen at the finals of a competition."

"Yes, it's terribly flat. And that jarring segue into their tango . . . I know we did better."

The fourth couple, the Pashniakovs, a solid pair from New York, had been taking second place to the DeMarcos at most competitions during the past two years.

"Oleg should be using more speed and attack in their jive although Kyra is doing well shaking her fringes."

"That's what Kyra does best. She belongs in a gentlemen's club." Terri squeezed Rick's arm. "But the Pashniakovs are definitely off their game tonight. Their rhythm is light, their choreography is disjointed."

They looked at each other sharing the same unspoken thought: The Pashniakovs could be had.

Last to perform, the DeMarcos were all showbiz and glitz. Cal wore a flashy black and scarlet-trimmed Latin outfit cut to show off his muscular arms and powerful chest; Svetlana's scarlet costume with shiny black sequins was even more daring than Terri's. From the start, they involved the audience with eye contact and facial mugging as they flashed through an original flawless samba and jive combo choreographed for expressive humor and spectacular lifts and drops.

Rick put an arm around Terri to console her. "Great choreography. No first place for us tonight."

"But we definitely beat the Pashniakovs for second."

"From your lips to the judges' ears."

"Cardinho, we have to find better choreography."

"I know. I wish I could be more creative in that area."

The audience loved the DeMarcos and gave them an extended standing ovation. The M.C. called all the finalists to the dance floor for the presentation of trophies and prize money. Rick and Terri stood at one end next to the Canadians as all six couples faced the Master of Ceremonies, organizers, judges, and TV hosts.

He squinted under the harsh lighting, and Terri gripped his hand in anticipation of the results. The first rankings would be for the Latin Division, and the second for their freestyle performances. Sixth place went to the Yamamotos, who made a lonely walk across the floor to receive their award from the judges. Tourkov and Sosnovskaya took fifth place.

Terri held her breath before the next number was called.

"In fourth place, Couple 259."

Terri and Rick glanced at each other. At the very least, they would take third, their highest placement to-date, but he could see from her expression third would not be good enough for her. Hell, it wouldn't satisfy him either.

"In third place, Couple number 187 . . ."

Although Terri and Rick recited a riff of expletives to each other while their supporters booed the decision, they did not expose their disappointment to the judges and the audience. Instead, she flashed a dimpled smile and he a broad grin when they walked across the floor to accept their trophy and prize money. It was no consolation for them to know if the knowledgeable audience had been polled, they would have taken second instead of the Pashniakovs.

The rankings did not change for the Freestyle. Terri dug her nails into Rick's arm when the DeMarcos received their trophy and prize money to a prolonged standing ovation, and she whispered to him in Portuguese, "I could scratch out their eyes."

CHAPTER 3.
JUNE IN JUPITER

Black nightwings.
Ferocious beaks.
Rows of spiky teeth.
Sharp talons.
Black nightwings enveloping her.
No fear.
Love and protection.
Then moonlight reflecting on a shiny strip of metal.
Cries of shock and pain.
Blood gushing.
Eyes of a madman.
Blade slashing.
Terror and flight.

erri awoke screaming . . . Rick held his trembling wife while she recovered from her nightmare. He knew its cause. Last month, her father had at last passed away in California at the Patton facility for the criminally insane, and old repressed memories returned to haunt her with dreams she would not share with him.

This much Rick did know. When Terri was twelve, her father went on an unaccountable murder spree. Before the police apprehended John Alves, he had butchered

Terri's mother and her three older sisters. Alves also murdered her maternal grandmother and two aunts from Brazil who had been visiting. Only Terri had survived because of her quickness. She eluded a fatal blow from her father's machete and fled into the street with a gash on the side of her neck. After that, she had lived in foster care with a family in West Los Angeles.

Without telling Terri, Rick had looked up the case on the Internet. All accounts agreed the court had been correct when it declared Alves too incompetent to stand trial. They described how he had stared into space with a permanent expression of fear while repeatedly babbling one meaningless word that most experts and news media preferred to pronounce and write as *Creeperee*. Whatever it meant, Alves had taken to his grave all the secrets that would have explained his reasons for murdering his wife and the other females of Terri's family.

She kissed his chest and sat up. "I'm all right now."

"Same nightmare?"

"Yes."

"Want to tell me about it?"

"I wish I could. It's always the same . . . a series of blurred images that frighten me. Guess I shouldn't watch any horror movies."

You never do.

Terri's black and red flamenco-style costume revealed plenty of shapely leg and thigh. When she spread her fringed black scarf high above her head to form a vee, the material and the extension of her long arms, hands, fingers, and sharp nails suggested the wings and talons of a black bird of prey, not his little bird.

In their spacious mirrored studio, Rick led Terri through their pasodoble for the fourth time today. The temperature inside had passed ninety-five, and the humidity had to be higher. Their temperamental air-conditioning unit had pooped-out last night, and the repairman was late as usual.

Terri cried out and aborted their routine. Her back problems had worsened, and she was still recovering from a virus. "Cardinho, I'm so sorry. We should have been on our way to Boston."

Rick comforted her until the pain subsided. Last month in California, they had lost second place by a single point. If Terri had been healthy, they would have outclassed the Pashniakovs next week at the Yankee Classic DanceSport Championships this week in Boston.

He compared his wife to a sleek speedy Ferrari, tops in design and performance but requiring continual fine-tuning. Her back frequently went out, and she often suffered pulled muscles. Four years ago after they won several American Smooth and Rhythm regional championships, she had needed almost a full year to recover from foot surgery. Her susceptibility to colds and viruses interfered with their practices and caused them to pass on many important competitions. He cupped Terri's face in his hands and kissed away her tears. God, how he loved his little brunette, loved her from the first moment of that first day he saw her fifteen years ago in Irene Kraai's classroom back in the tenth grade.

"I'm so disgusted I could scream. I'd give anything to stay healthy. Do anything. Anything, before it's too late."

Last October, Terri had not turned thirty gracefully and feared she was running out of time. Three years ago, they had taken a calculated risk and left American Smooth

to compete in the more prestigious International Standard Ballroom and Latin Divisions.

Because of their decision, they had faced extra years of working their way up the pecking order, often based more on exposure and previous reputation than current quality of performance. Newcomers had to pay their dues building reputations and creating favorable mind-sets among the judges for the next competition. Ultimately, their rankings would be based on technique, choreography, presentation, and intangibles such as their physical appearance and personality, and the bias of the scorers. One judge had suggested he darken his hair and eyebrows to accentuate his features.

They had no regrets. The wisdom of their move had been reinforced at their last competition when the PBS station telecasted only the International-style finals. On the plus side, they had progressed ahead of schedule with a chance to become national champions within the next five years, but that was not good enough for Terri. She wanted it sooner, and she wanted more than a national or even a world championship.

Her ultimate goal was for them to be *the* breakthrough couple and lift ballroom DanceSport to new heights of popularity in the United States expanding on the enthusiasm created by the TV shows *Dancing with the Stars* and *So you Think You Can Dance*, She wanted them to be superstars who didn't need B-list celebrities and snide Brit judges to tweak the ratings. She and Rick would host DanceSport competitions shown regularly on the major TV networks and cable sport channels, with challenges and tournaments sponsored by big corporations offering prizes in the hundreds of thousands. As dance champions, they would receive offers to endorse products, appear on talk shows, produce TV spectaculars, and appear in films.

Rick understood her impatience. He also wanted it all, and not only for the money and fame. Although revenge might be a less than noble motivation, his great fantasy was to rub some very nasty noses in the publicity of their success.

"Terri, let's think positively. We're going to Brazil for our first ever vacation, our first real honeymoon. Three weeks away from the studio will be a good rest for you, mentally as well as physically. We've been training and teaching day and night and can use a restorative hiatus." He also hoped for sage advice from Irene and Martin Kraai, who had been their mentors, best friends, Terri's surrogate parents, and his too from the day they had entered high school and taken seats beside each other in Irene's classroom.

"You're right as always, Cardinho. Then we'll be fresh and ready to give it our best shot at the Nationals in September. And after that, the Ohio Star Ball, Blackpool, and the World championships."

Rick sambaed towards the bar. "Ah, Brazil. Land of Carmen Miranda, José Carioca, the Bossa Nova and the Lambada, and luscious buns in string bikinis."

Terri followed him and squeezed his muscular behind. "The only tush you look at had better be mine."

"And a lovely *bunda*, it is"

"We'll be in Brazil during the middle of their winter, so we'd better take plenty of vitamin C with us and antiseptic hand wipes."

"Good idea. The Kraais told us everyone kisses and hugs there whenever they meet, even the children, and you know what germ carriers they can be. Martin came back from their vacations there with strep throat more often than not."

"Not to worry." Terri took a *Becks* from the refrigerator and opened it for Rick before pouring herself a cup of coffee. "I've already put our warmest clothes on my packing list because we'll be there during the middle of the Brazilian winter. We'll also need our summer things too. Florianópolis is subtropical, just like here in southeast Florida, "Remember that Irene wrote warning us to wear no jewelry."

Terri raised her hand. "Only our wedding rings."

Several of their students had pleaded with them

to cancel the trip. They told stories of tourists being robbed and assaulted as if crime had replaced soccer as the Brazilian national sport. Hotels even supplied armed bodyguards when guests went to Copacabana Beach in Rio. Their travel agent had reinforced those warnings and advised them to stay away from Rio and São Paulo. She had described them as big unmanageable cities saturated with crime, pollution, and gridlock.

They had shrugged off those negative accounts. In their letters and emails, Irene and Martin had described their destination, Florianópolis on the island of Santa Catarina, as a crime-free calm and tranquil paradise. True or not, after nine days with the Kraais, they planned to visit São Paulo, Rio, and Bahia despite the warnings and study authentic Brazilian dances at various *escolas de samba*, samba schools.

"Isn't it a weird coincidence that of all the places in Brazil, Irene and Martin moved to the island where I was born?"

"You'll handle it okay."

"I hope so. If they hadn't moved to Florianópolis, I'd never have considered going there."

And in Florianópolis, maybe we'll learn why your father went berserk.

"Cardinho, I've really missed Irene and Martin."

"I know, *passarinha,* my little bird, and so have I."

"Has it really been five years? We've hardly seen them since we moved to Jupiter, but I always felt they were an instant away if we needed them, but after they moved to Brazil and . . . " Tears came to her eyes. "I hope everything is all right with them."

"Of course it is. Otherwise they'd have told us to cancel our trip."

Rick didn't want to alarm her, but he also had been worrying about Irene, who had done most of the writing until last April. At first, her letters and emails had been upbeat, and descriptive. More recently, they had been brief with one continuing theme. Irene had begged them to come visit this summer before it was too late. Rick and Terri assumed *too late* meant that the Kraais were opting for their contingency plan: If, after living in Brazil for a year or two they didn't like it, they would return to the States.

The tone of Irene's last email, which they received late in April, had been morbid and dark without being specific. That was when they decided to sign with Skype so they could communicate with their friends at no charge by computer and microphone. They had Skyped the Kraais every week since then to ask Irene if there was anything wrong, but they talked only to Martin, who cheerfully assured them his wife was all right. They would have preferred to hear that from Irene herself.

Terri studied her profile in one of the mirrors. "Maybe I ought to get my nose done while we're there. Just a slight filing. Brazil is supposed to have excellent plastic surgeons, and Irene wrote there's a famous clinic in Florianópolis that charges about one-fourth the price we'd pay here in the States."

"No way. I love your nose exactly the way it is."

Terri said something in Portuguese, which he did not understand. "You'll need to attune your ears."

Rick conceded he was rusty in the language, slow of ear to brain, as he preferred to describe it, even though he'd taken two years of Portuguese from Irene in high school and another three at U.C.L.A.

"Okay, Terri, from now on, let's speak only Portuguese when we're alone." He set his beer on the bar and took her in his arms. "*Minha passarinha, eu te amo.*"

"I love you too, but *cuidado*, beware." Terri pulled Rick's face to hers, dug her nails into his neck, and playfully nibbled on his nose and eyelids. "Little birds can peck and claw."

CHAPTER 4.
WINTER IN JULY

The sky changed from clear blue to murky gray, the water from calm translucent azure to agitated opaque slate green at Sambaquí. Severe chilling winds from the south whipped across the bay, and frothing wave crests flung empty fishing boats against tin and aluminum shacks along the beaches. Violent gusts wrenched vegetation from the ground, tore branches from gnarled trees, and ripped tiles from rooftops.

He perched atop a massive weather-smoothed ocher boulder on the edge of a brooding cliff and watched the enraged surf below foam rabidly and crash maniacally against rocks along the serrated shoreline. He listened to the winds howl and whistle mournfully across the deranged landscape between crags, uneven hills, and clusters of small Monopoly-game board houses.

The natural violence, untamed ferocity, and raw beauty of the storm gratified him more than the most tourist-beloved sunny day on the island. He regretted that these turbulent south winds, sweeping northwards from the Antarctic past Tierra del Fuego, Patagonia, and the Argentine pampas to southern Brazil, lasted for only two or three days; then bland tranquility would return to the island until the cycle began again.

A powerful gust caused his companion to lose her balance on the slippery boulder, and he reached out to support her. "It will be dark soon. We should return to the house."

"*You are certain they are coming?*"

"*Yes, my love. They will come.*"

"*I have had second thoughts about the husband. He may resist. That will not be good. The others . . . they have so little patience.*"

"*I can manage them. Rick may not understand at first, but in the end, he will come around. And that will be good. Very good indeed.*"

Hate is ravening vulture beaks
Descending on a place of skulls

—Amy Lowell

FIRST WEEK IN BRAZIL

CHAPTER 5.
MARTIN KRAAI

ook, Rick, there's Florianópolis."

The Transbrasil 737 obligingly dipped a wing to give the passengers on the port side a better view. Florianópolis reflected soft gold under the late afternoon winter sun. Steep hills covered with homes sloped towards apartments and commercial buildings on the flatter central city and its shorelines. The bay was so tranquil its surface looked like glass. Two spans about the same length as San Francisco's Golden Gate Bridge linked Florianópolis to a densely populated mainland littoral.

The capital city for the State of Santa Catarina, Florianópolis had been named for Brazil's second President, Floriano Peixoto and was currently best known as the home of Gustavo "Guga" Kuerton, winner of the French Open a few years ago. The Kraais also had written that Santa Catarina's bureaucracy, university, and main airport were on the island, which had several dozen exceptional beaches and no heavy industry.

"It's more beautiful than Irene and Martin described."

"So it is." Rick preferred looking at his wife, so lovely and sexy in her scarlet and black trimmed Sergio Tacchini. Last week when they phoned the Kraais to let them know the specific date of their arrival, Martin had advised them to wear warm-ups or running suits for comfort and to protect their money and valuable documents during the trip. He'd also urged them to stay with him for the entire three weeks of their visit to Brazil. When they asked about Irene, he changed the subject.

"How's your back, Terri?"

"Still holding up. What about your tush?"

"My buns of steel? Okay, if I remember to shift buttocks"

The 737 flew past the city and circled over lush green sub-tropical vegetation and flat marshlands surrounding the airport. Rick checked the right pocket of his jacket to be sure no one had stolen his wallet, passports and other travel documents. If they ran short of cash, Irene and Martin would give them Brazilian currency, which they would pay back by depositing a check in the Kraais' U.S. account.

After the landing and a long taxi that stopped about a hundred yards away from the provincial airport terminal, they stepped onto the tarmac. Terri took a deep breath and adjusted the oversized tinted glasses on the bridge of her nose. Rick unzipped his jacket and figured the temperature to be in the high seventies with moderate humidity. While they walked towards the terminal, he squinted through his sunglasses at the mob of people on the upper level balcony calling out to relatives and friends when they spotted them.

"Terri, can you see Irene or Martin?"

"Not yet."

"I hope they haven't put on so much weight we won't be able to recognize them."

In their letters, the Kraais had praised the food and described how their eating habits had changed to accommodate three full meals a day, snacks between, and late dinners. Back in Los Angeles, Irene had to swim and work out to maintain her figure, and Martin had been fifteen to twenty pounds overweight.

They entered the small baggage claims area separated from the main terminal lobby by a glass partition, and Terri pointed out a lean and fit man in a beige shirt and gray shorts who was waving directly at them. "It can't be."

"I think it is." Rick gestured thumbs-up and waved back. "He's grown a mustache."

Martin Kraais spoke to the guards and pushed past them. "Terri. Rick." He kissed her on each cheek and wrapped Rick in his powerful arms for a hug and pats on the back, the classic Brazilian *abraço*. "Welcome to paradise."

Martin's appearance left Terri speechless. He was sixty-six, and when they last saw him and Irene at the Kraais' farewell dinner a little over a year ago, he had been paunchy and pale, with dark bags under his eyes, the look of a burned-out urban high school teacher. After a year in Brazil, he had become robust, more muscular, and deeply tanned. His nose seemed slightly longer and sharper than Terri remembered, and she saw no pouches under his eyes. He also appeared taller. Was that an illusion caused by his weight loss? Stomach flat with no love handles, Martin was even leaner than in the photos taken when he'd been a GI stationed in Germany during the early sixties. When they had last seen him, Martin had been graying. Although still bald on top, his dark brown hair showed no trace of gray.

Terri assumed he had grown his thick mustache to blend in with the local gaucho types. Rick's clean-shaven face was among a slim minority at the airport. She found her voice. "Martin, you look great, at least thirty years younger."

"At the very least," Rick agreed.

"I've never seen you looking so fit. Are you on some kind of special diet?"

"No, Terri, just the opposite. I'm eating much more than I did in L.A. It's the food here. No additives, less fat. You know, it's great to see you kids again."

"And you, Martin. Like Rick says, you're looking fantastic." Terri searched past him through the glass partition. "Where's Irene?"

"With all your luggage, we knew there wouldn't be room for another person in the car."

Terri pouted. "I'm so anxious to see her."

"Tell me, how are things going with your dancing?"

Subject changed again. She patted the small black traveling bag slung over her shoulder. "We brought with us a slew of DVDs from our most recent competitions. My back is still going out on me, and I was so weakened by a virus and strep throat, we had to pass on some prestigious competitions."

"Well then, we'll have to do something about that."

"As it is, I won't be ready for serious competition until September, which is why we thought now would be the best time to visit. Martin, I'll do anything to have a healthy body. Anything."

"Then we'll make sure you spend time at Caldas de Imperatriz, the thermal baths on the mainland. They're exceptionally therapeutic. I'd like to do even more for you kids. And I will." Martin moved towards the exit when Rick recognized the first piece of their luggage. "I'll bring the car around and meet you outside."

Terri squeezed Rick's hand after he left. "I'm having a really bad feeling about Irene."

"I know, and there's something strange about Martin. It's more than his changed appearance, but I can't figure out what it is."

CHAPTER 6.
A PERSISTENT UNPLEASANT ODOR

ice wheels." Rick carried their heaviest luggage to the curb outside the terminal where Martin stood next to his Chevrolet Monza, all black with tinted windows.

"Made in Brazil. It's got almost two decades of age, but it's been well-maintained and loaded with so many extras you might equate it with the old Caddy Cimarron."

The trunk could not accommodate all their luggage, and Martin placed the largest piece in the back seat. Terri could barely squeeze inside next to it. Rick settled in the front passenger seat. Martin was right. There would not have been room for Irene.

"Aren't you belting up?"

Martin twisted an end of his mustache and started the car. "No, but you go ahead, Rick. It's considered unmanly in the south of Brazil. More significantly, it identifies you as a gringo, an outsider. So does an automatic transmission. A gaucho, a real man shifts manually."

"And a real woman like Irene?"

Martin did not answer Terri's question. As he drove away from the airport, he went into a long-winded description of the idiosyncratic Brazilian economy.

Whenever Terri interrupted to ask about Irene, Martin continued as if he hadn't heard her, "The Brazilian currency is relatively stable vis-à-vis our dollar. Not like the old days when inflation got too high and they dropped three zeros, added the word *new*, and often renamed it. *Cruzeiro, cruzado*, or as it is now, the *real*. With dollars and the knowledge when to make a financial move through the black market into the Brazilian economy, one can live extremely well with more bang for the buck than in the States."

Rick glanced back at Terri. She seemed about to cry in frustration. Why was Martin avoiding the subject of Irene? Had something happened to her? He wrinkled his nose at a foul smell and stifled an urge to retch. "Martin, what's that peculiar odor?"

"I don't smell anything. Do you, Terri?"

"Only Rick's after-shave."

"Most likely it's our leather, which is treated in cow urine. It also nauseated me the first week or so after we moved here. You'll get used to the odor. Just lower your window until you do." They rounded a bend in the narrow highway between steep hills and the water. "And this is Saco de Limões."

"Bag of lemons," Terri translated.

"Yes, and to the left is the Baía Sul, the ..."

"South Bay," Rick finished for him. He watched small fishing craft, yachts, and recreational powerboats glide over the calm waters, then he turned to his right. "Those hillside houses have a wonderful unobstructed view of everything, but they seem more like *favelas*, shanties."

"This is not the most desirable part of Floripa. That's what we natives call the city, Floripa. Many poor fishing families live there. As you'd expect, real estate speculators would like to buy them out for the view and pay good prices too, but those stubborn *pescadores* won't sell. And who can blame them? After all, where would they go?"

Traffic in both directions intensified. Martin kept to the left along the shoreline instead of veering to the right, which, he explained, would have taken them into the center of town.

Rick decided to stop asking about Irene for the time being. Terri must have come to the same conclusion. Her voice had a forced cheerfulness. "We were remarking on the plane during the approach how much Florianópolis resembles San Francisco."

"Yes, bridges and steep hills with incredibly dramatic views. But without pollution, crime, and earthquakes."

Rick took in more sights. "It looked as compact as San Francisco from the air. What's the population?"

"More than four hundred thousand inhabitants. Over a million tourists visit during our summer season, and we get thousands during the winter."

Rick instinctively braked when Martin blasted his horn and a rusty Volkswagen Beetle almost sideswiped them He never enjoyed being a passenger. "It's absolute anarchy on the roads here."

"Let me assure you ... it is relatively tame here compared to driving in the big cities. But true, even here, a horn, nerves of steel, and total aggression are the tools necessary to ensure survival on our Brazilian roads."

"Do you use gasohol?"

"No, I prefer petrol, even though I pay a premium for it. In the long run, you get more kliks to the liter and a quicker cold start in the morning with good old gas."

The boulevard widened with complicated merges and turnoffs. They circled around a bus terminal and passed at the base of a steep hill worthy of San Francisco, a tall building of gray concrete and glass, which Martin identified as the *Hotel Diplomata.* "Those two hilly suburbs across the Baía Norte are Bom Abrigo and Estreito."

"I'm more interested in hearing about Irene."

Rick noted that Terri's sharp tone had no effect on Martin. Their trip definitely was not off to a good start.

Martin drove in the right lane for the next two and a half miles past architecturally creative condominiums facing the bay. "As you can see, these condos can vary in width from a mere twenty-five feet to well over a hundred. Some have more than seventy-five hundred square feet of living space. They take up an entire floor and require two elevators, one for social and the other for service."

Rick almost retched again at the pungent odor despite the open windows. "That seems to be the trend in southeast Florida as well."

Terri pointed at an eleven-story building where each apartment had an outdoor swimming pool and view facing the bay. "That's my favorite."

"My good friends, the Silveiras, live there. They own the *cobertura,* the two-level penthouse unit. You'll be meeting them."

Terri peered out her window for a better view. "Why didn't you and Irene buy here?"

Rick did some rapid calculating. "Probably too expensive."

"No, we could have swung it. Although their currency has been relatively stable since it became the *real,* the dollar stretches very far in Brazil if you know how to play the game. We were tempted to purchase here until we discovered all the problems connected with the so-called *condominio-fechado,* the closed condominium. The entire process is extremely complicated. Remind me in a few days to explain it after you and Terri settle in. Anyway, we wanted a home at the beach, on the sand by the water."

After Martin drove them past the Governor's mansion, the highway made a ninety degree turn away from the bay. "We're facing east now. You see all those large homes on the steep slope to your right? That's Trindade, an exclusive neighborhood. You might call it the Bel Air of Florianópolis. My very good friends Zé and Rosa Zimmermann live there. They have a seven-bedroom suite mansion. You'll be meeting them as well."

He turned north on a four lane stretch of highway that curved through rolling hills, and continued, "If you take that road to the right for about eight miles, you'll hit Lagoa da Conceição, another beautiful community, and a few miles beyond the lagoon is Joaquina. The beach there has spectacular dunes, and it's the site of international surfing championships. But I'm partial to the northern beaches. You'll see everything eventually."

In spite of the island's beauty and surface normality, Martin's radically changed appearance, his refusal to discuss Irene, and that persistent foul odor troubled Rick, and, he assumed, Terri as well:. He had smelled urine treated leather each time the Kraais had returned from their annual trip to Brazil with new wallets, belts, purses, and shoes. No, whatever he was still inhaling smelled more like rotten meat.

Rick turned in his seat to face Terri and touched his nose, his expression a big question mark. She did not look at him and concentrated on the changing landscape so she would not pick a fight with Martin over Irene's absence.

CHAPTER 7.
URUBÚS

nder the late afternoon sun, she watched the young mother and her two boys play on the littoral rocks below. She glared at them with hatred, palpable hatred and malevolence for her own grandchildren.

Those disagreeable, hyperactive little wretches. Blond and fair like their mother. So gringo. In no way do they resemble my beautiful son.

And that woman! Physically healthy, robust, never ill, in the prime of life, while I am condemned, imprisoned in this decaying wreck of a body. It is so diabolically unfair, a deliberate nasty trick of fate, which must be rectified, rectified as soon as possible.

Martin's proposal, unfortunately, is only half a solution. A more comprehensive outcome is required. Perhaps matters shall be resolved now that his young friends have arrived.

While Martin drove Terri and Rick through green hills and lush valleys, he continued to avoid speaking about Irene.

"... and that road to the left takes you back to Sambaquí."

Terri tensed. "That's where my mother was born."

"Shall I detour now and take you to her house?"

"No, let's do it another time. I'm not quite ready."

"Another time then it shall be. You should know that Sambaquí is a government-protected historic and archaeological site. It was the burial ground of the original Indian inhabitants of this island before the Europeans came. They planted their dead vertically."

Martin braked and swerved to avoid hitting two vultures in the middle of the road tearing out chunks of viscera from a dog hit by a car. The predators ignored their intrusion as Martin edged past them along the soft shoulder

"Our *urubú* is a variant of the black vulture unique to this island and better scavengers than any garbage company, and more efficient too."

"They're so incredibly beautiful." Terri laughed at herself. "*Puxa vida!* Oh, wow! I never expected to hear myself saying that about vultures. What do you think, Cardinho?"

Rick studied them. Larger than the turkey buzzards of Florida, these *urubús* had the same blue-black sheen of Terri's lustrous hair, matte gray faces, slender blue-gray beaks, and almost-human expressions. Their dark brown eyes suggested greater intelligence than basic birdbrain. He could not think of them as beautiful but conceded they were indeed striking and regal. They lacked the specific vulturine features that usually repelled him: fleshy red caruncles and lappets; wrinkled, bristly reptilian heads.

"Not my idea of a pet, Terri, but I agree that they're more impressive than the buzzards we see in Jupiter, although, our Florida vultures maintain a more respectful distance."

"You'll get used to them." Martin accelerated past the 80-kph speed limit. "They serve a useful purpose, ecological food-chain and all that, especially along the beaches, because so many dead fish and penguins are washed ashore."

Rick grimaced at the image of vultures feeding off lovable Disneyesque penguins.

Martin slowed when they approached a police station on their right. Wrecks of cars and trucks littered the vacant land on either side of the one-story building, an obvious warning to careless motorists.

Terri stroked the back of Rick's neck. "I'd prefer it if you didn't drive here."

Martin again accelerated beyond the maximum speed limit. "He'll do all right. All it takes is the usual defensive driving and blatant aggression with heavy use of the horn."

The highway curved through more unimproved land. To the right and beyond were ramshackle farmhouses and grazing lands for lean cattle and goat and between them stagnant swamps and marshes. They saw workers in green-scummed semi-tropical mire clearing bulrushes and reeds, and Rick imagined mosquitoes and other bloodsucking bugs feasting on exposed skin.

Farther along, Martin called their attention to men in small boats casting nets in the middle of neat rectangles of water. "Shrimp-breeding is a profitable business on the island."

To their left beyond marshy breeding grounds for teeming insects and vermin, they saw green vegetation below a dentated ridge of purple and chocolate brown cliffs topped with high brush and palm trees. High above, vultures floated downward in a circular pattern.

Terri admired their grace and silhouettes. "They seem more like gliders up there."

"Our *urubús* make use of thermal air bubbles rising from the ground as it heats up. Like a smoke ring, hot air rises from the center, and they glide inside the ring."

"You've learned a lot about the vultures since you moved here, Martin. Is there a reason why?"

"No, Rick. Like you and Terri, everyone is intrigued by them at first. Then they become part of the landscape."

Terri pointed to the left. "Is it all wilderness over there?"

"Yes, from Sambaquí to Ponta Grossa, the northwest point on the island."

They drove for several more kilometers through open countryside until they reached another turnoff. Instead of continuing straight along the main highway from Florianópolis to Canasvieiras, another northern beach, Martin turned right and drove along a winding hill to Ingleses. When he slowed at the crest, Rick and Terri gasped at the view below.

The road ahead of them dropped sharply towards a compact coastal town with a wide expanse of crescent-shaped beach facing the Atlantic Ocean to the north ,bracketed by sharp promontories at either end. At the bottom of the hill, small homes and typical beach community stores, real estate trailers and shacks, small markets, and yards filled with construction supplies lined the last flat kilometers with massive unspoiled dunes and unimproved land behind them.

After they passed condos, hotels, and restaurants, the highway dead-ended at the beach. Martin turned right onto a narrow two-lane road he identified as the *Estrada Geral*. It snaked between small convenience shops, condos, and sprawling beachfront homes on the left, and on the right hillside estates, and more enormous unspoiled dunes. Beachgoers were returning to their cars, bikes, and homes, a normal day's-end at the seashore the same as those anywhere in the USA, except that pairs and larger groups of *urubús* watched them from eaves, mailboxes, and roofs along the road.

"We have arrived."

Martin turned left across the road onto a beige and rust swirled terrazzo driveway and stopped in front of bronzed metal garage doors set in the middle of a red brick wall. His house was typical of the large beachfront homes they had passed, with ten-foot high walls and no windows facing the road.

Terri stretched when she got out of the car. "Your house is very impressive, and we have a reception committee too."

Rick saw them too. A pair of handsome black vultures unmoving perched as sentinels on the roof.

Martin sounded his horn twice and joined them on the pavement. "You really ought to look on the bright side."

"Which is?"

"If they don't bother you, Rick, you know you're alive."

"Where is Irene? Why isn't she here to meet us?"

Martin did not answer Terri, and the garage doors opened. A man at least seven feet tall dressed all in black walked towards them. He was of indeterminate age with dark brown hair falling to his broad shoulders. His smooth skin, an unusual sienna tone, was tightly drawn over his hairless acromegalic face. Its enormous size, generous nose, and heavy jaw made him appear as if he were hewn from stone and reminded Rick of the giant heads on Easter Island.

"This is Paulo Costa. Lico, we call him. He works for Sônia Batardi."

"Irene's best friend from her school days in São Paulo."

"That's right, Terri. He's her *faxineiro*, general handyman, chauffeur, and bodyguard."

"Bodyguard? You wrote us that the island is crime-free."

"It is, relatively. Sônia has loaned Lico to me until I get my new house in order. He sleeps in that small apartment over the garage. He'll take your luggage to the guest suite."

When Martin stepped out of hearing to exchange a few words with the *faxineiro,* Terri moved closer to Rick. "That station wagon in the garage? Martin could have driven it to the airport and brought Irene with him. And where is she? Why didn't she come out to greet us?"

"Whatever the reason, we damn well ought to find out in the next few minutes."

"Yes, we'll insist on it."

Lico crammed himself into the Monza and drove it into the three-car garage next to the station wagon. Martin unlocked a narrower copper metal door at the far right side of the wall and led Rick and Terri into a courtyard separating the garage from the main house. They walked a stone pathway along the eastern wall past TV security scanners. The rectilinear two-story house of rusty brick and red tile was trimmed with chocolate brown wood beams. Its high walls sloped downwards towards the beach so as not to obstruct any view.

Rick pointed at a black vulture watching them from the wall. "Do they stay here all day and night?"

Martin paused on the broad front steps before opening the ornately carved double front doors set in the middle of his home's eastern side. "No, as I told you, our *urubús* are diurnal. They'll soon be returning to their roosts until daybreak. You'll get used to them."

Terri fixed her eyes on the vulture without blinking. "I'm already used to them."

CHAPTER 8.
REVELATION

hey absorbed the last of the afternoon sun as it balanced briefly on the western slopes of Ingleses. The heavier older one turned to the younger. "I had expected no less, of course, and now that I have seen her, I cannot adequately express how pleased I am that she is so perfect of face and form."

"Yes, your plan should proceed smoothly."

"Provided my son wants her."

"Will he?"

"I can never be certain about Ivo. I shall encourage him, of course. We may know as early as tonight."

"If Ivo chooses her, be prepared for conflict. Martin will not be pleased. It is not what he wants for her."

"I can manage him. I always have."

"That is true, but then what do we do about the husband?" The eyes of the Younger narrowed. "He is too blond, too handsome. I do not like that type of gringo. He should be eliminated immediately."

"No, we must wait a bit longer."

"But you have so little time."

"Time enough to carry my plan through to fruition."

Martin punched a code to disengage his security system and unlocked the front door. He brought Rick and Terri into a spacious two-story foyer, complete with bench, guest closet, and an adjacent powder room. "My new house is sixteen meters wide and twenty meters long excluding the garage, about six thousand square feet of living space, *mais ou menos*, more or less."

Rick's sense of foreboding intensified. Why did Martin say *my* house and not *our* house?

"Where is Irene?"

Martin again ignored Terri's question and continued speaking as he took them to the right into the living room. "... *dois ambientes*, two ambiances, ten by six meters."

The great room divided in two by the placement of plush furniture, half formal, half casual, had ceramic floor tiles of a pleasing brick tone, fully stocked wet bar, fireplace, gaming area, and a high-tech entertainment center set between floor-to-ceiling jacaranda bookcases along more than six meters of wall. Although the plush slate blue leather furniture and accessories were new, Terri and Rick recognized familiar paintings on the walls and oriental rugs scattered over the tile floor that the Kraais had shipped from their home in L.A..

The beach-facing part of the house was rounded at the edges, which softened the rectilinear construction. Bronze-tinted sliding doors opened to a patio the width of the house and five meters deep. Outside, a barbecue area and lawn was protected by brick walls, and a metal gate opened to the sands.

Adjacent to the living room, a formal dining room had the same view across the patio and lawn to the water. The oval table, buffet and hutch, and twelve armchairs were of Brazilian rosewood, the latter covered with burnt orange and pale blue silk upholstery. The patterns of the jacaranda wall paneling suggested a Rorschach test.

"I paid forty-five thousand dollars for the land and another hundred and fifty thousand for construction. You know that's a steal by American standards, but more than three times what they promised me as a fixed price two years earlier.

Terri stepped in front of him. "Martin, this is all very impressive, but I can't stand the suspense. I insist on knowing. Where is Irene? Is something wrong?"

He escorted Terri to a sky blue leather sofa, asked Rick to sit beside her, and called out for someone named Eva. An aged, leathery *empregada* in black entered carrying a large tray with a bottle of beer for Rick and two demitasses of *cafezinho.*

After the servant returned to the kitchen, Martin settled in an armchair opposite them. He raised his small cup of coffee in a welcoming toast and encouraged them to drink. Rick found the beer to be refreshing and tasty, with a name no less German than most American brews, *Kaiser.* Terri sat on the edge of the sofa and left her coffee untouched.

Martin lit a cigar and brushed his mustache with the back of his hand. "I didn't know how best to tell you. Not even when you phoned to let me know you were coming. It isn't easy for me now. I was afraid you'd cancel your trip. You see, there was a fatal accident. Irene is dead."

Rick stared at Martin, unable to speak, and Terri let out a piercing primal scream. "No! I can't believe it. Not Irene."

Rick placed his beer on the table, put an arm around his wife who sobbed uncontrollably, and held her hand as those three words sunk in: Irene is dead. He felt sorry for Martin. The Kraais had been inseparable, best friends to each other, exactly like him and Terri. His mouth went dry. "Tell us, Martin, what happened?"

"She drowned."

"Drowned? When?"

"The end of April."

"April? That was three months ago. Why didn't you tell us?"

"Rick, I was in a terrible state. I couldn't bring myself to phone or write the bad news. I should have, but I continued to procrastinate. I knew you were involved in important competitions."

"Martin, Terri and I, we're your best friends, like family. Closer. Your own flesh and blood children couldn't love you and Irene more. You should have told us. We'd have dropped everything and flown here."

"I know that, but I was thinking of the two of you. I didn't want bad news to interfere with your chances for success at the competitions. In any case, you wouldn't have made it in time to attend her funeral. I was expecting your visit this summer. That's another reason why I waited. I wanted to tell you face-to-face."

Terri had difficulty speaking. "I still can't believe Irene is dead, and drowned of all things. She was an excellent swimmer, an exceptional athlete. You must be awfully lonely here in your new house. It's so big for one person."

"I'm adjusting." Martin hesitated for a moment and toyed with his cigar. "There's something else. It will probably shock you as much as Irene's passing. I married again."

Rick felt his wife trembling. Terri, who almost had been murdered by her father, had loved Irene as much as any child could love its birth mother. So had he. He'd have to be strong and in complete control for her emotional well-being.

"I'm confident you'll accept Maria Lourdes. I married her only two weeks ago, and I apologize that she is not here to greet you. Lico told me there was a problem in the kitchen, and Maria Lourdes had to go marketing for some odds and ends. She'll be back within the hour. Tonight, we're throwing a party in your honor. You'll be meeting our dearest friends."

Terri shook her head. "That's impossible. We can't face anyone now."

"She's right, Martin."

"I understand how you feel, but it won't do any good to stay in your room and brood."

That was exactly what Rick wanted, to be alone with Terri, to brood and rethink their plans. "Martin, we're exhausted."

"If you're typical of travelers to Brazil, you'll be over-tired and unable to sleep anyway. Be thankful you didn't fly from L.A. to Floripa, as we did, twenty-six hours airport to airport. By the time you unpack and shower, you ought to have your second wind. It'll do you good to be among people who also knew and loved Irene, friends who are prepared to love you as well."

Rick drank his beer and wished he'd asked for something stronger. "What happened exactly? How did Irene drown?"

"No one knows. She went for her daily swim, and hours later her body washed ashore."

Terri sniffled. "I can't believe Irene is dead. Where is she buried, Martin? I want to lay flowers at her grave, light candles at the nearest church."

"She was cremated. We scattered her ashes out at sea."

"Cremated, no grave?" Terri looked at him horrified and shrank against Rick. "Irene . . . there's so much I never said to her."

"It's always that way." Martin stood. "Now, then, you probably want to freshen up. Come with me."

CHAPTER 9.
MARIA LOURDES

é Zimmermann turned their black Santana sedan onto the road to Ingleses. "Rosa, this sudden change of plans bothers me."

"She knows what is best, and it is the perfect solution to both her problems." His wife jabbed her elbow into his ribs. "Cuidado, Zé, a truck is coming."

"I see it. Let us all meet them first, and then decide. Perhaps there is another way."

"Turn on your lights. There is no other way."

"How can you know that? They only just arrived."

"We have intuition. Watch out for that Corcel."

The delegado accelerated and cut into the right lane ahead of the Brazilian-made Ford. "But Martin adores them. He has told us more than once that they are like his children. He would never allow it."

"He will if he has no choice. Remember what happened to Irene."

"At least we tried, gave her every chance."

"A waste of time. I was right about her too."

"In my opinion, we may be going too far this time. I predict . . . there will be trouble."

"We can deal with it. We always have. Get into the left lane. I do not understand why you have this love affair with the right."

In the guest suite, Rick held Terri while she cried to exhaustion. He was too stunned to let loose his own emotions. Added to that, their best friend had placed a wall between them despite his surface geniality and hospitality. He believed Martin had not told them the entire story. His reasons for withholding the news of Irene's death for almost three months didn't wash. His uncharacteristically high-strung monologues seemed intended to prevent them from asking more questions.

Terri wiped her eyes. "Oh, Rick, I feel so guilty we didn't come sooner when Irene was still alive."

"We couldn't know." He opened the closet. Their empty bags had been stored in one corner, their clothes hanging in perfect order. The rest lay organized in dresser drawers.

She unzipped her jacket, raised an arm, and sniffed her armpit. "I've never smelled so gamy."

"It may not be you." Rick detected something else, the same odor that had nauseated him in the car. Urine-treated leather, Martin had said, but he could find no leather in their bedroom, excepting their own American made items.

When Terri went into the bathroom, he looked out the window to the east. It was night black outside, and the house next door was unlit. The temperature had dropped markedly. He shut the window and turned on the small 1200 BTU room heater Martin had left for them explaining that only his master bath upstairs and the kitchen and laundry room downstairs had central gas.

He took in every aspect of the ample guest room. He figured it to be about fifteen-by-thirty feet with closets at either end, a double suite that could accommodate more visitors if they closed the accordion doors. The floors were of the same high quality rust-colored ceramic tile he'd seen downstairs, and on the walls the Kraais had hung colorful serigraphs by Araújo, a naïve Brazilian artist, and a small surreal oil by Roni Brandão, more typical of Irene's taste.

He brooded over her drowning and Martin's strange behavior. The Martin Kraai they used to know would have called them immediately to report Irene's death. They were like family, better than family. The Kraais had been their best friends too, responsible for him and Terri meeting, for introducing them to ballroom dancing, for just about every stage of their development over the past fifteen years, and for that loan so they could make a down payment and open their own studio.

No, Martin's secrecy and instant marriage to a stranger did not add up. Rick speculated Irene might not have drowned. Perhaps sharks or some other awful creature of the sea had gotten to her. Because tourism was their main industry, the local authorities would cover-up something like that.

"It's all yours." Terri came out of the bathroom wrapped in her scarlet terrycloth robe, kissed him for being so thoughtful, and stood next to the small heater. "Remember what Martin said. Switch off the gas when you're through."

Martin had shown them how to turn on the pilot for the individual small propane gas heater when they needed to use the sink, bidet, and the electric shower. Rick had never trusted propane tanks, not even for barbecuing, and it helped that he and Terri did not smoke. He took his turn in the guest bathroom of cheerful yellow tile and aqua ceramic fixtures and used some of the bottled water Martin had left for them to brush his teeth. He plugged in his adapter and shaved before undressing. The shower's feeble pressure permitted at best an intermittent trickle of hot water when he switched on the electricity.

Shivering afterwards, he headed straight for the small room heater. By then, Terri had dressed in a bulky canary yellow cable knit sweater that she wore over a vermilion shirt, faded denims, and yellow sneakers. He put on layers of clothes to get warm: T-shirt first, black merino turtleneck, and a flannel blue and black plaid shirt, tucking all into his jeans. He added his thickest wool socks before lacing his black high-tops.

When Terri bent to remove articles from the bottom drawer, she suffered painful back-muscle spasms. "I wonder ... maybe I can get someone to make a Macomb for me while we're in Brazil and improve my health."

Rick massaged her back. "We could just as easily ask the Haitians to work some voodoo for us when we return to Jupiter." Although something nagged at him to stay until they found out the truth about Irene's death, he was ready to write off their entire trip to the Brazil as a disaster and make an immediate U-turn. "Terri, tomorrow we're taking the first flight out of here to São Paulo, Rio, Bahia, or even back to Florida if you prefer."

"Yes, please. Let's get away from this place. And what shall we do with these?"

Irene had requested they bring an odd mix of supplies, all specific brands: *Crest* toothpaste with fluoride, *L'Oreal* hair coloring, *Neutrogena* soaps and oils, *Animal* perfume, and two dozen paperbacks, mostly mysteries.

"I guess we should give these gifts to his new wife although I don't know if she understands English."

"To hell with his Maria Lourdes, whoever she is. Rick, something is terribly wrong. Irene and Martin always gave us the impression that if one died the other couldn't have gone on living. He's positively cheerful."

Rick placed on the dresser the bottles of *Johnny Walker Black* and *Biscuit VSOP* he had brought for Martin. "I agree. He doesn't seem to be all that broken up about Irene's death. Maybe moving to Brazil changed everything between them. Remember, we haven't seen them in over a year, and not all that much before that after we moved to

Jupiter five years ago. And Irene's last letters were awfully bleak, as if she had a premonition something horrible was going to happen to her."

"Nobody changes that quickly, Rick, especially not Irene and Martin. I know they say life is supposed to go on, but something just isn't right. I still find it impossible to believe Irene drowned. She was an experienced and powerful swimmer. My God, she swam for Brazil in the 1964 Olympics."

"Perhaps some tricky local riptide pulled her under, or she no longer had enough stamina."

Do you really believe that?"

"No."

"I don't feel like going downstairs. Martin should have known that we wouldn't want to be among strangers. It was wrong for him to make a party."

"He probably didn't want to be alone with us."

"He wouldn't be alone. He has his Maria Lourdes. I can't accept it. How could he have married again, and so soon?"

Rick could not imagine what Martin's new wife was like. He saw only Irene at their mentor's side, the way it always had been. "Maria Lourdes must have gotten to him in a weak moment."

"You may be right." Terri set her jaw, and her eyes flashed the same fiery determination he'd seen every time just before a major dance competition. "All right, let's go downstairs. I want to check out this Maria Lourdes thoroughly before we leave. And, we shall leave tomorrow. You can bet the farm on that."

"And I want to confront Martin and insist he tell us everything."

When they heard a tapping at their door, Rick and Terri looked at each other, and she said, "*Entra.*"

Martin entered with a slender young woman dressed in a gray sweater, black wool skirt, and black leather boots.

"My wife, Maria Lourdes."

Terri coolly nodded instead of hugging and kissing Martin's new wife. The moment was too awkward for her to go through the traditional Brazilian *abraços e beijos*.

Rick forced a smile at Maria Lourdes for Martin's benefit. It was eerie. She could have passed for Terri's sister, although not quite as beautiful. Still, Maria Lourdes had similar features, with the same lean build, full breasts, dark olive coloring, and shiny blue-black hair that hung like a cloak over her narrow shoulders. If Martin's new wife was typical of Brazilians, Terri would definitely blend in with the native population.

Maria Lourdes took Terri's arm and said in melodious Portuguese, "Come, our friends have arrived, and they are most eager to meet you."

Martin thanked Rick for the scotch and cognac, and they followed the women, "You'll be at a disadvantage until your ear becomes accustomed to the local dialect. Unlike in São Paulo and Rio, very few speak adequate English here. American tourists rarely come to the Island."

That would make it difficult for him to ask Martin's friends about Irene. "Then if I have a problem communicating, only you and Terri will be able to help me?"

"Sônia Batardi, Irene's best friend from her school days, is fluent in English and many other languages. You've nothing to worry about. You'll do just fine, and I expect Terri will adapt instantly to our *catarinense* dialect because it had been spoken in her home before her father went insane."

CHAPTER 10.
A GATHERING OF FRIENDS

In the living room, the first person Rick noticed was towering Lico who tended bar, still all in black, black as any *urubú.*

Martin and Maria Lourdes took him and Terri to a graying woman whose enormous size and shapeless layers of home-crafted brown and beige wool coverings created the illusion she had been poured over the entire couch. Her complexion was sallow, and she had a distracting mustache and scattered bristles of dark hair on her chin. A young man in a dark blue running suit stood behind the dowager and massaged her shoulders.

Martin seemed to genuflect before her. "*Doutora* Sônia, let me present Rick and Terri Hamilton, whom I treasure as if they were my own children. My friends, this is Dr. Sônia Batardi, who, as you know, was responsible for our discovery of this island paradise."

Sônia stared at them through thick glasses, wall-eyed and without expression, while she crocheted and cooed to the yelping, foul-smelling feces-brown miniature pinscher curled in her lap. Rick inhaled more than the odor of unwashed dog emanating from the monstrous woman. An asphyxiating putrescence reminded him first of mildewed rugs rotting in Florida humidity, and then something more like that disagreeable odor in Martin's car and the guest suite.

Could she be the same ageless pretty and thin Sônia they had seen in photographs, the same Sônia who had been Irene's best friend since their school days, the same woman Terri was supposed to resemble? He could not imagine fastidious and elegant Irene Kraai ever associating with this filthy malignant personality.

Maria Lourdes introduced them to the young man standing behind the couch. Sônia's son, Ivo Batardi, had the type of face that suggested if he removed his glasses, nose, eyebrows, and mustache might come off with them. Rick thought his kisses on Terri's cheeks were more familiar than necessary.

Ivo continued to leer at her and welcomed them to Brazil in Portuguese as if giving official approval of their visit. "You will see, dear friends. It is paradise here."

Terri backed away from him and clung to Rick. "That's what everyone says."

Rick knew his wife did not enjoy large parties and meeting strangers. She came to life only on the dance floor, when they were alone, or with their most intimate friends, like Irene and Martin. But now there was no Irene. He figured Terri must be thinking the same thing. She seemed ready to cry again. He squeezed her shoulder. He didn't know what else to do at the moment, except if Ivo made a move on her, he'd demolish the presumptuous lecher.

"Louisa!" Ivo snapped his fingers at a Tyrolian-quaint young woman going through Martin's CDs and DVDs at his media center. Then he sighed and gestured apologetically for Terri's benefit. "She is my wife."

Louisa's floral patterned pale blue and yellow peasant dress and braided blonde hair seemed out of time and place with Rick's image of Brazil. He caught Sônia watching her daughter-in-law with overt hostility when she came over for introductions. Poor Louisa had acquired the mother-in-law from hell.

While Terri and Maria Lourdes chatted with Louisa, Ivo twirled an end of his mustache and took Rick aside. "It will be my pleasure to show you everything Floripa has to offer, specifically the Relax Clubs. The women here are more beautiful and unspoiled than those in São Paulo."

"Rick is too happily married for that nonsense." Martin led him away from Ivo and back to Terri, Louisa, and Maria Lourdes.

"What happened to Sônia? She's so unlike the photos you and Irene showed us."

"A tragedy, Terri. And if her behavior seems odd to you, it's because she's taking medication for a severe burn that nearly killed her. She was unaware of a gas leak in her bathroom and lit a match."

Rick seriously considered taking cold showers from now on regardless of the temperature.

Martin and Maria Lourdes took them across the room to another grouping of leather chairs and curved sofa sectional where the women were seated and the men stood apart and made the introductions: "This is Flávio Vysocki from São Paulo, and that lovely young woman in the gray dress on the couch is his wife, Gabriela."

Flávio was a pale blue-eyed blond in his thirties, snub-nosed, heavy-set, and almost as tall as Lico. He had on a forest green corduroy shirt, loose blue jeans, and beige docksiders. His nervous glances towards Sônia interested Rick.

"Flávio is the best architect in the entire State of Santa Catarina, if not all of Brazil. He designed and built my house."

Rick awkwardly complimented the architect in Portuguese while Terri fluently exchanged pleasantries with Gabriela, another dark brunette who could have been mistaken for her sister and even more like Maria Lourdes' twin. *Is everyone related?*

Martin turned to a man with thinning curly brown hair and an impressive mustachio, then pointed to the small, stocky, yet even more sharply featured young woman seated next to Gabriela. "And this is *Doutor* José Zimmermann and his wife Rosa. Zé is the *delegado*, literally deputy sheriff, but more accurately Chief of Police, for the 7th District, which covers Ingleses, Canasvieiras, and Jurerê. All the Northern beaches. He's originally from Blumenau, a city more German than many in Germany proper, that you must visit while you're here. And Rosinha is one of his detectives."

"*Prazer*, pleased to meet you." Rick shook hands with Zé, a tanned body builder whose muscles bulged through a snug tomato red polo shirt. He noted an uncanny resemblance between Zé and Martin. They could pass for brothers.

Rosa Zimmermann wore a shapeless olive-drab woolen sweater, black slacks, and high-heel pointed boots. She made it clear to Rick that she wanted no *beijo* from him. Just as well. She had the sharpest nose and beadiest eyes of all the dark women. She also was the plumpest, with pitted sallow skin. If Terri and these women had truly been sisters, Rosa would have qualified as the ugly one. And she emanated a smell as malodorous as Sônia's.

Rich reviewed his theory that the cops might have covered up the cause of Irene's death so that tourists would not be frightened away, but if Martin's best friend was the local police chief, he most certainly would have told him the truth.

Zé went into an unasked for monologue about his efficiency. "On those extremely rare occasions when some foolish gringo commits a crime, we immediately seal off the bridges so no one escapes."

Rick understood most of Zé's Portuguese. "They do the same in Palm Beach."

"But here it is perfectly crime-free," Ivo interrupted. "I have never felt so safe since we moved here. When I lived in São Paulo, I was afraid to leave for work. I did not know if I would find my wife and children alive when I came home. Here, we do not even lock our doors or windows."

Rick resolved to ignore whatever Ivo had to say. Sônia's son was the type who had an obvious tendency to exaggerate, even lie, in order to seem important. The same as Martin's house, all the expensive homes he had seen during the drive along the Estrada Geral had high walls, metal gates, and, high-tech security systems.

"Can't let our dearest friends die of thirst." Martin led them to the bar where Lico had laid out an assortment of fruit juices and mixers next to a bottle of clear liquid made from sugar cane, which smelled strong enough to be a gas substitute for cars. Rick recognized it as *cachaça*, the basic ingredient of the Brazilian national drink Martin and Irene used to bring back from their trips to Brazil. Although he preferred beer, he understood they expected him to try the traditional *caipirinha*.

Martin gave him and Terri the choices of sweet or sour, with countless varieties in between, and recommended the *batida paulista*: *Cachaça*, ice, the white of an egg, and lemon juice with the glass moistened so that sugar adhered to the rim; or, he could substitute coffee for lemon; or coconut milk for a sweeter drink.

Rick saw no way out. "*Uma batida paulista, por favor.*" He remembered to open his mouth wider this time when speaking Portuguese. Irene had repeatedly complained that Americans barely moved their lips and resembled ventriloquists when they spoke foreign languages.

"Terri, what will you have?"

"A glass of coconut milk, Martin. No alcohol, please."

After Lico mixed, poured, and served, they raised their glasses for *saudes*, toasts to everyone's health. As expected, Rick found the taste similar to a rum sour. He put on his best Good Neighbor Policy-Alliance for Progress smile. "*Gosto.* I like it."

That pleased Ivo, obviously a rabid Brazilian chauvinist, and the others who assured Rick he was *muito simpatico*, except Rosa. He figured she probably had a lousy disposition and the cop's attitude that everyone was guilty of something. No, it was more than that. He sensed she had taken an instant dislike to him.

He turned around when Ivo went into a tirade against his wife, which Sônia watched with overt pleasure. "What is he screaming about, Terri?"

He's criticizing her for just about everything. Shoddy housekeeping, her appearance, lack of firmness with their children."

"Definitely not a healthy marriage."

"And none of our business, Cardinho."

"I can't believe his mother was Irene's best friend."

"I know. Remember those photos she used to show us? Even the ones taken just a couple of years ago, Sônia was thin and youthful. She can't be more than sixty. She and Irene were classmates. What do you think happened?"

"Like you said, not our business." He glanced around the room at Martin's guests. "But before the night is over, I expect we'll know more about what happened to Irene."

Her eyes moistened, and she bit her lower lip. "It seems so strange to see Martin without her. Maria Lourdes seems sweet, but she's so unlike Irene who was tall, blonde, and blue-eyed."

"Maybe that's why he's chosen her. No way would she remind him of Irene."

"I still don't understand it. Irene and Martin were lovers and best friends, inseparable too. The way we are. Rick, please, don't let anything like that ever happen to us."

"Never."

Two more couples arrived, and Martin and Maria Lourdes introduced them to Terri and Rick. Nelson de Andrade, a slight, feminine-featured graying man in his forties sported a 1930s movie style mustache and cut an elegant figure in his all-gray ensemble: Cashmere sweater, silk shirt, flannel trousers, and calf-leather shoes. Fátima, his pregnant wife, had on a drab green wool dress and was physically interchangeable with all the other women, except for her mustache, which almost rivaled her husband's. The de Andrades were travel agents, and Nelson promised to make a list of the best samba schools for them when they visited Rio, his hometown. Terri and Rick reassured each other. First thing tomorrow, they would go to his agency and arrange for the earliest flight out of Florianópolis.

The last couple, Edmur and Valéria Silveira, had on matching tan warm-ups. Stocky curly-haired Edmur was in his forties, with the inevitable gaucho mustache. He was Martin's realtor, originally from Pôrto Alegre. Rick wondered if it was significant that all the men had come from other cities while their women were natives of the island.

After a closer look at Valéria, Rick saw another common denominator among the dark sharp-featured women. They seemed to be of similar ages, late twenties to early thirties, he figured. Each resembled Terri physically, all completely unlike Irene and Louisa.

Maria Lourdes linked an arm with Terri's as if they were indeed sisters and sat with her among Gabriela, Valéria, Fátima, and Rosa. It was obvious to Rick that the other women deliberately excluded Louisa from their circle, and he went out of his way to chat with her until Martin took him away. Even with his limited Portuguese, he learned that Ivo's wife was well educated, with a hunger to speak to someone about classical music and literature.

During cocktails, Rick communicated in Portuguese as best he could. The men instantly accepted him because he was Martin's friend. At no time did anyone mention Irene by name or even refer to her. It was as if she had never existed. She existed all right in memory and the void her absence created. He could not stop thinking about Irene and how she ought to have been the hostess tonight. He glanced over at Terri, who had become the center of attention, probably answering questions and asking more, he expected. She seemed to be in better spirits because the women were receiving her as if she were a long-lost sister.

But what should he to make of Sônia? Everyone deferred to her well beyond normal respect. The Kraais had always been in awe of her intellect. She was a respected anthropologist, ethnologist, and a published expert on legends and mythology. Respect and awe aside, why had Martin damn near groveled during the introductions? He wasn't the only one. Ivo positively slobbered over his mother, and the other men also paid court to her.

Lico, the enigmatic *faxineiro*, interested Rick as much as Sônia for reasons other than his odd reddish-brown coloring, great height, and features of no recognizable ethnicity. A man of proud bearing, at the very least he treated Martin and the other men as equals and was subservient only to Sônia. Lico repeatedly looked towards her as if expecting a command. That had to be one hell of a story.

Eva, Martin's *empregada*, brought in a tray filled with assorted hors d'ouevres, and Rick liked–the black and vermilion *mariscos* best, the local variety of clams, and one tasty concoction he could not identify. "Martin, what's this dish?"

"Sônia's own recipe, a seafood cake."

"*Eu gosto muito*, I like it very much," Rick called out to Sônia. Uncomfortable under her unwavering gaze, he motioned for Terri to come over to him. It took several minutes before she could get away from the women.

"Have you found out anything more about Irene?"

"Not yet, but everyone here is trying to be so nice. They all knew my family." Rick wondered if that was a good thing. "And we're getting more invitations than we'll ever be able to accept. The Silveiras want us for dinner Friday night. Remember? Martin showed us where their condo is, the building with a swimming pool on each floor we passed on the Baía Norte. And Ivo invited us for a *feijoada* this coming Saturday. That's the Brazilian national dish. Irene always wanted to make a proper *feijoada* for us in L.A. but couldn't find all the ingredients."

"I remember, but we can't accept their invitations if we're leaving tomorrow."

"I know that, but I didn't want to say anything and have to explain why. You know they'd all pressure us to stay."

Martin and Nelson joined them. The travel agent spoke too rapidly for Rick to understand, and Terri translated, "The de Andrades are inviting us to their daughter's fifteenth birthday party at their club a week from Saturday night. It's the same as a debutante's coming-out, like the Mexican *quinceañera*."

Rick thanked Nelson. "Unfortunately, we're scheduled to leave here a week from Thursday." First thing tomorrow, they would make new reservations for the first available flight. He could not yet articulate his sense of urgency to get off the island and dark feeling Martin and his friends would do everything to prevent them from leaving.

Martin winked at Terri. "I'm sure we'll be able to talk you into staying longer."

She smoothly avoided committing herself. "Ivo invited us to a *feijoada* on Saturday. Does he live nearby?"

"About fourteen miles back toward the city, in Sambaquí. And we're invited too. In fact, wherever you go, don't be surprised to see all the same faces. Social life is quite incestuous in Floripa. For example, on Sunday, we'll be throwing a *churrasco* for you, a Brazilian-style barbecue, to which everyone here is invited."

When Terri returned to the women, Flávio maneuvered Rick into a corner. The architect's eyes were those of a haunted man. Although he spoke slowly in generalities, Rick understood it had something to do with the *urubús*. "Are you telling me the vultures got to Irene's body while she was still alive?"

Before Flávio could say more, Zé took hold of his arm and pulled him away for what Rick suspected to be a rebuke.

Will we ever learn the truth about Irene?

CHAPTER II.
AN ODD QUESTION

fter a multi-course dinner of rice, black beans, and the local seafood, the men and women went to separate sections of the double-ambience living room. Terri and her new friends sat in a semi-circle around Sônia. Louisa busied herself going through Martin's CD and DVD library. The men sat at a hexagonal green felt-covered gaming table by the bar for poker, cigars, and brandy. Martin smoked his cigar and walked with Rick outside along the perimeter of the lawn.

Rick, who did not smoke, sipped from a snifter of cognac and waited for his friend to speak. The night air was chilly but bearable because he was adequately dressed and filled with good food and drink. The tide made a light rustling sound as it washed the sand. A breeze wafted an invigorating aroma of salt water. The constellations and half moon were clear and bright. For the first time in his life, he saw the Southern Cross in a place other than the flags and stamps of Australia and New Zealand. North, south, east, and west continued to elude him.

When they reached the metal gate to the beach, Martin stopped and drew a deep breath. "So, Rick, what do you think of our paradise?"

"It's really something." Rick hoped Martin missed his deliberate ambiguity.

"And how do you like my friends?"

Rick thought it best to be diplomatic. "Zé, Flávio, all of them . . . they're nice guys. You all seem to be part of an extended family, and Maria Lourdes is a lovely young woman."

"I knew you and Terri would accept her once you got over the surprise." Martin looked towards the house. They could see the women conversing. "She seems as if she's already one of them."

Rick agreed but did not necessarily believe that was a good thing. Nothing specific. Just a feeling. Gut instinct. "First thing tomorrow, I'd like to go over to Nelson's agency and change the date of our flight out of here."

"Excellent. I told Maria Lourdes that once you kids saw Floripa, you'd want to stay longer."

Rick did not want to reveal their plans to leave as soon as possible. "Level with me, Martin. Is there something you haven't told us about Irene's death?"

"No, there's nothing else. And is there anything new with your family?"

Rick noted he changed the subject away from Irene again. "Status quo."

"Sorry to hear that."

Rick did not like to be reminded of his family. "All bridges are burned, the foundations demolished."

Martin saluted Rick with his drink. "That's what I always liked about you, respected you for, even when you were a callow teenager. You're an independent bastard, totally inner-directed."

"Yeah, I gotta' do what I gotta' do no matter what others think."

"Well, as they say, the best revenge is living well."

"Not if those who harmed you are also living well or better."

"Good point. Irene and I, we used to remark how much we enjoyed watching you and Terri grow together and mature into self-sufficient, talented adults. I suppose we liked to think we had a little to do with it."

"More than a little, Martin. I don't know where we'd have been without the two of you. Damn, I can't believe Irene is . . . "

"And you still have no regrets you didn't get your degree and go into one of the professions?"

Because Martin would not discuss the circumstances of Irene's death, he had no choice but to go along with the flow of conversation. "Only one regret, that it would have saved me the trouble of always explaining why a bright lad like myself didn't finish college."

"College degrees aren't worth what they used to be unless you go into one of the professions or have to pass through the Human Resource gauntlet if you want to work for a large corporation."

"I know degrees count for zilch in the dance world."

"Rick, be completely honest with me. How serious are Terri's health problems?

"We're missing too many important competitions because of them, but I'm more worried about her emotional state. Her dad passed away in April."

"Yes, I received your e-mail."

"It brought back old memories and nightmares. I can't get her to talk about them though."

"Understandable. She'll come around."

"There's more, though. Terri's been in a nervous state since last October when she turned thirty. She fears time is running out on her and that another serious injury will force her to call it quits before we've achieved our goals."

"Yes, she said you had to drop out of a big competition last month."

"Nothing new. You know that Terri's health has always been erratic. She's so damn susceptible to colds and viruses. We took care of her feet, but her back can spazz-out at any time, like it did just before we came downstairs. Doctors have yet to recommend a treatment or medication that works. Sometimes a visit to the chiropractor temporarily fixes the problem.

"Rick, as you know, we will do everything possible to improve Terri's health during your visit."

"The thermal baths you mentioned at the airport?"

"That and more."

"Like some exotic plant extract from the Amazon?"

"Close enough. I promise ... you'll soon be seeing changes in her stamina."

"Whatever works, but even if nothing does, I appreciate all you're going to do for her."

"I'm delighted to hear that. And what about you? Are holding up okay?"

"No physical complaints. My health and stamina are fine."

"Is there anything related to your dancing you want to improve?"

"Technically, we're as good as any couple, but I'm not as creative as I'd like to be, need to be. Even if by some miracle Terry did have perfect health, we'd still probably lose placement points because our routines are not all that original or spectacular. We'd have to find a way to improve our choreography if we want to become world champions. It hurts us most during the open part of the competitions."

"Open?"

"Free-style routines."

"I see, and who are the best choreographers?" Martin listened to Rick recite their names. "Felipe Gotelli? I've heard of him. An Argentine Italian, I believe, who is reputed to be the supreme tango maestro."

"And more. Gotelli would never work with us. It's not only his high fees. He's completely booked creating tango and DanceSport routines for the wealthiest of clients, new ballets, and Broadway shows."

"Perhaps you may encounter him while you're here. He has a beach home in Jurerê."

"Another of your miracles?"

"For you and Terri, anything is possible."

CHAPTER 12.
"IT IS PARADISE"

Rick preferred to go inside, but Martin wanted to continue their conversation. "And how is your studio doing?"

"We're taking on almost more than we can handle thanks to the new ballroom dance craze." Rick described the TV shows, *Dancing with the Stars* and *So You Think You Can Dance.* "As you know, we run an honest establishment with no gimmicks, phony promises, or ten thousand dollar contracts filled with penalty loopholes to bilk gullible lonely widows."

"And there must be plenty of them in Florida."

"There are, and those with money can be too demanding. We'll never prostitute ourselves to please unreasonable cash cows. We also do everything ourselves. No second-rate assistant teachers or barracudas to steal our students."

"What's the going rate these days for lessons?"

"We charge seventy-five dollars for a full hour."

Martin whistled. "That much?"

"A hundred, sometimes more, for specialized instruction. When Terri is healthy, we can combine to give ten to fifteen hours of lessons a day, and we teach five, sometimes six days a week."

"That can add up to big bucks."

"It may seem that way, Martin, but we're not getting rich. We pay out plenty to our coach for lessons in style, technique, presentation, and choreography. We also have to cover the cost of her airline tickets and meals. Tatiana lives in Montreal and flies to Florida for a week each month to train us and our most advanced students. Then there's our costumes. At least Terri makes her own. Otherwise we'd be paying in the thousands for them. Even so, the materials she uses for her ballroom gowns and sexy costumes for Latin don't come cheap, and she has to create new dresses and accessories every year. I have to shell out more than a thousand each for my tuxedos and Latin suits and much more for all the shoes we go through in a year."

"What about the prizes you win?"

"They're never enough to cover all we lay out for transportation, hotel, meals, and competition fees. And, we're paid meagerly for one-night exhibitions and the routines we've done on Caribbean cruises. Martin, we're like any other small business. Medical bills are high because we have no group insurance. Terri makes several visits each week to her chiropractor, and I need see my masseuse almost as often for deep-muscle treatments. Bank loans are taking another big bite of our income. We increased our debt load last year when we bought the adjacent bay to double the size of our studio, and there's still the mortgage on our condo. Even though it tripled in value because of the real estate boom, we do not want to risk refinancing it. Because of the recent run of hurricanes, our insurance rates, condo fees, and assessments have skyrocketed. Still, we're fortunate to be earning a good living at something we enjoy doing. That's why we were able to pay off your loan so quickly."

"It's good you did. We didn't think we'd need it, but the hundred thou' came at the right time."

Rick looked at Martin surprised. Not rich, the Kraais had always been comfortable, with an adequate liquid reserve. Although they had retired from teaching on a meager percentage of their salaries, the sale of their house in L.A. two years ago had netted them a profit of several hundred thousand. Martin also had liquidated his late parents' home in the Richmond District for another nine hundred thousand.

"What happened? Was it a bad financial investment?"

"Worse, it was a lifetime emotional investment in family gone sour." Martin flicked his cigar ashes over the gate onto the sand below. "Irene's never recovered from the betrayal."

"What are you talking about?"

"You remember how she used to speak with so much love for her first cousin, Margarita Fonseca, who lived in São Paulo?"

They had met Irene's millionaire cousins several times whenever they visited L.A. and stayed with the Kraais. He remembered Margarita as a short and pudgy overly made-up woman with pretty features on the surface but of ugly temperament. A spoiled brat with no intellect and of limited education, she spent her time mostly in conspicuous spending. Irene had worn blinders regarding Margarita; treating her as the kid sister she never had, and Martin had kept his mouth shut for his wife's sake. Margarita's husband, Mauricio, was even worse according to Martin, a typical Brazilian son-in-law, the type who postured as a successful entrepreneur without ever succeeding at anything. Margarita had controlled the money and consistently humiliated her husband in front of everyone by handing him cash to pay for meals in restaurants and purchases in stores.

Rick remembered how, over the years, Martin and Irene had helped the Fonsecas transfer dollars from Brazil to accounts in the States and Europe. The Kraais also put dollars in the Fonsecas' U.S. banks before each trip to Brazil and then received Brazilian currency at the most favorable black market rate. He listened and hurt for Irene while Martin narrated the appalling details of the betrayal.

"We transferred more than five-hundred thousand dollars to Margarita's New York bank to pay for the bulk of our construction and furnishings and to purchase a Brazilian car. Then, after we arrived in Brazil, we discovered that Margarita's twenty-two year old son, Rodrigo, who had signature access to all his parents' bank accounts, had embezzled our money to finance his drug habit and a major buy."

"The bastard."

"Despite their assorted multi-million dollar bank deposits and savings in the U.S. and Switzerland, the Fonsecas refused to make good the theft. First, they lied that no such transaction had taken place. Then Margarita told us it was our problem to collect from her son, that she and Mauricio were not getting involved, and never to communicate with them again. You can imagine how their cruelty devastated Irene. She never got over the maltreatment and betrayal by her favorite cousin. Those thieves behaved as if we were the criminals when we asked them for our money." Rick knew Martin was not the type to let people get away with hurting his wife and theft of his money. "What did you do?"

"Legally, we were in deep guano. We had signed nothing. We simply transferred the money to their account in the States, as we so often had done before with faith and trust. Even with a notarized, signed document, can you imagine the cost of dealing with lawyers in two countries, the time and energy it would take, and more money for bribes? Economically, we were wounded, but not ruined."

"So they got away with it."

"Not quite." Martin laughed nastily. "There is a God after all, it seems. Margarita and Mauricio, their son, Rodrigo, and daughter, Janine, all died in an auto accident a few months later."

Rick's heart ached for Irene. He looked out towards the surf, as if he might be able to see where she had drowned. "What happened to Sônia must have been shocked Irene as well."

Martin glanced towards the house. "Yes, that was another disappointment. Not that it's Sônia's fault. She had a severe disfiguring burn all over her body from that accident. Like I told you, one of those buboes, propane gas cylinders, leaked and exploded when she used her lighter. Sônia was fortunate to have survived, but she requires much medication to numb the pain. Even the thermal baths don't always help her. Then there's the obvious problem between Ivo and Louisa."

Rick did not want to get into unnecessary gossip. "Was Irene depressed at the time of her drowning?"

"You're thinking she might have committed suicide. True, she was unhappy here and wanted to return to the States. But no, Irene was not suicidal. She went out for a swim, as she did every morning. The water was calm, I've been told. I spent the day on business in the city. A police patrol found her body later that afternoon on a deserted stretch of beach at the far end of Jureré. She apparently had a stroke, drowned, and washed ashore. Zé made sure they conducted a thorough autopsy."

"Rotten luck. You'd been planning this move for years."

"Yes, rotten luck. Irene, for all her intellect, was one hundred percent Brazilian when it came to certain beliefs. Before she drowned, she'd become convinced someone had made a *macumba,* a curse, against her."

"Who and why?" Martin did not reply. "You won't mind if I say that Terri and I were surprised you'd married again."

"Maria Lourdes was very supportive."

"Then you won't be returning to the States."

"No, this is my home now, although I keep most of my dollars in the U.S. and I'll always be an American citizen. Rick, you and Terri are still very young. You haven't reached your prime yet. I'm in my sixties, yet I really believe I've discovered my fountain of youth here."

"That's obvious. What is it? The water? The air? The food?"

"It is paradise, as you'll soon discover. Come now, let's go back inside and join the others."

Rick accepted a beer from Lico and ate more seafood cakes while he scanned the living room. On the surface, it was a typical social evening, a normal gathering of friends for dinner, gossip, and cards. Yet, everything seemed askew, off-angled and shadowy, like an expressionist film noir. Was he in a state of shock over Irene's death or punchy from a long trip and lack of sleep? Most likely the latter, he concluded.

Terri, on the other hand, seemed to be in better spirits, chatting with the women as if they were longtime best friends. Well, whatever, he'd go with the flow for the rest of the night. Tomorrow, he would be able to think more clearly after some much needed sleep.

CHAPTER 13.
"THEY'RE COUSINS."

Black wings extend overhead.
All light obscured.
Matte gray faces.
Slate blue beaks.
Humid breath.
Essence of decay.
Unearthly hissing and other malevolent sounds.
Sharp talons.

ick awakened in the stifling bedroom and reached out for Terri. She wasn't there. He swung his legs over the edge of the bed and took his wristwatch from the nightstand. It was almost eleven in the morning. Where was she? They had to leave the island today.

He massaged his throbbing temples. He couldn't remember coming upstairs last night and falling asleep. He never had an opportunity to ask Terri what she'd learned from the women and to tell her about his conversation with Martin.

He forced himself to stand, peeled off his damp pajamas, and opened the window and wood shutters. The weather must have already reached eighty degrees. Not a cloud in the sky, it was a gorgeous mid-winter day. He heard growling. In the yard of the house next door, a trio of sable brown Dobermans were fighting over a large meaty bone. On the roof, a pair of sleek black vultures perched like carved medieval gargoyles. Maybe he'd heard them arrive while sleeping, and the sound of their beating wings had contributed to his nightmare.

Terri entered wearing a two-piece *fio-dental*—dental floss—string bikini bathing suit, kissed Rick, and handed him a mug of coffee. "Morning, Cardinho."

"When did you get up?"

"Seven-thirty."

"Why didn't you wake me? It's already past eleven."

"You needed the sleep, and you drank more than usual."

"You may be right. I don't recall saying good night or going to bed. Did I do or say anything to disgrace us?"

"Not a thing." Terri went to the window. "It's a glorious day. Last night the women told me we could expect radical changes in the weather."

"Then it's best we fly out of here today." He noted her lack of response. "Where's Martin? We'll need a ride into the city."

"He had business to take care of in Floripa, and Maria Lourdes went over to the mainland for a dental appointment. We're on our own until dinner tonight."

"Then we're stuck here for another day?"

Yet again she did not respond. "How soon will you be ready for your breakfast, a walk on the beach, and a swim?"

"Give me a few minutes."

When Rick joined Terri on the patio for coffee, orange juice, and breakfast rolls, the glare bothered his eyes, and he put on his sunglasses as a vulture landed on the low wall between the lawn and the beach.

"So incredibly beautiful, isn't it?"

"If I heard Flávio correctly last night, he implied that the *urubús* may have gotten to Irene before she was found. That's probably why Martin had her cremated."

"Rick, I have to tell you. I'm no longer resentful that Maria Lourdes has taken Irene's place."

He worried something strange was going on with Terri. She either ignored his questions and comments, or she changed the subject, the same as Martin did when they arrived.

"After speaking with Maria Lourdes, I've begun to feel like we're old friends. She even called me *filha* several times . . . the way Irene used to."

"Daughter? That's odd. She must be close to your age. Did Maria Lourdes tell you how she met Martin and Irene?"

"Sônia introduced them. They're cousins."

CHAPTER 14.
THE OLD MAN, THE SEA,
AND THE URUBÚS

The tide washed across the sands of Ingleses, covered their feet, and receded. "Now that I have met this blond adonis, senhor Rick, I am convinced that we should do something about him. This day!"

Sônia shook her head. "Rosa, you are always so impatient."

Maria Lourdes stepped over a penguin carcass. "I agree with Sônia. We must give Rick a chance. Martin will control him."

"You are too emotionally involved. Martin was wrong to invite them. You should have discouraged him, Maria Lourdes."

"I tried, but he wants to help Teresinha."

Rosa kicked the remains of a large fish. "Senhor Rick asks too many questions. He may discover everything and interfere."

Sônia silenced Rosa with a regal gesture. "He will learn only what I want him to know. In the meantime, Rosa, do nothing unless I give permission. Ivo has yet to decide if he really wants Teresinha. And we have more immediate problems to deal with. Do you not agree, Gabriela?"

"Yes, my Flávio is getting worse."

Sônia faced Sambaquí. "And there is still the matter of that woman."

Before they stepped onto the beach, Rick turned his attention towards the shanty on the west side of Martin's house. Its tin roof rested on unstable aluminum siding. The grounds teemed with three generations of shabbily dressed men, women, and children repairing nets and caulking a large rowboat beached on the sands in front of their yard.

"Martin's neighborhood isn't so exclusive, after all."

"They're *pescadores,* an *açoriano* fishing family."

He wrinkled his nose. "What is that odor? It smells like a sewer. I didn't notice it last night. The wind must have shifted. I guess the *pescadores* have outdoor plumbing."

"I thought so too, but they're not the problem." Terri pointed at Martin's neighboring house on the east side. "It's coming from there. Martin told me all about it when we had coffee earlier this morning. Unlike in the States, there's no central sewer system on the Island. Each homeowner is responsible for constructing his own *fossa grande,* septic tank or great sump, which must be replaced every two to five years. He's already registered a complaint with the authorities, and they told him it will be taken care of, eventually."

"*Amanhá,* tomorrow."

"And see that large tower in the center of his neighbor's house, and the one like it in the middle of Martin's home, all rusty brick and resembling a castle keep? He explained to me that every home here also needs its own *caixa d'agua,* water tower. There's no central aqueduct system or water-well in Ingleses."

Rick saw Lico watching them from the walkway along the side of the house. All in black again, black like the vultures, except his skin was the color of the red Brazilian soil. One more mystery he preferred not to dwell upon.

They sidestepped a column of inch-long black ants about to march across their feet when they walked out the gate onto the warm sand. Rick stopped to take his first close look at the black vulture that had not moved from the wall. This *urubú* was typically shiny blue-black with matte gray face and beak, and, he guessed about three feet tall. It paid no attention to them and faced out to sea, its keen brown eyes searching the water's edge for carrion.

Terri stretched out her arms and took in the entire crescent shaped beach. Extravagant homes, fishing family shacks, and glass-front condos extended in both directions to the steep cliffs that embraced Ingleses in geological parentheses. "Well, which way do we go?"

He squinted into the bright sunshine through his dark glasses. It seemed that winter in Brazil, the equivalent of January in the States, was no different from Florida during the Season or southern California most any time of the year. Along the strand, individuals, couples, and entire families sprawled out on choice locations of sand, jogged, or walked along the beach for exercise. At the far section of beach to the west, a half-dozen surfers rode the waves while their girlfriends in string-bikinis watched them from the shore.

Nearby, two children no older than seven or eight were building an impregnable mound-castle near the water: It was a classic Moment of the Child, that pristine time of joy and innocence, with glistening tranquil sea, womb-warm sand, and bright benevolent sun. Rick remembered when he played at his own small section of beach in Santa Monica, and he yearned for those lost self-absorbed childhood days until the reality of the *urubús* intruded.

Not far from the children, a pair of vultures waddled towards a plump penguin that had been deposited on the sands by the waves. Scattered along the entire crescent of beach, more *urubús* stood in pairs, threes and fours or perched on the houses. Each occasionally spread its wings as if to absorb the sun's rays. They seldom moved out of the way when humans approached, and then never very far.

He pointed at a small island, over which more *urubús* were circling. "Wonder if it has a name."

"It does. *Ilha Mata-Fome*, literally the island of hunger-kill."

Rick focused on the vultures. "That could have several meanings."

"Martin said that not too far away from us, on the eastern side, there's another small island off shore, *Ilha das Aranhas*, Island of Spiders."

Rick thought they should have named Santa Catarina, Ilha dos Urubús. He placed an arm around Terri's shoulder, and she snuggled against him as they strolled to their right towards the oldest section of Ingleses, dominated by the spire and cross of the local *igreja* about four hundred meters away.

"Terri, I'm completely disoriented. I need to get a fixed point regarding north and south."

"I know what you mean. We'll have to get used to the sun traveling across the north." She let the tide cover her legs to mid thigh. "Rick, it's warm, like the ocean in south Florida. And clear too. I can see all kinds of fish swimming by."

"And almost as many washing up on the beach, penguins too. I never noticed they had potbellies until now. That ought to satisfy these vultures."

"Last night, Sônia told me the penguins are fatter these days because of global warming, and fish have become more plentiful because water temperatures have increased around Antarctica."

"That ought to please the *urubús*." He stopped when Terri performed some stretching exercises. "How's your back?"

"Almost one hundred percent." She gripped his arm. "Rick, I have to stay healthy. I must, if we're ever going to be champions."

"You will."

She looked out to sea. "Maybe they've got some magic potion, some exotic substance here in Brazil to help me. Don't most of the miracle drugs come from rare plants found in the Amazon rain forest?"

"So they say, but they're probably harvested for export to the big pharmaceutical companies. While we're here, and I hope for no more than another day, we may be vulnerable to exotic diseases."

At the airport, Rick had seen signs alerting everyone to the dangers of dengue fever, and they had already been bitten by more than their fair share of exotic bugs that, he prayed, were non-toxic. Even now on the sands, he was careful to avoid stepping on bug-eyed, creepy-crawling little monsters and those large black ants. He preferred to believe they were pacifists and not armies of *marabunta* like the ones he'd read about years ago in *Leinengen versus the Ants.*

Terri stroked his back. "I wish you'd taken a shirt. There's no smog here to filter the sun, and you're certain to get a severe burn."

"Next time." Rick wasn't concerned. His initial sunburns usually developed into a light metallic tan. "Some very impressive homes here."

No two were alike. The architecture ranged from cold gray concrete and glass to warm brick or painted stucco. He figured the typical house covered about six thousand square feet, and all had well-manicured, broad expanses of lawn. Between them on unimproved parcels of land were the shacks and sheds of fishing families. Ingleses appeared to be a community in transition, on the verge of becoming an exclusive beach resort with many of the native fishing families clinging to their property to the bitter end.

Halfway to the church, they stopped near one of the aluminum shacks intrigued by a leathery, bearded old man in tattered shorts. He stood as motionless beside a lifeboat as one of the *urubú* sentinels and squinted out to sea. A half dozen men ranging in age from early teens to late forties sat behind him on a long bench in front of the shack. When the old man motioned with his hand, the fishermen sprinted to the boat, pushed it into the water, and rowed about a hundred meters. A black vulture descended and perched on the prow. The men paid no attention to it while they cast their net and harvested an abundance of fish.

During their return to shore, one of the men placed a large fish in the *urubú's* beak, and it flew away. The fishermen beached their boat, divided their catch, which they placed in ice-filled coolers, and returned to the bench for a smoke, soft drinks or beer. They watched the old man again peer out to sea, ready to move at his next signal.

Rick took Terri's hand, and they continued their walk. "That's more Hemingway than Hemingway."

"Yes, it's another world here."

"Possibly the end of the world. Or world's end. Although on the surface it's postcard-perfect, I sense a bleakness . . ."

"That's because you're a city-slicker."

"Maybe." A pair of *urubús* stared at them unblinking as they passed a partially devoured penguin. "These vultures remind me of most of the women we met last night, dark, sharp featured, and always watching."

Terri laughed and squeezed his hand. "Now I know you're hallucinating. I didn't want to tell you because of your enormous vanity, but they all thought you were very good looking."

"Seriously, what do you really think of Maria Lourdes? You've been able to communicate with her."

"She's very gracious and concerned about our comfort. She absolutely adores Martin."

"Were you able to learn what he does with his time? He was vague with me last night."

"When I spoke with him this morning, he told me he's dabbling in real estate. That's why he spends most of his days traveling all over the island."

"I never figured Martin to be an entrepreneur. He always said that when he retired, he'd write some serious novels."

"He explained all that to me. By the time Martin and Irene sold their house and his parents' home in L.A. and began building here, he'd been bitten by the real estate bug. He says he's doing very well."

They left the beach and went a block to the old *igreja*. Rick froze when they stepped inside the church and saw what appeared to be a half dozen vultures scattered among the pews. He recovered when he realized they were old women in black. His mind raced with bizarre connections: *Urubús*, these old women, the dark women he met last night all merging into one, then separating again.

"Is something wrong, Cardinho?"

"No, I've been thinking about Irene." He went with Terri to light candles for her, and they prayed silently to help deal with their grief.

During their walk back to Martin's house, Rick studied the vultures and listened too. He heard a familiar noise, the same unpleasant sound from his dream, which now sounded more like a sucking of air.

Which of these vultures is male? Which is female? And who spends the night doing what and which way to whom?

CHAPTER 15.
TIO RICARDO

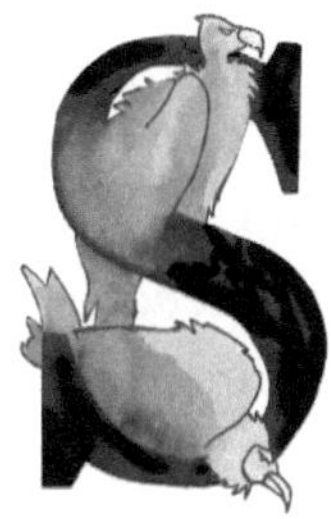*he spent much of the afternoon thinking about Teresinha's beauty, gracefulness, and sexual appeal, everything she could have desired for her son. If Ivo truly were attracted to Teresinha, he would not be able to keep his hands off her. If he wanted Teresinha, she would give Rosinha permission to dispose of Rick, Martin and even Maria Lourdes too if they interfered.*

But first, she intended to deal with that woman.

As the philosopher wrote, nothing can be more pleasurable than to plan the destruction of an enemy, and then get a good night's sleep.

"Fantastic. Delicious" Terri attacked her second portion of bloody rare *picanha*, a special Brazilian cut of lean beef.

They sat on benches at a long table in the barn-sized restaurant, *Ataliba*, with the Kraais and the Batardis who had brought Tinho and Jairzinho, their hyperactive blonde sons. The restaurant, which was on the mainland off the north side the bridge, served meals *rodizio* style, all-you-can-eat. Waiters circulated among the patrons with skewers of beef, pork, chicken, links of sausage, and gravy soaked rolls. In the middle of the restaurant, one could choose from an abundant buffet of pasta, *farofa* (a type of manioc), rice, potatoes, black beans, salads, vegetables, soups, and desserts.

Rick thought Sônia to be no less repulsive than last night, oily-flabby, covered in unclean layers of brown wool, emanating a foul odor he had yet to identify, with nasty little Bubi in her lap. He tried not to stare at the bristly mustache and hairs on her chins. The woman had told everyone where to sit and placed him between Maria Lourdes and Louisa, so Teutonically fair and buxom in a faded blue and yellow flowery print dress. She was starved for serious conversation, but every time they attempted to converse Sônia or her son interrupted.

At first he had been annoyed that Sônia wanted Terri seated next to her pathetic unpleasant creep of a son. Ivo's dark brown shirt was partially unbuttoned to expose scattered hairs on his narrow chest above his bowling-ball beer belly. If he made the slightest move on his wife, Rick intended to set him straight physically. He soon realized that Ivo ignored Terri and instead ogled and flirted outrageously with every young woman in the restaurant.

"*Tio* Ricardo!"

"*Tio* Ricardo!"

"*Por favor, Tio* Ricardo"

Rick stood, bent his arms, and flexed so that seven-year-old Tinho and five-year-old Jairzinho could hang from his biceps yet another time. The boys yelled and laughed when he lifted them off the floor. He had been roughhousing with the children from the moment the Batardis had arrived at Martin's house. His exposed sunburned arms stung from the boys' hands. He had on a loose, black cotton short-sleeve shirt, white denims, and thongs. Terri was tan and lovely in her fuchsia and baby-blue striped cotton sundress, a cheerful contrast to the blandly attired Batardis and Kraais.

He thought the boys were adorable in their identical gold trimmed navy blue warm-ups, which, Louisa had explained, was their school uniform. He felt sorry for them because they craved masculine attention. Their father had completely ignored them until now when they wanted to play. He ordered the boys to stop bothering Rick, who tried to assure him it was all right.

Ivo slapped Tinho, the eldest, who ran crying to his mother, and he ranted at Louisa for not controlling their sons. Rick observed Sônia watching them pitilessly. What did she have against Louisa? And why was she so unloving towards her own grandchildren? He caught Terri's gesture warning him not to get involved, although Ivo deserved to be reminded what a blow to the face felt like.

Terri was deep in conversation with Maria Lourdes, whose raven black hair fell loosely onto her navy blue sweater. Uncanny how much they did look like sisters. From what she had said this morning, Terri no longer felt as he did that it was unnatural to see Martin with a woman other than Irene. He worried that he and Terri were no longer on the same page about leaving Florianópolis as soon as possible and that things did not seem right. He'd also never seen her eat so much meat.

Martin ordered more beer. "So, *meus amigos*, what do you think of this restaurant?"

Terri waited until the waiter had served her third portion of meat. "I've never experienced anything like it. Although there are some *rodizio* style restaurants in southeast Florida, we've never tried any of them.

"Terri isn't much of a meat eater. At least she hadn't been until this evening. Rick raised his glass of *Brahma chopps.* "Great draft beer."

Martin touched glasses. "Yes, Brazil has the best beer outside of Germany."

Ivo slapped the table. "Brazilian beer is better than German beer."

Martin stood and patted his flat stomach. "Time for more rice and beans."

Rick intended to get some answers from Sônia while Martin was away from the table. "About Irene's death . . ." he began in Portuguese.

"We will speak English. I can always use the practice." Sônia shifted her bulk on the bench, fed her min-pin a piece of bloody beef, and stared at him through thick glasses. "Irene's death was quite distressing to us, and she was so looking forward to your visit. Irene talked about you and Teresinha often. It is as if we know everything about you."

"*Idiota!*" Ivo yelled more invectives at his wife. "Look at their behavior."

Louisa cringed under his verbal assault not knowing what to do. Rick saw Tinho and Jairzinho playing with other children and running between the tables. None of the diners or staff seemed to mind. Ivo left the table ostensibly to reprimand his sons but instead moved closer to speak with a slender attractive brunette at the dessert buffet.

Rick noted she was another young woman who resembled Terri. Were all the women on this island inbred?

He resumed his conversation with Sônia "Then you don't think there was anything unusual about Irene's death?"

"Why should there be?" She did not take her eyes from Ivo and the brunette.

"The vultures . . ." He deliberately let his voice trail off.

Sônia removed her glasses and studied him as if he were a scientist's impaled insect. "It was an accident. Irene drowned."

"She was an accomplished swimmer."

"And believed she had the stamina of her youth. Unfortunately, there are limits that prevent immortality and even an exceptionally long life. I advise you to forget about Irene."

CHAPTER 16.
TOURING

he following morning they rose early because Martin and Maria Lourdes wanted to take them on a tour of the beaches before going into the city. Rick sat the front passenger seat, Terri and Maria Lourdes in the back. Another day had begun with no independence of movement for them, no opportunity yet to see a travel agent. At least Martin had sprayed the interior of his car with room freshener.

They passed through a mix of subtropical and temperate plant life in combinations of pale to vivid greens growing in the rich red soil. Every few kilometers, the coastal landscape changed from wild coast to broad beach, to communities of luxurious homes or fishing family shacks, to solitary beaches of massive dunes, to inlets and grottoes beneath serrated ocher rocks and cliffs. The island was a scenic dichotomy: rustic isolation, and the conveniences of a teeming city; luxury condos overlooking palm-lined avenues facing the bay, and *favelas* scattered all over the island; broad beaches, and isolated rocky coves. *Calma e tranquilidade*, calmness and tranquility everyone said; but Rick sensed that what one saw on the surface was illusion.

"I think you made the right choice," Terri said as they drove away from the open, unspoiled beach of high dunes and outstanding surfing at Joaquina on the eastern side of the island. "Although it's beautiful here and everywhere else on the island, I like Ingleses the best."

Rick agreed with Terri and added that the diverse beaches and the countryside had one thing in common, the ubiquitous *urubús.* They hovered above, fed off carrion on beaches and roads, or perched on rooftops, walls, and gates.

Martin blasted his horn at a car moving too slowly ahead. "There's a beach for everyone's taste, from open sands to rocky coves. In my opinion, we're sitting on a commercial time bomb waiting to explode. Once we get the attention of developers from the major industrial countries, Florianópolis will become *the* vacation spot of the world."

The drive to the Baía Norte took them to a steep hill for a last spectacular view of Lagoa Conceição. Ten minutes later, they reached the western side of the island. Martin made a sharp left between the condos facing the North Bay and drove into Florianópolis Central. Traffic was heavy, the sidewalks filled with people.

Terri touched Rick's shoulder. "There's so much life on the streets, not at all like Jupiter."

"You'll become even more enchanted with the Island as the days pass," Martin said. "I always have the feeling I'm in a big city, even if Floripa is small in area. I'm having it both ways. I've bought back the last thirty or forty years. You're younger, of course, and don't have my perspective, but I find it no more primitive here than the beach communities in California when I was a child and teenager. And I have the most modern luxuries too. It's all a trade-off wherever you live, except I think I've come out far ahead."

Rick looked at the rooftops. "I guess all this activity explains why we don't see any vultures here."

Martin sounded his horn to ward off a Volkswagen Golf veering into his lane. "I suspect our *urubús* fascinate you more than you care to admit."

"I know I'm impressed by them," Terri said before he could reply. "They're absolutely magnificent creatures."

Maria Lourdes squeezed her hand. "I have always thought so too. Our men should be as good looking." The two women giggled together in the back seat like loving sisters.

Martin reminded them that the city was a triangle. If they continued straight along the base of the hills, they would end on the Baía Sul heading towards the airport. He turned right onto a wide boulevard, and drove to the top of a steep hill. He pointed out a massive multistory supermarket across the street that took an entire block, *Angeloni's*, which was where the women would be shopping after lunch. That concerned Rick who did not like the idea of being separated from Terri, even if for a few hours on this strange island.

"And where will you be taking my husband, Martin? It better not be one of those notorious Relax Clubs I've heard about."

Martin chuckled. "Not today."

Terri's eyes narrowed. "Not ever!"

"Of course not, an pay no attention to Ivo's fantasies. I'm going to take Rick over to Nelson de Andrade's travel agency to convert some of your dollars into *reais*. He gives the best black market rates on the island."

Rick looked back at Terri. "Great, and I'll have him change our tickets."

"I knew you'd want to stay longer."

Rick did not argue with Martin. He and Terri had already decided to change their reservations to the earliest possible departure date, and then present him with the accomplished fact to avoid unnecessary arguments and more delays.

"Rick, after we see Nelson, I have to stop at my bank. It's around the corner from Ivo's store, and the women can meet us there. As you kids will soon discover, everything in Florianópolis is in easy walking distance, a matter of minutes. It's really the good life here."

After Martin parked his Monza on a side street, they ambled two long city blocks down a steeply angled hill worthy of San Francisco towards the gray concrete and glass *Hotel Diplomata* on Avenida Paulo Fontes. "We do plenty of walking here. I hope you don't mind."

Rick was conscious of emissions from carburetors that had no anti-smog devices. He took Terri's hand "Be careful. These steep hills can injure your back."

"I won't let them. I feel too good, and Maria Lourdes told me we're going dancing tonight after dinner."

"If we're still here."

"I doubt if we'll be able to get a flight out of here today."

Rick reluctantly agreed. It would be mid-afternoon by the time he saw the travel agent. They would be spending another night on the Island, so they might as well make the most of it and watch the native Brazilians dance. He took in the sights and sounds of the city. It was a pleasant eighty-plus degrees with a refreshing breeze and little humidity. Except for the bureaucrats who wore jackets and ties, the locals dressed casually. Martin had on a brown short-sleeve shirt, khaki shorts, and thongs. Maria Lourdes wore a white blouse, slate blue shorts, and tennis shoes. Terri had followed her suggestion to dress for the weather and put on her red and white blouse and shorts ensemble.

Rick chose to wear an aqua long-sleeve shirt with his white denims because he needed to cover his severe sunburn and let it heal. He remembered to place his wallet in a front pocket. Martin carried a dark brown leather purse slung over his shoulder, as did all the other men on the streets. He did not miss the contradiction: Macho mustaches, gaucho attitudes, and purses.

Terri must have been reading his mind. "Martin, be sure Rick buys a purse like the one you're carrying. I think they look neat."

94

CHAPTER 17.
MARIA LOURDES' SURPRISE

Rick drank his beer and looked out the window of the twelfth floor restaurant of the *Diplomata*. Their table for four had an unobstructed view of the bay, bridges, and mainland. The sky was clear blue, with cotton-white protean cloud formations, the water azure and calm. Service by the staff in gray tuxedoes was impersonally obsequious and efficient. Terri chose the same entree as Maria Lourdes, shrimp Grego, breaded individual large shrimp and cheese. Rick's shrimp Bahama had a flavorful cream sauce.

Martin trimmed the fat off the edges of his thin steak. "Now that you've seen most of the island, I hope you can understand why I've decided to live here permanently."

Rick watched sailboats take gentle breezes and glide across the Baía Norte's clear surface. What lay below its depths? Whatever it was, something there may have killed Irene. It would be futile to express his feelings to Martin. Instead he repeated the familiar cliché, "As the Brazilian Consul in Miami told us, Florian . . . excuse me . . . Floripa is so beautiful it hurts."

"Maybe you'll retire here one day."

"That's a long way off, Martin. We've just turned thirty."

"You and Terri could live six months here and six months in the States. Follow the sun. Lead a life of perpetual summer and early autumn."

"We have that all year in Jupiter."

"But we have no hurricanes here. Strong winds, but no hurricanes."

Rick wondered just how powerful those winds were. "Anyway, we have to train, compete, teach, and run our studio."

"And these aren't exactly easy commuting distances," Terri added.

"There's also the political instability."

Maria Lourdes shook her forefinger at Rick, its nail longer than Terri's, "You must remember that Brazil is a large country, larger than the continental United States. Other states may be depressed economically, but Santa Catarina is thriving. Although the larger cities are polluted and crime-ridden, we are not New York, Washington D.C., or Detroit. Florianópolis is not Rio or São Paulo."

Rick gaped at Maria Lourdes. He had been listening so intently to everyone's Portuguese he thought he'd been translating accurately until he realized she was speaking perfect unaccented American English. How could it be? Martin had told them Maria Lourdes had never traveled beyond Santa Catarina. Even if she'd had extended conversations with Irene and Martin during the past year, how could she be familiar with so many disparate communities in the United States?

Terri was equally astonished. "Maria Lourdes, you didn't tell me you spoke English."

Rick looked at Martin. "You never mentioned it either."

Maria Lourdes paid no attention to their reactions and went on in English, "I know why you think the Brazilian Government is unstable. That's a result of reading all the biased reporting in the *Los Angeles Times* and other

American newspapers and magazines."

Martin gestured for the waiter to bring them another round of drinks. "Maria Lourdes is right. Remember how Irene used to get upset because they never wrote anything positive about Brazil or even report that the Brazilian President had met with our President?"

Rick was accumulating a novel-length collection of unanswered questions. How could Maria Lourdes have known what had been written in the only major L.A. area newspaper? Had Irene and Martin given her more than English lessons and included a thorough indoctrination in every aspect of life in California. Unlikely, even if Maria Lourdes had an exceptionally retentive mind and an eerily imitative talent. If he closed his eyes, he could hear Irene talking.

If Terri wasn't going to question her more aggressively, he damn well would. "Maria Lourdes, where did you learn to speak such perfect American English?"

"I'll give you a perfect example of relative governmental stability," Martin interrupted. "Remember that couple who rode the elevator with us and got off at the eleventh floor?"

Rick remembered. The man had been short, dark, and sharp-featured, more Indian in appearance than Azorean and his wife a well-groomed bleached blonde dressed in an ambiguous international style.

Martin had a self-satisfied smile. "He's the Governor of the State of Santa Catarina. He's residing at this hotel while his mansion is being renovated. Did you see any bodyguards or an entourage of toadies?"

"None." Rick was not interested in the Governor. He wanted to know more about Maria Lourdes' fluency in English. "Getting back to . . ."

"Our Governor doesn't need security." Martin raised his glass. "I tell you, my young friends, this is paradise."

CHAPTER 18.
"ASK SÔNIA."

 aria Lourdes arrived after lunch. Terri left with her, and promised Rick she'd learn about the woman's sudden mind-boggling fluency in English. In the meantime, Martin deflected all his questions about Irene and Maria Lourdes during their short walk into the center of town. Shoppers filled the sidewalks, and Rick was amused by clusters of men at the corners arguing and gesturing during their midday *cafezinho* break. Teams of women in starched green and white dresses swept the streets. Attractive policewomen in immaculate khaki uniforms patrolled in pairs and directed traffic.

All the remaining clichés Rick had held regarding Brazil were obliterated during their walk through Florianópolis. He often thought of countries in colors. Mexico was cheerful white, green, and red; Spain somber burnt gold and black. Brazil ought to have been primary splashes of gold, green, orange, and aqua. If the beaches and vistas on the steep hills of the island were spectacular, the local inhabitants generally gave him an opposite impression. Many appeared as drab as the populations of wintry eastern European countries when they were under control of the communists.

They passed arcades, bazaars, and several square blocks where no autos were permitted. If he not heard

Portuguese spoken, Rick would not have believed he was in Brazil or in any other specific country. For every dark, sharp featured man or woman he saw a fair blue-eyed blond or redhead. Florianópolis was as much a melting pot as any major city in the States, except for one image he'd held regarding Brazil. With few exceptions, everyone was white.

"Martin, I thought Brazil had a higher percentage of blacks."

"It has, and plenty of people of mixed blood too."

"Where are they?"

"Mostly in the north and the big cities of course."

"Why not here in the south?"

"*Quem sabe?* Who knows? Perhaps the climate here doesn't agree with them."

"Physically? Or is it a racial thing?"

Martin shrugged. "I suspect they're less comfortable in the southern states, which are the most non-Portuguese European parts of Brazil settled mostly by Germans, Italians, and Slavs."

"And I'm curious about Lico."

"Really?"

Rick thought Martin's comment sounded like forced nonchalance. "I can't get a handle on his ethnicity. Is he from some obscure indigenous tribe?"

"You'll have to ask Sônia. She found him years ago."

"Found him?"

"I told you. Ask Sônia."

"I will." Rick knew he had touched a nerve, given Martin's harsh response. He hoped Terri would have more success with Maria Lourdes.

Martin took him into an enclosed mall. "The locals call it a *shopping*." When they entered a men's clothing store to buy his purse, he said, "Rick, let me bargain as if I'm buying it for myself. The *catarinenses* have a love-hate attitude towards tourists. They need them as a necessary source of income and complain that they cause too much traffic congestion. Everyone here delights in *exploitado*, the local pastime of gouging all strangers, most specifically the Argentines, who cheerfully overpay, always in dollars. The *catarinenses* literally pick them clean."

"Like the vultures along the roads and beaches?"

Martin stroked his mustachio. "Yes, you might say so. During our summer season, the Argentines will pay an average of one hundred dollars a day, in U.S. dollars, to rent a small room or shack at one of our beaches, and considerably more for an apartment or condo. Entire families will give up their homes to the tourists and sleep in tents or out in the open while they earn enormous sums of rent. For the rest of the year, everyone works as little as possible, and not even the most generous bribes can encourage them to move."

Rick sniffed the stores leather goods: Wallets, belts, and purses. The odors were unpleasant, but milder and different from the mystifying pungency that had nauseated him in Martin's car and emanated from Sônia and the other women.

The Brazilian system of retail sales bewildered him. After he self-consciously selected a black leather purse, Martin haggled the price down, took a receipt from the saleswoman, and guided him to a bulletproof cage. He paid the cashier and received another receipt, which he handed over to the saleswoman for the merchandise. Apparently, no salesperson could be trusted to touch money or credit cards in Brazil, family members too if Irene's cousins were typical of the country.

They went across the arcade corridor to Nelson de Andrade's travel agency. Martin's friend looked natty in a lightweight pastel green blazer, soft canary yellow turtleneck, saffron yellow cotton trousers, and pale gold leather loafers. His mustache was neatly trimmed and nails buffed to mirror-reflection.

Nelson seated them at his desk and ordered one of his employees to bring them *cafezinho*. Rick saw photos of Fátima and two dark girls on the desk. "Your daughters are very pretty."

"Thank you. Maria Elena is six now, and Josefa is four." He rapidly counted through two thick wads of currency and handed them to Rick. "Your five hundred dollars worth of *reais*."

"Nelsinho has given you the best black market rate in Floripa," Martin assured him, then said in English, "You don't need to count it. He is honest."

Although Rick wasn't all that sure about Martin's assessment, he did not want to offend his host. He stuffed the *reais* into his new purse and placed their tickets on the desk. "Senhor Nelson, my wife and I wish to change our travel plans. We are scheduled to leave next Thursday, but we want the next flight available to São Paulo, Rio, or Bahia."

"What are you saying, Rick? Have we offended you and Terri in some way that I'm not aware of?"

"I'll explain later, Martin."

Nelson punched his computer keyboard and read the LCD display. "I am sorry, senhor Rick, but all flights are filled, even through next week."

"Every one?"

"Yes, it is now the peak of our winter season." He studied the tickets. "However, I will confirm your flight to São Paulo for next Thursday. Let us hope they do not cancel it at the last moment."

God forbid!

Martin lit a cigar. "Don't look so unhappy, Rick. I really want you and Terri to stay with us longer. So does Maria Lourdes."

Nelson smiled at Rick. "Yes, everyone will be delighted if and your lovely wife extend your visit with us."

Rick next suffered through a long half hour at Martin's bank, Sudameris. The transaction, which would have taken a few minutes in the States, included yet another *cafezinho* break and gossip with the manager.

After banking, they walked along Rua Deodoro, one of the streets where autos were prohibited, and crossed the gridlocked Rua Tenente Silveira to Ivo Batardi's lingerie store. Rick thought it poorly situated in the middle of a busy street, which had limited parking, and too narrow, with barely enough room for a modest window display. He could not imagine how Ivo made a living, even if all his stock were sold in a month. It could be a front for a more disreputable business or plaything for a spoiled mama's boy. How convenient for a womanizer to specialize in lingerie.

He thought that the small store had an unnecessarily high overhead, unless all worked on commission. The cashier and two of the saleswomen were middle-aged, wearing cheerless colors and cheaply made-up. The youngest salesgirl wore a clinging white linen dress, and he recognized her as the woman Ivo had spoken to in the restaurant last night.

They heard shouting, and Louisa and her two boys hurried down the stairs in tears chased by Ivo, his face crimson, his expression murderous. He shook his wife one last time and cuffed the oldest boy before they moved outside and continued their quarrel on the street.

Rick understood the words *estúpida, idiota* and *filha da puta* among the Pórtiñol abuse spewing from Ivo's mouth. "Maybe we ought to leave, Martin."

"No, it's normal behavior for them. It's been going on for years. They really love each other."

He could not believe what he had just heard. What had changed the mentor he had known all these years?

An abusive family situation created no big concern for Martin who used to react with a strong sense of outrage at the slightest misdeed. He and everyone else had forgotten Irene's existence, and there was Maria Lourdes' inexplicable fluency in English and familiarity with American geography and politics in Irene's voice?

Normal behavior, Martin had said. Just what the hell is normal in Florianópolis?

CHAPTER 19.
PECKING ORDER

e must do something about Flávio immediately."

The delegado saluted Sônia. "Consider it done. And senhor Rick, too?"

Martin was horrified. "No, Rosa, Not Rick. Terri will never cooperate if you harm him."

"Why do you protect the gringo?"

"Terri loves Rick. And I owe him." Martin kicked at the sand. "He must not be touched, no matter what."

"That is not up to you."

Sônia had enough of their bickering "I shall decide. I, and no one else!"

"Will someone tell that woman to stop it?" Sônia screamed when Lico carried her into the upper level of the Silveiras' condominium. "Tell her to stop that dreadful noise now."

Louisa froze at the piano in the media and gaming room, which included a fully stocked bar, pool table, card tables, and two rows of beige leather lounge chairs facing a wide-screen wall-size HD-TV and media center. Rick thought her Chopin etude had been concert level quality, and he was disgusted but not surprised when Ivo did not defend his wife.

"Tell her to get away from that piano. Now!"

When Ivo moved towards her with his hand raised, Louisa left the piano and ran downstairs. No one followed.

Valéria broke the silence. "Now that Tía Sônia has arrived, we can watch our new friends dance."

Rick held his breath when he kissed Sônia's unappetizing oily cheeks. After he inhaled again, he cupped his hands over his nose to absorb the mild fragrance of his aftershave instead of the woman's rank essence.

Lico placed Sônia in the front and center lounge chair. Ivo asked his mother if she was comfortable, if she was close enough or too far away from the screen. Martin offered to fetch a pillow for her back. Edmur brought over a tray of canapés. Zé handed her a bourbon and soda. Sônia impatiently waved them away and demanded that Terri sit between her and Ivo.

Rick scanned the room. Despite the gaucho posturing of the men, Sônia was the leader of this clique, deferred to, respected, and feared. Even Martin shrank in her presence. Zé, Edmur, Nelson, Ivo, and Martin, with variations on the same theme, were physically alike. Their women too, except Louisa. Ivo's wife who was definitely an outsider, never spoken to, never allowed to contribute. Sônia referred to her as *that woman* and harshly addressed her as *you*. Why was she so abusive and hateful to her daughter-in-law and grandchildren?

Flávio is another outsider. Always staring at me. What is it he wants to get off his chest?

Rick briefly locked-in with Lico's deep-set eyes. The goliath in black stood by the bar, inanimate as sienna stone. Rick concluded he was more than a *faxineiro*. There was nothing subservient about him. He shook off the thought, and worried he might be overreacting to Lico's mysterious presence. At least he had no unpleasant scent.

Rick turned towards Terri who was in animated conversation among the women. Was she having the same thoughts and reactions?

After Edmur inserted one of their dance DVDs in his player and the lights dimmed, Rick went outside past the swimming pool and barbecue area and rested his arms on the railing. He watched the play of lights from traffic below and homes across the bay. He had too much on his mind to enjoy the view: How Irene had died; how and why Martin had changed; and Maria Lourdes' fluency in English. Terri had told him that when they went shopping together this afternoon, Martin's wife spoke only Portuguese and avoided explaining how she learned to speak perfect English.

They were trapped. They would not be able to fly out of here before next Thursday. Every flight was booked solid, so he'd been told. All the car rental agencies in Florianópolis had told him the same thing it was the height of the winter season and none were to be had. Would he have been more successful if Martin had not come with him? Maria Lourdes did offer one of their three cars any time he and Terri wanted to drive around the Island on their own, with Lico as their chauffeur.

Tonight, they were the Silveiras' guests of honor, surrounded by the same people who had greeted them the evening they arrived, the same people who would be at Ivo's *feijoada* tomorrow. He should not have been surprised. Irene and Martin had complained after every trip that everyone in Brazil operated in a tight incestuous circle of family and friends.

But Martin is no longer complaining.

Rick heard giggling as a body leaned against his back and a soft breast pressed into his elbow. Antônia and Stefania Silveira, Edmur's nubile daughters, had been flirting with him from the moment he and Terri had arrived. Seventeen-year-old Antônia was a tall, robust flaxen-haired freckled blonde with bangs, and fifteen-year-old Stefania a luscious honey blonde whose hair was curled in baroque ringlets.

Martin had explained the contrast between the girls, who did not resemble either parent, and their three swarthy younger brothers. They were the daughters of Edmur's first wife, a blonde of German-Ukranian origins from Londrina in the State of Parana, who had died shortly after they moved to Florianópolis.

An accidental drowning, Martin had said.

The girls insisted that Rick show them some dance steps although Stefania was more interested in just being in his arms. They also pleaded with him to attend Stefania's debutante ball a week from tomorrow night. He told them they could learn some steps by watching the DVD, and he escorted them inside.

When the screen went blank, Terri and Rick received applause and effusive congratulations with a few exceptions. Sônia sat in silence with an unpleasant face. So did Rosa whose expression suggested she had been sucking on lemons. Ivo decreed that International-style professional dancing was out of step with Brazil, because *that* was no way to dance the samba.

The tinkling of the dinner bell ended his harangue, and they went downstairs into the dining room. Lico carried Sônia to her chair at one end of the table. Louisa sat between Zé and Nelson, her eyes swollen from weeping, her face flushed. She would not look away from her plate.

Stefania and Antônia competed with each other for Rick's attention throughout the meal, and Terri winked to let him know she took no offense. She was flattered rather than jealous when other women found him attractive, provided they did not disrespect her.

The men tried to include Rick in discussions of the daily exchange rate between the *real* and the dollar and the value of real estate on the island. Martin too, the same

Martin who had never talked high finance back in L.A., the same Martin who used to express his contempt for all non-entrepreneurial money movers. Tonight, he casually threw around six and seven figures in U.S. dollars. How was he surviving economically? It wasn't only the cost of his home at Ingleses. He had monthly expenses, which, everyone said, were high in Floripa even for Brazil.

All Martin's friends lived luxuriously. The Silveiras' condo had amber swirl marble floors, rosewood and jacaranda paneling, and gold fixtures in the bathrooms. Valuable antique carpets and furniture filled each room, and the kitchen was computerized. The basic apartment downstairs covered more than seven thousand-five-hundred square feet and covered an entire floor reached by two elevators, one for social, and the other for service. It had five full bedroom suites, a sumptuous master suite and bathroom complete with hydro massage, wet and dry saunas, and separate maids' quarters. This upstairs media room led out to a patio and swimming pool, all with an unobstructed view of the Baía Norte.

Rick could not begin to guess how much money Edmur and Valéria had invested in it. Martin had told him that another unit available on the fifth floor was being offered for a million two hundred thousand U.S. A bargain by American standards, except that was for only the unfinished walls and air space. Everything else would cost extra: Tile, carpeting, walls, installation and hook-ups of wiring and fixtures, creation of closets, all the bathrooms, kitchen, and laundry room.

Then there was the problem of furnishing the condo. By the time the buyer completed an apartment, it could run to over several million dollars, and all that might take as many as three years, sometimes as much as five to complete, with all the hassles involved in synchronizing work schedules, dealing with craftsmen and laborers, and obtaining permits.

Where did all their money come from?

The Silveiras' condo also impressed Terri. "Valéria, your home is *lindíssimo*, very beautiful."

"Thank you."

Maria Lourdes exchanged nods with Martin. "Would you like to have an apartment like this, Teresinha?"

"If we had the money to afford one, we'd pay off our mortgages, stop teaching, and close the studio. Then Rick and I would spend all our time training with the top coaches to become national and then world champions."

"All that may happen sooner than you think." Everyone looked at Sônia who had spoken for the first time at the dinner table.

"Your performance was indeed inspirational," Edmur said. "Tonight, we must show you the night life of Floripa and go dancing."

Not everyone wanted to make the rounds of the local *boites*. The Zimmermanns went home immediately after dessert. When Lico carried Sônia to the elevator, she ordered Louisa to come with her. Ivo had a previous engagement. Rick guessed he had a rendezvous with the young saleswoman. Antônia lamented that she had already made a date with her boyfriend, and Stefania, who was bitterly disappointed that her parents would not let her go, pleaded one more time with Rick to stay for her party next week.

While they waited for the elevator in the social hall, Flávio took Rick aside. "We speak . . . in privacy, yes?"

He was pleasantly surprised that the architect spoke English although it was halting and thickly accented. "And I have many questions for you. But when, and where?"

"*Segunda-feira*, Monday." He handed Rick his card. "*Onze e meia horas*, eleven-thirty in the morning."

The address was his construction site on the Baía Norte. "Is it about Irene?" Flávio's expression indicated an affirmative. "Will you tell me more about her, how she died? Martin won't . . ."

"I can say no more here." He paused and made sure no one else could hear. "*Faça o favor*, please, tell no one. And forgive me, *senhor* Rick . . . *especialmente*, especially not your wife."

CHAPTER 20.
SAMBAQUÍ

 er pain had intensified, but today was too important to risk taking the mind-dulling medication. *"Ivo has made his choice. It will not be Teresinha, but I still need her to resolve my other problem."*

"Then what do we do with her gringo *husband? Eliminate him?"*

She glared across the veranda at Louisa and spit. "No, it must be that woman! Let the plan unfold, Rosa. See how Rick reacts. If Teresinha can convince him, good and well enough."

"Don't you think the view from here is even better than the one Martin has in Ingleses, Rick? It's so much more interesting."

"There's hardly any beach."

"Yes, I prefer plenty of sand too."

Terri and Rick stood on a huge ocher boulder ten feet above the water at the edge of the Batardi compound. Cotton-soft white clouds broke the monotony of the pale blue sky above the aqua and turquoise bay. Directly across from Sambaquí, buildings gleamed white in Estreito on the mainland, while to the left, they had an unobstructed view of Floripa's magnificent condominiums eight miles away along the curved littoral of the Baía Norte. Below them, the tide receded to create clear pools between rocks and stones that trapped small fish along with seaweed and other detritus before the water rushed in again.

Rick felt the unfiltered sun sear his face, burn through his lime green shirt and yellow shorts, and sting his arms and legs. He thought seriously about walking back across the lawn to the veranda and sit under the shade of the canvas awning. The temperature was in the eighties with only an occasional gentle breeze to ameliorate the increased humidity.

He appreciated the vivid hues of butterflies and hoped he would not be a feast for the exotic insects, common bees, and flies humming and buzzing across the veranda and along the perimeter of the yard over cactus, succulents with shoots of bright flowers, hedges, and clumps of blossoming shrubs. He drank his second beer, convinced that no other place on this planet had so many different spectacular views and radical shifts of terrain in so confined a space. Unlike the broad open beaches of Ingleses, Joaquina, and Jurerê, Sambaquí's shoreline had serrated rocky inlets and twisted trees with gnarled roots exposed between boulders and stones at the water's edge. To swim here, one had to tread carefully among treacherous layers of rocks before plunging into the water.

Unlike Martin's home and Edmur's condo, Ivo's misshapen two story house was a tear-down of rotting wood and peeling paint. He could afford much better. Why did he choose to live among so much filth and disarray?

Rick turned around to see what the others were doing, the same others they saw every day and night. Sônia sat alone with her ill-tempered min-pin on a frayed couch in the center of the veranda and crocheted. No matter the weather, day or night, she wore the same shapeless layers of brown wool. Ivo mixed *caipirinhas* at his makeshift veranda bar. He had two physiques, the muscular legs of a soccer player, and above his "sack of marbles" Speedostyle black bikini, a beer belly and skinny-flabby torso and arms. Ivo repeatedly touched his groin, and Rick suspected he was adjusting a sock or possibly a potato. Martin had written that many Brazilian males used falsies at the beaches to exaggerate their manhood.

Rick had not appreciated Ivo's suggestion that Terri purchase a *fio-dental* bathing suit or an even briefer style he called *C pacol*, which, he said, went places dental floss could not reach. The Silveira girls, Stefania and Antônia wore the latter. They posed provocatively and flirted with him.

Each woman had brought an *empregada* to the feijoada, and they were busy setting the tables, one inside the house for adults and another across on the lawn for the children. Terri calculated that even in Brazil it had to be terribly expensive to entertain and feed so many people. In the driveway, Lico waxed and polished Sônia's stately black Ford LTD, black as the vultures, black as his clothing, the ideal chauffeur for a vulturemobile.

On the lawn between the veranda and the rocks, Zé moved his lounge to face Nelson and Edmur. As best Rick could understand, they were arguing whether some local soccer star was over the hill. Flávio, who was waiting for Ivo to finish preparing his drink, caught Rick's eye. He cocked his head indicating he wanted to continue their brief conversation from last night, which was impossible at this moment.

Below them, at the water's edge where gentle waves immersed their feet, Martin and Maria Lourdes stood trance-like on a large rock. Perched on an adjacent boulder, a pair of black vultures also looked across the bay towards Estreito.

"*Umbigo!* Belly-button!"

"*Tio* Ricardo!"

An army of children charged towards Rick and Terri and interrupted their quiet moment. He roughhoused with off Ivo's sons, the Silveiras' three boys, and the Zimmermanns' five-year-old twin girls. "Here we go again, Terri. Round two."

"They adore you, and who can blame them? You're a natural daddy." Her eyes softened. "You ought to have been a father by now. It's all my fault."

"We agreed. Our life is too busy for us to be decent parents."

"Yes, I know, but after we become champions, everything will be different. I promise."

Ivo announced it was time to eat. The *empregadas* took charge of the children. The adults went into the dining room and filled their plates from a buffet.

Sônia saw Terri wince in pain when she sat at the long wooden table. "Your back is still hurting you?"

"It began giving me trouble last night while we were dancing."

Martin gestured a thumbs-up. "You should have seen them, Sônia. Their mambo was so exciting everyone stopped to watch them. Plenty of cheering and applauding too. Then at the very end of their routine, Terri's back gave her trouble."

"We shall definitely do something about your health problems while you are here, Teresinha. But first you must enjoy my son's *feijoada*."

Terri and Rick remembered that years ago Irene had described the components of the classic *feijoada*. Black beans were the foundation, its main ingredient. The cook then added white rice, pork, sausages, cured meats, bacon, tongue and other parts of the pig including ears, feet, and tail. In the north, some included vegetables and orange juice. Like any other national dish, no two recipes were alike. Only the method of serving was uniform among the individualistic Brazilians. The *feijoada* had even inspired Hector Villa-Lobos, Brazil's greatest composer, to create in honor of their national dish: *A Spontaneous Piece in Four Parts: Farina, Meat, Rice, and Black Beans.*

Ivo's cook had placed the white rice and cooked meats on a buffet separate from the beans with a tongue in the center. Martin advised Terri and Rick to first pile the beans on a plate, then the meats, and drown them in a rich bean sauce followed by another sauce of lemon, pepper and thinly sliced onions. Maria Lourdes showed them how she placed the white rice, kale, lemon rinds, thin slices of orange, and *farofa,* farina ground from the manioc root, around the edges of their plates.

Rick thought the meal was too heavy and cholesterol-rich, and the swarms of assorted bugs annoyed him. Apparently, Ivo did not consider it necessary to add screens. Terri surprised him. Her appetite seemed limitless as she went through three heaping helpings.

Ivo pointed at Rick's half-eaten portion. "You do not like my *feijoada?*"

"It's good, but I ate too many of Sônia's seafood cakes before lunch." He found them to be rich and addictive, which was probably why they did not allow the children to have any.

Screaming hysterically, Jairzinho ran in from the outside to his mother. Ivo left the table and moments later brought in a three -foot snake he had decapitated.

Terri shuddered and looked away. "I hate snakes."

"Yes, it is best to be wary of them," Sônia fed Bubi a sausage. "According to government statistics, there are more than twenty thousand snake bites annually in Brazil, about five thousand of them fatal."

Terri cringed against Rick when something large and brown insect zipped past the table at eye level. "What was that?"

"One of our flying cockroaches," Martin said. "You have them in Florida, I believe."

Rick watched another zip by. "These are twice as large as our palmetto bugs. I should have brought a baseball bat. One flying cockroach coming in, high and inside."

Terri grimaced. "Do that back home, and you'll have to clean up the mess. Yuck!"

Martin laughed with them. "If you're that squeamish, I know one part of Brazil you definitely won't want to visit, Mato Grosso."

Terri scanned the open door and windows for more flying cockroaches. "If it isn't a big city or on the ocean, you're absolute right."

Sônia spoke in English "Actually, Mato Grosso is quite an educational experience. It contains countless specimens of unique flora and fauna although one must be alert to the insects and vermin that swarm at certain times of day and night. Many years ago when I was a young graduate student, I went there on an expedition for the University of São Paulo to make contact with the Xavante, a tribe of primitive Indians. I especially remember how disagreeable the *tabanidas* were. They are less than two centimeters long, similar to the horsefly, but have a snout like a hypodermic. Of course, the best defense against them is either to wear thick clothing or move into the bright sunlight. Clothing makes one sweat, however, and then sweat-bees, about the size of honeybees, swarm all over you. They do not sting, nor do other smaller species of the bee, which enjoy crawling up our nostrils. But brushing away an army of sweat bees often disturbs the honey bees and aggressive wasps, which deliver the most painful stings that can swell one's face to monstrous proportions. If, on the other hand, you remain still, you might be attacked by minute fruit flies that find our eyes, nostrils, and mouths attractive. Other tiny creatures prefer entering our ears and make dreadful fluttering noises either on or near the tympanum. Yes, it can be a most disagreeable experience and might drive one mad. Of course if you run, brush them away, or move at all, it brings on the sweat again, and with it more swarms of sweat bees and wasps."

Terri shuddered. "How does one escape?"

"I think we'd need something like an astronaut's suit." Rick's surprise at Sônia's sudden volubility and use of English had turned to suspicion. He believed her description of Mato Grosso was more than a pedantic lecture. Was it a warning, or was she laying the foundations for them to accept something sinister?

Sônia fed her whining min-pin more sausage. "It is possible to walk out of their area, but then one encounters the exceptionally voracious *pium*, who live only in the sunlight. Their bites can result in lumps many times larger than the little beasts. As the sun goes down, the *pium* leave only to be replaced by the *maruim*, barely invisible midges. You never feel their bite. The effect becomes evident later in the evening. A severe itching and irritation. Pink to red welts, up to a quarter inch in diameter."

"Like the no-see-ums we have in Florida, only worse according to your description."

"Much worse. I can assure you of that, Teresinha. I have been speaking of daylight. After sundown, the usual hordes of assorted insects smash against the lights and drop to drown in our coffee, soft drinks, and beer. If you are foolish enough to go for a walk at night, you will encounter sand-flies small enough to go through the mesh of most mosquito nets. They deliver painful bites. And there are the ticks. So, as you see, in spite of our giant flying cockroaches, snakes, and oversized ants, life here is paradise compared to Mato Grosso and the big cities. And it's safer to swim in our ocean."

Rick took her bait. "Because there are no piranhas in salt water?"

Sônia shook her head. "No, I was referring to the *candirú,* a parasitic fish that thrives in the Rio das Mortes. They are around five centimeters in length, more or less two of your inches, exceptionally narrow, and attracted to urine. They will burrow into human orifices, which discourages nude swimming."

Rick's scrotum contracted "As bad an image as sliding down a banister that turns into a razor."

Terri crossed her legs. "How do you remove them, Sônia?"

"With extreme difficulty, usually by amputation or cutting, as they have spines on the side of their head which dig deeply like fish hooks into their victim when agitated."

The conversation at the table resumed in Portuguese, and if Rick concentrated from the beginning, he could follow the subject. He had his own topics and questions. Flávio might answer some of them if they were ever able to speak alone. For the moment, he thought Sônia might explain others because she was more sociable today.

"Martin told Terri and me that the Indians who lived here were buried vertically."

"That is true, Rick, and their burial grounds are protected by law as archaeological treasures. In any case, that was before the white man came."

He had asked that specific question because he remembered what he had learned years ago about the Zoroastrians in a comparative religions course. They also had buried their dead vertically in Towers of Silence to be food for vultures. The Indians of Sambaquí and *urubús*—was there a universal connection? He thought it best not to voice those speculations for the time being.

Flávio spoke for the first time. "*Senho*r Rick, *antes dos* Tupí, before Tupí . . ."

Sônia silenced the architect with a murderous glare, and Rick wanted to know what had upset her. "Tupí?"

Martin looked at Sônia as if asking for permission to reply, and he must have received it. "They're the basic linguistic and racial stock for nearly the entire continent of South America, the Guarani being the most well known of the Indian tribes."

"And who lived here before the Tupí?"

When Sônia and Martin did not answer Rick, Flávio broke the extended silence. "*Uma raça,* a race . . . *mais inteligente,* very intelligent, yes? *Antes* written *história,* before . . .*"

Sônia cut him off. "Of course they were Tupí. And it is really of no consequence." She waved her hand to signify an end to the conversation and closed her eyes.

Ivo went to his mother and asked if she needed anything. Lico motioned for him to leave her alone.

Lico's peremptory dismissal of Ivo reinforced Rick's instinct the colossus was more than a *faxineiro*. He sensed a psychic and emotional bond existed between the strange colossus and Sônia.

CHAPTER 21.
A DERANGED HOUSE

fter the *feijoada*, Terri and the women chatted at the table, and Rick prepared to siesta in one of the comfortable lounges next to Zé, Nelson, Edmur, and Martin who were already asleep. He was unable to nap. His stomach had expanded as if he'd swallowed the entire *feijoada*, and he could hear Ivo berating Louisa yet again for not controlling the boys while Sônia crocheted on the veranda and observed the abuse with overt approval.

When Flávio stepped onto an ocher boulder, Rick left his chair without disturbing the other men and walked to him. A pair of vultures soared above, and Flávio flinched. He moved closer to Rick and glanced towards the men. Martin had awakened and was staring at them.

"*Senhor* Rick, *Muito urgente*, most urgent . . . you must leave Florianópolis. It is not Brazil. It is not of this planet. Today, *Doutora Sônia, não disse nada* . . . she said nothing about her *importante* discovery in Mato Grosso."

He paused, and whispered something that sounded to Rick like *Kee-roo-pyr-ree.*

"What did you say?"

"*Os urubús . . .*"

"Rick!" Terri called from the veranda. "Come join us. We're all going for a walk."

Flávio took hold of his arm. "*Não fala* . . . do not tell your wife. Lembra, remember, *segunda-feira*, Monday, I explain all."

Martin approached them. "What have you two been talking about?"

"Architecture, the local variety."

"So specialized a subject? Your Portuguese must be improving." Martin placed a fatherly arm around Rick's shoulder. "But now you're going to see the most unusual structure on the island, yet. We're going to Sônia's house."

Lico drove ahead with Sônia. Martin walked with Rick on the one-mile stroll along the narrow coastal road. Terri and Maria Lourdes followed several yards behind the men. She had linked arms with Maria Lourdes. Rick wanted to know what they whispered about so seriously. Flávio had begged him not to tell his wife about their meeting on Monday. Were these dark women also asking Terri not to tell him their secrets? Would she?

Martin also looked back at her. "Terri, are you sure you want to see the house that belonged to your grandmother and where your mother was born?"

"Yes, Martin. I didn't think so when we arrived on the island, but now I believe I can deal with it."

The accessible part of the main road ended before massive wrought-iron gates. Martin led them to the left and down and a steep descent towards the water and over rocks until they approached a sprawling, shapeless tri-level house of natural stone and weather-stripped wood. Surrounded by gnarled arthritic trees, it nestled flush against the craggy base of a vertical cliff. Sônia's LTD was parked at the bottom of the road leading from the iron gates.

Martin held the door open for them. "I know you'll find this to be a most unusual house."

Rick thought *unusual* was an understatement. One side of the living room was the cliff itself. The other angled and paneled walls had been covered with impressionistic idealized landscapes signed *Whitby*. Each canvas included vultures circling high above against the sky. Opposite the cliff wall at the other side of the living room, a half dozen steps of natural stone led up to an open dining room and beyond to the kitchen where Lico was preparing *cafezinhos*.

Martin and Maria Lourdes led Terri and Rick down another six steps to a corridor. "Sônia went to siesta in her office. Come, we'll you show you the rest of the house."

Rick heard Terri say to Maria Lourdes, "You were right. It's definitely the most extraordinary house I've ever seen. I like it."

"Think of it as your home. Your mother was born here. She married here. And here you were born. It has been in the family for many generations."

Rick thought he might go mad if he had to spend even one night here. Had living in this house led to the homicidal madness of Terri's father? Each of the four bedroom suites had a private bathroom of marble, tile, and scalloped baroque fixtures of gold, with plenty of rust and mold too. Despite Terri's reaction, Rick viewed the house as a rotting corpse. Windows leaked air. So did misaligned doors. Paint peeled away from walls and ceilings. Warped paneling and mildewed furniture fabrics intensified the atmosphere of corruption and decay. From what he had seen so far, inside and out, he thought that this deranged mausoleum perfectly suited Sônia, but never his wife.

Alone with Martin in one bedroom, Rick saw a photograph of a handsome sun-bronzed lean young man standing by a partially completed landscape. "Who is he?"

"Roger Whitby, the artist who did those landscapes for Sônia you've been admiring. He was an exceptionally gifted artist from London with a great future."

"Was?"

"A most horrible death. Inexplicable too. Roger was an experienced athlete who loved to scuba and climb. He preferred to paint the outdoors and spent hours exploring the hills and cliffs behind this house. One day, he fell to the rocks below. Those landscapes on the walls . . . they are typical of what Roger painted until he started to see things."

"What things?" *Urubús and eviscerated corpses?*

"We don't want our wives to see them."

Martin opened a closet and took out several portraits of a ghostly, anguished creature uttering a silent scream, whose humanoid face floated in a dark abyss. Whitby's signature on the canvases looked as deranged as his subjects. Rick felt every hair on his body stiffen as his genitals tightened in primal self defense. He could not believe the painting was a self-portrait of Whitby himself, unless the artist had been taking LSD at the time. The subject was not human in a realistic sense. It was, instead, a rendering of a tormented creature, mammalian to be sure, but with disturbing humanoid characteristics. Its twisted mouth was open wide in a toothless scream from the depths of a limitless maw. Its pulpy eyes reflected some ultimate horror better not seen or imagined. Yet, Rick could not take his eyes away from the gruesome paintings.

"They make Munch's *Scream* seem like a shout of joy. I wonder what the artist really saw. Or do you think these are self-portraits and he was going mad?"

Martin shrugged and placed the canvases back in the closet. "Who can know the mind of any artist."

"How did Sônia end up with so many of his canvases?"

"Whitby lived here and paid his rent with the paintings." Martin held Rick's arm. "No, don't open that door. Sônia will not want to be disturbed."

CHAPTER 22.
AN APPETITE FOR FLESH

ick struggled not to show his impatience to get away from the island at the *churrasco*. Martin's Brazilian-style barbecue. It was no different from Ivo's *feijoada* and the evening at Edmur's condominium: The same couples, their children, and the *empregadas*; the same conversations about Formula One racing, *futebol*, real estate, and the *real's* relationship to the dollar.

He'd had enough of the same behavior too: Sônia crocheting with Bubi in her lap; Ivo belittling Louisa; more roughhousing with the children; Antônia and Stefania flirting; Flávio prevented from coming near him; Terri in intense conversation with the women; *urubús* soaring, feeding at the shoreline, and watching; and Lico the only exception, unusually slow of movement and tiring today.

Will Terri ever have enough of this sameness?

He went out of his way to speak with Louisa inside the house. Ivo's harassed wife understood much of his mix of English and gringo-Portuguese. She pointed out books in Martin's library she had read in her native language and told him that Mozart and Chopin were her favorite composers. He still could not understand why Sônia despised her shy, well-educated daughter-in-law and her grandchildren as well. It was unnatural. So was everyone's refusal to explain how Maria Lourdes had learned English, and much more. Today when Martin started to answer Rick's questions about Sônia's husband, Rosa elbowed him hard in the ribs to end the conversation. Martin was not his own man. How had that happened? He had never been the type to let anyone walk all over him. Maybe Martin had been lying about Irene's death because he was afraid of something, afraid of these insular *catarinenses*.

He watched Terri eat multiple portions meat as if her hunger for flesh had become insatiable. He no longer believed she shared his eagerness to get away from the island. He had trouble reading her, and she did not share her thoughts about Martin and his friends. He'd also begun to feel he was losing his wife to these women thanks to the relentless segregation of the sexes.

Rick had observed another kind of segregation: Louisa and her sons, Flávio's isolation, Edmur's daughters too—all of them blonde and fair—like himself and Irene.

After the meal as everyone prepared to go into siesta mode, he saw a larger number of vultures alighting along the walls. Terri came over to him. "Cardinho, I hope you won't mind. Maria Lourdes, all the women, they've invited me to spend the day tomorrow shopping with them, and afterwards we going to visit the thermal baths. It's some thirty kilometers to the south on the mainland."

"That's great. Those baths are supposed to help you." Terri's absence would give him an excuse to meet Flávio in town without arousing Martin's suspicions.

"Oh, and Martin said he'd be delighted to drive you into Floripa Central if you'd like to spend the day there."

CHAPTER 23.
BAÍA NORTE

artin savored a Cuban cigar in the passenger seat of his Monza. "You see? It is very easy to drive in Brazil."

Rick comfortably handled the wheel of Martin's car, and traffic along the four-lane highway to Florianópolis Central was light as he cruised at 80 kph. *No noticeable odor of urine-treated leather. Have I become used to it?*

A good twenty minutes away from Florianópolis, he decided the time had come to end their small talk. "Martin, we've known each other for fifteen years. You've been more than a best friend. You've been a father to us. Terri and I, we owe you so much."

"It is I who owe you. I owe you a life, Irene's life. That afternoon when you rescued her from those scumbags, it gave us an extra fourteen years of a great marriage. That's when we made a firm decision to do everything we could for you. And Terri."

"You paid us back many times over. The moral support. That altruistic no-interest loan for our studio."

"True, it wasn't good business. Potentially risky, and we didn't even become silent partners. Still, it worked out okay in the end."

"Better than we expected."

"I never told you, Rick, but it was an emotional decision that went beyond paying you back for saving

Irene's life. I'm still outraged that your family won't accept Terri and your careers as professional dancers. We wanted to give you kids a head start so you'd make a success of it sooner and prove to your family how wrong they've been."

Rick doubted they would change their minds. His natural mother had died of ovarian cancer when he was seven. Shortly after the funeral, his father, a successful corporate attorney, married a wealthy widow with two sons and passed away eight years later when Rick entered high school. He left everything to his second wife. When Rick started going steady with Terri, his stepmother and older stepbrothers insisted he stop seeing her. Geographically challenged, they regarded Terri as a generic Hispanic and worse, the daughter of a crazed murderer who carried his bad blood. After graduating high school, he and Terri moved into an apartment, which gave his stepmother an excuse to disinherit him. His stepbrothers, one a lawyer and the other a real estate developer, also severed relations.

"Rick, I really want to do more for you, especially in the matter of Terri's health. Maria Lourdes is worried about her too. That is why she's taking her to the thermal baths today. You'll see an improvement tonight. Guaranteed. There's something very special about this island."

Rick could not have agreed more although not the way Martin intended. "Are you all right?"

"I'm thriving in paradise."

"Is there anything Terri and I can do for you?"

Martin alerted him to reduce speed as they approached the highway patrol checkpoint with wrecked cars on the side of the road. "You really want to know how I'm adjusting to Irene's death. What can I say? It was a shock. I felt the loss. Still do, although I love Maria Lourdes. It's a different life for me now. Am I making sense, Rick?"

"I guess so. But you're not in some kind of trouble, are you?"

"Why would you think that?"

"Being in a foreign country, alone on a strange and remote island."

"Believe me, Rick, I am not alone. I have Maria Lourdes and many fine friends. I'm leading a very good life. A life of choice. Understand this. When Irene died, it was as if I also died with her. Death, however, can lead to rebirth. Yes, I have been reborn here. I want you and Terri to share . . . " Martin paused.

"Share what?"

He shook his head. "Too soon, it's still too soon."

They drove the rest of the way in a heavy silence, broken only by Martin's directions. He told Rick to park on the steep hill above the *Hotel Diplomata*. After they got out of the car, he pointed beyond the busy street towards the southeast. "This is Rua Tenente Silveira. It will take you past Ivo's store. You remember where it was?"

"Yes, in the center of town."

"I'll meet you there around four o'clock." Martin grinned at him "You look like a native with your purse. All you need to complete the image is a mustache although you're so blond I doubt if anyone would notice it."

Rick self-consciously adjusted the strap over the shoulder of his cobalt blue short-sleeve cotton shirt and made sure he had a small wad of *reais* in the front pocket of his white denims. "I hope to speak like one as soon as possible."

"You're doing fine. I recommend *Democrata's* for lunch. It's a block past Ivo's store, on the same side of the street. Great steaks. Good wine list too."

"I might give it a try." Rick intended to dine elsewhere, anywhere to avoid running into Martin and his friends."

Martin got back into the Monza. "Then, *até breve*! See you shortly."

"*Até breve*."

He watched Martin drive off, or attempt to. The Monza moved about ten feet before coming to a stop. Traffic was bumper-to-bumper, pedestrians shoulder-to-shoulder on the sidewalks.

Rick walked several blocks to the crest of Tenente Silveira before looking back. No sign of the black Monza. He back-tracked to where he had been dropped off and walked in the opposite direction from the *Diplomata*, past *Angeloni's* supermarket, to the major intersection of Avenidas Des. Amo Hoeschel and Rio Branco. He had studied a map of the city after Terri left with Maria Lourdes and felt adequately oriented even though the street names changed every few blocks. If he went to the right, he would reach Central again, a block behind Ivo's store. To the left and a shorter distance away was the Baía Norte.

Before proceeding to Flávio's office, he went into a travel agency near the intersection. The owners confirmed what Nelson and all the others had told him last Friday. It was the height of the winter season, and all flights were booked.

Ten minutes later, Rick stood in front of a nearly completed twelve-story condominium along the strand on the Avenida Rubens de Arruda Ramos not too far from the Silveiras' apartment. He went up a wide flight of black-and-white terrazzo stairs to amber-tinted glass front doors and entered a massive marble and wood lobby where an elderly armed security officer sat at a desk. After a difficult exchange between his *gringo* Portuguese and the guard's *catarinense Pórtiñol*, he was able to translate that Flávio had neither come to work this morning, nor had he left any message for him. He used the guard's phone to call the architect's office and received the same response from his secretary.

On his own because Flávio obviously would not be meeting with him today, Rick walked along the Baía Norte deep in thought. Had everyone been right about the architect, that he was unstable and unreliable? No matter, he and Terri would be leaving on Thursday. Three more days. Three long days and longer nights.

An enticing aroma of garlic wafted by and reminded him he was hungry. He saw a half block away *Macarronada Italiana*, a restaurant Martin had pointed out as one of the most popular in Floripa. He hesitated outside and watched a gang of ragged preteen boys swarm over cars driving into the angled parking slots. The urchins opened doors, offered to clean windows, and promised to protect the automobiles from theft and vandalism for tips.

Other young entrepreneurs hawked flowers among customers dining on the outdoor patio of the restaurant and inside. They tugged at sleeves, interrupted meals, and successfully begged more money from the patrons. Their *exploitado* had no effect on business. The restaurant was filling to capacity for lunch.

Rick felt a hand on his arm. He tightened his grip on his purse and turned around. A small boy handed him a package wrapped in butcher paper the size of a small book. From Flávio? No sign of him anywhere along the strand. How had he been identified? "Who gave this to you?"

The boy shrugged his ignorance, and Rick gave him a generous tip. He went inside the restaurant and selected a table in the deepest recess with an unobstructed view of the entrance. He would not be surprised if within minutes Martin and his friends joined him for lunch.

Paranoia city! He tried and failed to understand why his instincts told him that would be so terrible, aside from more repetitive conversation. After ordering beer and cannelloni *quatro queijos,* four cheeses, Rick unwrapped the package. It contained a small cassette player and tape but no note.

He scanned the restaurant to see if he recognized any among the patrons. *Good, all strangers.* He asked himself again who could have identified him for the boy outside. Flávio, most likely. Then, would it not have made more sense for him to have left this package with his secretary at the construction site? And if it had been Flávio, why hadn't he included an accompanying message? No, it had not come from the architect unless he was incapable of acting rationally. Then who else? Obviously Martin or someone from his crowd. But that didn't make sense either. Martin and his friends had done everything possible to prevent him and Flávio from speaking alone.

Rick had enough of his own dithering. He set the volume at low and placed the player against his ear. He almost gasped aloud when he recognized Irene's voice:

CHAPTER 24.
"THIS IS NOT BRAZIL."

July 17th

Am I going mad? Only three weeks in Brazil, and already I've come to believe that someone has made a *macumba* against me.

Who? And why?

All those years of retirement planning down the drain. And it's my fault. I let Martin talk me into moving to Florianópolis. He's loved it, wanted to retire here, ever since we visited Sônia after she moved here eighteen years ago. I hate it. No! Worse than that. I fear it. I am alone, no one to confide in. No one understands. Martin thinks it's homesickness, but I know better.

Yes, someone definitely made a *macumba*. I should have heeded the signs. They began at customs in Rio the moment we arrived. We had all the necessary documents, medical records, even police forms verifying we weren't criminals. Yet, they confiscated our passports as if we were indeed undesirables and demanded a document, which didn't exist. A simple document in which Martin swears I am his wife and we have no children or other dependents. The Brazilian Consul in L.A. still swears that no such form is required. Martin had to be given special clearance so he could rush over to the U.S. embassy for the document. That kept us in Rio an extra six hours.

Written on the flag of Brazil are the words *Ordem e Progresso*. Order and progress indeed! Brazilians have always referred to their country as *the land of the future*. A foolish fantasy!

Why didn't I resist moving here? How could I have forgotten why I emigrated to the United States more than thirty years ago and proudly became a citizen? Now, I'm constantly reminded about the dark side of Brazil. The poor quality of health. Signs warning of dengue fever. Louisa's boys have worms, and they're upper-middle class.

And everywhere that maddening Third World mentality. Tunnel vision. Lack of imagination and initiative. Inability to innovate. Absurd literalness. Yesterday, I went inside a new hotel in Ingleses and asked the clerk what time they began serving dinner. He said seven-thirty. Martin and I arrived at eight, but the restaurant was closed. My fault, of course. I should have asked if it was open in the winter. It would never occur to a Brazilian to volunteer information. If one were to ask, Do you have the time?, the inevitable reply would be a very serious, Yes.

Brazil is no longer my *patria amada*. The beloved homeland has lost its morality and become a nation of liars and thieves.

Rick could not begin to imagine the intensity of Irene's pain when she described how her favorite cousins had stolen their money. One thing he did know. She expressed more pain and hurt from the betrayal than Martin had conveyed.

August 1st

He says no, but I know my husband. Martin is planning some form of revenge against my cousins. How can I stop him?

August 18th

Not only have we been betrayed by my family, we're repeatedly lied to by Sônia Batardi, once upon a time my best friend. How she has changed! For the worst! Sônia is a monster. And she lives in a home designed for monsters. She and her oedipal clone, Ivo, do everything they can to prevent Louisa from establishing her pediatric practice.

Rick wondered why no one told him Louisa Batardi was an MD. Of course, he hadn't asked.

Sônia advised that we buy land on a beach facing north, and assured us all was calm and tranquil there, that the south winds would come about every ten days and last for only three days at most. Lies, all lies. Sônia failed to warn us about the north winds, which are more violent in intensity.

Worse than the winds, those ubiquitous vultures, blue-black and matte gray, and so secure among themselves, waiting and watching. For what? For whom? For me?

At least Ingleses has the best beach on the island, of that, Martin and I are in total agreement.

Rick heard the anguish in Irene's voice as she described in detail her maladjustment to the Island. When the Kraais first arrived on the island, they had lived in a rented house at the other end of Ingleses, a big four bedroom brick house that on the outside seemed like a rock against the elements. It was a Brazilian-built house, however: No insulation between poorly laid roof tiles and the rooms below; misaligned windows letting in howling winds, mosquitoes, and large repulsive flying cockroaches; inefficient electric showers; and gas cylinders that had to be replaced monthly if one wanted hot water on demand.

October 4th

Impossible! You can't bribe anyone here for better or faster service, because during the Brazilian summer the Argentines come by the hundreds of thousands, pay everything in U.S. dollars, and are shamelessly exploited by the natives who regard all mainlanders as *gringos*. Then gorged and sated, totally without ambition, the *catarinenses* laze around the rest of the year."

October 11th

The winds. Always the winds. Maddening winds from the south, from Patagonia and Antarctica, the bottom the world. No place to hide.

"Am I becoming phobic? I'm even beginning to doubt Martin, my husband, the man I've loved and lived with for the past thirty years. Martin seems preoccupied. And Sônia is so completely changed. Over the past two years, she's become obese, sloppy, filthy, increasingly bitter and sarcastic. The result of her accident and severe burn? Without photos it's impossible for me to remember her slim good looks, her taste and style. All that is past. She leaves all decisions to her worthless son and openly despises Louisa, whom Ivo married without her permission. She even hates her grandchildren. *That woman's brats*, she calls them, never Ivo's, and lavishes unnatural affection on her son and that yelping unwashed mutt of hers.

And Sônia's *faxineiro*. Lico! What am I to make of him? Why can't Martin see he's different? His height and elongated body, the peculiar head, unusual complexion, and those deep-set eyes. Sônia says Lico is *açoriano*. I do not believe her. Unless certain myths are true, that the Azoreans were survivors of Atlantis, and he's some kind of throwback. Now isn't that ridiculous? Lico of Atlantis? I'm not that far over the edge, yet.

October 16th

I've met a charming artist from England who is renting a room from Sônia in Sambaquí. Roger Whitby paints the most beautiful landscapes. I may purchase one if the price is right.

October 22nd

Martin has never been happier. He thoroughly enjoys the company of friends we've met through Sônia. He's always with the men discussing soccer and real estate thanks to the local gaucho custom of segregating the sexes at after dinner. I find the women quite boring. They gossip, play silly card games, or shop. Very limited. All of them. Louisa is the exception. She is well educated and might have something to contribute, but she's completely cowed by her husband and Sônia, who is medicated most of the time.

One of the women is Sônia's cousin. Maria Lourdes Céspedes is a rather pretty version of the local dark, sharp featured women of Portuguese origin. She reminds me of Terri. But physically only. I don't like or trust her, or any of them . . . their men too, except Flávio, our architect. But then he's a *gringo* too. Like me, from São Paulo.

October 29th

Horrible news. I received a phone call from my cousin Sérgio. He told me his sister Margarita, her husband Mauricio, and the children . . . all the Fonsecas are dead. A motor accident on the road to São Sebastião. Did I really wish that terrible a retribution for them? It seems Martin did. He is so very pleased. Did he have anything to do with the accident? If so, how? I wonder. No, a silly thought. Impossible. Should I go to the funeral?

November 5th

It was painful to be among family, but it was right that I went. Sérgio refuses to believe it was an accident. He is going berserk over what happened to Margarita's overseas accounts. Big money missing. I think the Fonsecas may have robbed him even worse than they did us. Sérgio has another suspect. He did not make a direct accusation, but I got the distinct impression he thinks Martin may have been involved. I cannot believe such a thing.

January 4th

A new year, and I have never seen Martin so fit. I wish I could get him to shave that awful gaucho mustache. But it's more than his physical appearance that has changed. Ever since I came back from the funeral, he's been secretive, more distant, as if he's become another person.

The same way Terri seems to be changing? Rick thought.

January 7th

When I think about it, I'm astonished at how completely Martin has adapted here. Unbelievably, he speaks a purer *catarinense Portiñol* than I, whose *paulista* dialect marks me permanently as a *gringa*.

January 15th

Martin made changes in the construction of our house last November. He told me only today. It'll be larger, more luxuriously appointed. But where will the money come from? Martin says he has it. I must believe him.

February 1st

Summer. A season in hell. Unbearably hot and humid, and no air conditioning. Windows must stay open to catch the slightest breeze. That brings in the bugs, their bites. I hope by mid-year we can live in our own house. To be truthful, though, I want to return to the good old U.S. of A!

Is that *urubú* on our back wall staring at me?

February 18th

Compared to big metropolitan centers like São Paulo, Rio, and L.A., the Ilha gives a false illusion of calm and tranquility. In reality there is much crime here. Drug trafficking is rampant. Citizens of Paraguay, Uruguay, and Argentina need no visas to cross the borders. Gangs of young men from those adjacent countries and other parts of Brazil come here to sell drugs, rob tourists, and burglarize homes. Even murder. They seduce maids fresh from the farm, then use them to gain entry. Zé and Rosa are fatalistic about it. Maybe they're taking big payoffs. How else could they afford their enormous seven-suite home in Trindade, and an equally luxurious beach house at Canasvieiras, plus other investments in real estate.

Martin seems preoccupied. I've never known him to be so uncommunicative.

March 3rd

The vultures! Now I am beginning to understand. At first I thought I might be going over the edge, that they were watching me. And not only the vultures. Sônia, Maria Lourdes, Rosa, Gabriela, Fátima, and Valéria. Lico too. They monitor my every move.

And there are secrets.

It is an island of vultures! But the *urubús* are more than a metaphor for the avaricious *catarinenses.*

And I am a prisoner!

Rick stopped the tape. Prisoner, Irene had said. That was exactly how he felt.

CHAPTER 25.
THE GROTTO

March 11th

Yesterday, it was so hot at Sônia's house in Sambaquí that I went for a long swim in the Baía Norte. I scubaed along the cliff and discovered an underwater entrance to a labyrinthine grotto.

Very unusual markings on the walls. Not erosion. More like glyphs, maybe some unknown ancient writing. Perhaps written by the mysterious inhabitants of this island who were here before the Indians. And more. I also saw some wall drawings. Very disturbing. Sônia might be able to make sense of all this, but I no longer trust her. I shall return here alone better prepared.

March 14th

I climbed above the grotto. Thought some exploring there might bear some fruit. At the top of the cliff, I saw Roger painting furiously. A man possessed. His appearance horrified me. I hadn't seen him in several months. He is emaciated, unshaven, and wall-eyed. A lunatic's face. He gathered his materials and fled from me, but not before I caught a glimpse of the canvas. No landscape this time. Was it a monstrous distorted self-portrait, or an accurate depiction of a creature he saw and wished he hadn't?

March 27th

Roger Whitby has disappeared. No opportunities yet to go back into the grotto. I am either watched or the water is too rough.

March 29th

Distressing news. Roger Whitby fell from the cliff to the rocks below at the entrance to the grotto. The *urubús* got to him. Police gospel according to Zé.

April 5th

At last, I was able to get away. I penetrated deeper into the grotto, this time with my flashlight. More unsettling discoveries. I dare not go farther. I need to know more about the history and lore of this island, and the origins of the *urubús*.

This evening, I saw Roger's last canvases at Sônia's house. Grotesque. Indescribable. Can't bear to look at them. They should be destroyed. No, amend that. They should be kept for evidence of his madness or what may lurk somewhere on the island.

April 15th

I've gone to the grotto again, this time with my throwaway camera, and, God help me, I discovered what really happened to the Fonsecas. I wish I hadn't.

Taking photos of my discoveries for proof, but I can't show them to anyone here in Floripa. Must have them developed somewhere else.

Terri and Rick wrote that they'll visit us in July after our house is completed. I wish they were here now. No, better if they don't come."

Rick suspected that if Irene had indeed written them not to come, Martin may have prevented the letter from being mailed, her e-mails from being sent.

April 20th

Although Flávio promised our house would be finished by the first of May, we must wait another two months. Even so, Martin and Lico are transporting all our belongings . . . books, rugs, paintings and graphics, and furniture we brought from L.A. . . . to the new house.

I'll have to be careful where I secrete my notes and this tape. Better that I keep them with me at all times. I must fly to São Paulo. Once there,

I'll have the photos printed and leave them with my cousin, Sérgio. I'll also need to create a valid excuse for my trip, something that Martin and the clique will accept.

April 23rd

No one questioned my reasons for visiting São Paulo No problems getting the photos developed. Studying them. Although they are not all that clear . . . need a better camera . . . they're still horrifying and puzzling. But the implications . . . I prefer not to think about them. I purchased the best digital camera I could find for my next trip into the grotto . . . about time I joined the twenty-first century. I placed the photos in an envelope and left them with Sérgio.

Irene's photos are in São Paulo!

Rick decided, no matter how much Martin might object, he would go there while Terri spent time at the baths. From what he'd heard Irene say on her taped diary, it was essential he meet with her cousin. Sérgio Posner had her photos of the grotto, and, perhaps, answers to some specific, very important questions.

April 25th

Received an e-mail from Rick. Terri's father mercifully passed away at last. And just when I've learned why he went berserk and murdered all the women in her family. I've also discovered what his babbling meant. *Creeperee*, as the journalists wrote it. If they only knew what he was really trying to communicate.

My God! I cannot confide in Terri. It must be Rick alone. I must alert him to the danger he faces. But will he come this summer? And, what if something happens to me before then?

Martin, has gone into Florianópolis Central on business, and the women . . . I cannot think of them as friends . . . they have gone to the thermal baths on the mainland. No one is around to spy on me, to question my actions.

Despite my instinctive fears, I cannot pass up another opportunity to explore the grotto. The tide is out, and although it is midday, the Baía Norte is mirror-tranquil, evening glass as the Malibu surfers would have described it. California. How I wish I had never left my Golden State.

Am I like those horror film characters I despise for being absolute fools when they enter a dark house in which a sadistic slasher has already killed several people? No matter, I must return to the grotto.

I swam about a hundred yards inside the grotto to a limestone wall and climbed onto a narrow walkway leading into its maw. I had to remove my scuba gear, goggles, and fins and leave them on the path. I unzipped my waterproof bag. This time I brought a powerful halogen lamp and a newer digital camera with beaucoup pixels, far superior to the one I used before. This time I'll have clear irrefutable photographic proof for the skeptics. But I can never show them or describe my discovery of the grotto to Martin or any of the women. Or anyone else in Floripa. That's why I've booked a flight back home to the States without telling anyone.

Now I'm deeper into the grotto. Although I'm no geologist, I am convinced its interior is not the result of natural erosion. My instincts also tell me it was not created by humans. I am trying not to imagine the vile creatures that most likely did construct it and their purpose for doing so.

Yecchh!

Blind albino creatures that have never seen daylight are scurrying away. Just as well. They're absolutely repugnant. Even more disgusting are those drawings along the grotto walls, but I must photograph each one to prove they could not have been drawn by humans.

Rick heard a shrill scream and thought it might be the moment when Irene died. Then he heard her breathing heavily.

I thought I'd illuminated another person in the grotto. Not a man, it was that grotesque albino humanoid I'd previously encountered. It's more afraid of me, I think. It's crawling away. I should go back, but curiosity is impelling to proceed farther than I've gone before.

I am now stepping through a mouth of stalactites and stalagmites, half-expecting them to chomp on me. Illusion born of primal fears?

Looks like I've entered another chamber.

Rick heard her gasp.

Gruesome paintings along the walls. Odors are making me nauseous. Overwhelming putrescence. No matter, I must photograph these monstrosities and repellant narrative panels. Then I must get out of here, off the island, and hurry back to L.A.. There I'll be safe. Martin can have his paradise.

I sense a presence behind me. I . . .

End of narration.

Rick calculated dates. Irene's body was found two days later. So Martin had said. He pushed away his food. He had consumed only a few bites of pasta, and they lay in his stomach like an anvil. His beer was now warm and flat. What was he to make of her diary?

"I cannot confide in Terri," Irene had said.

"Do not tell your wife," Flávio had said.

Why?

Rick could relate to Irene's anxieties concerning the island: The brooding atmosphere at the beaches;

omnipresent *urubús*; a suspicion he was being watched; and mistrust of Martin and his friends.

What had Irene seen in that grotto?

Who or what had taken her life?

He rewound the tape, listened to it again, and took out his map of the island. No indication of any grotto around Sambaquí. *A deliberate omission?* He considered going for a swim to look for it.

Sure. Very wise. A plunge into the unknown. And then what?

CHAPTER 26.
THERMAL REACTION

eresinha accepts."

"I knew she would. We must do the same for Rick."

"If we can, Martin. Sônia may not wish to restrain the others much longer."

"Please, Maria Lourdes, ask her to give Rick more time. He still has not the slightest idea."

"And when he does understand, will he consent?"

"He will do anything for Teresinha."

"I hope you are right. Fortunately, Rosa and Zé are occupied with more pressing matters at the moment."

Deep in thought, Martin did not attempt to make conversation on the drive back to Ingleses. That was fine with Rick. He had plenty to sort out himself, and he could feel Irene's tape burning through his purse.

Her familiar voice had unleashed a tidal wave of reminiscences that carried him back to an earlier time and place. Irene would forever be inseparable from his first memories of Terri. Most importantly, on that first day in their 10th grade English class, Irene had seated him next to shy and withdrawn Terri Alves, and they had fallen instantly in love with each other.

Because Terri was fluent in Portuguese and closely resembled her best friend, Sônia Batardi, Irene accepted her as if she were her adored natural child. Terri, in turn, came to love Irene as much as the mother she had lost, and Martin, who taught History at another high school in the city, as the nurturing father she'd never experienced. The Kraais liked Rick and regularly invited him and Terri for dinner, films, and live theater. Those were great times. Conversation with Irene and Martin was always educational no matter the subject. Rick and Terri learned much about life, history, fine arts, and especially Brazil, which the Kraais visited every year.

Every year—and that puzzled him. Irene knew Brazil inside and out, warts and all. How could she have miscalculated so? Was there something about her background he had missed? He recalled what he knew. Irene had been born in São Paulo, an only child, to an upper middle class family of Central European origins. She had been university educated in business. After representing Brazil as a swimmer in the Olympics where she took an honorable fifth place in the 800 meters freestyle, she'd gone to work for *Varig Airlines* in public relations.

Irene had met Martin shortly after she was transferred to L.A.. By the time they married, both her parents had passed away. Martin then convinced Irene to quit Varig, take some college courses and get a California teaching credential so they could lead a comfortable life with plenty of free time for traveling. They used to visit Irene's family in São Paulo every summer with side trips to Rio, Bahia, and Buenos Aires, the last for Argentine tango lessons. After Sônia moved to Sambaquí, they would spend about a week in Florianópolis each year as well.

Rick remembered Irene saying often that although she enjoyed visiting family and friends she would never again want to live in Brazil. Was their move all Martin's doing?

When they arrived at the house, Martin muttered something about working upstairs in his study and left him alone. Rick changed into warmer clothes and waited for Terri on the veranda. The *empregada* brought out a beer and a plate of seafood cakes, which he nibbled absentmindedly, while *urubús* soared high above the cliffs and the small island of Mata-Fome in the purple dusk.

Terri returned from the thermal baths after dark with a stack of packages. Her eyes sparkled, and she was hyperactive.

Rick sprang from the lounge. "Terri, you look fantastic. How's your back?"

"What back?"

He moved to kiss her, almost retched, and backed away in disgust. "Your breath . . . what the hell have you been eating?"

"Must be the meat and sauce we had for lunch."

"What was it, carrion?"

She gaped at Rick, then handed him her packages and ran up the stairs. He followed her into their suite and placed her packages on their bed.

After Terri vigorously brushed her teeth and rinsed with mouthwash, she stepped back into the bedroom, pirouetted, and stretched. "I can't remember when I've felt so good. You'll have to go there too."

Rick had not seen his wife this excited about her physical condition in years. He was tempted to test her back and run through some of their most difficult routines here and now in the guest suite, but he had too many questions. "Did you learn more about Irene's drowning and how Maria Lourdes leaned to speak English so well?"

"Everyone insists Irene's drowning was an accident. I believe them. That's all it was, an accident. And I never had a chance to ask Maria Lourdes about her ability to speak English. Anyway, we had lunch with Louisa. Maria Lourdes wanted me to get to know her."

Rick was surprised the women had included Louisa. "Did you know that she's a doctor?"

"Yes, a pediatrician. *Puxa vida*! Imagine! She's an MD, an accomplished musician, incredibly well-read, and indestructibly robust too. Never sick. I can't tell you how much I envy her. If I had Louisa's health, we'd already be champions."

"We'll get there."

"And I was so surprised and delighted when Sônia, Gabriela, Fátima, and Valéria met us at the baths. The entire gang. And they all use the diminutive of my name, Teresinha. Oh, Rick, everyone here is so warm and friendly."

"They'd have to be idiots not to like you." He continued to stare at Terri. She was ebullient, on a super-high. Could the baths really have worked miracles in just one day?

"We also stopped at a fantastic crystal and china store on the mainland a few miles across the bridge." Terri showed him her purchases, a pair of enormous beach towels and a half dozen beer glasses she had selected especially for him.

At first glance, they appeared to be as fine as Baccarat. The rims, however, were not well finished and had some sharp edges. He did not mention it to Terri. She didn't drink beer and need never know. "They're great, *Passarinha*."

"I knew you'd like them, so I ordered complete sets in the same pattern for wine, water, and champagne. They'll be ready for us in a week at their main store in Blumenau. We can drive up there for the day."

"One week? But we're leaving on Thursday."

She put her hands on his face and kissed his nose. "I know you too well. You're angry that I want to stay longer."

"Confused is a better word. I remember that you were ready to leave the moment we learned Irene had drowned."

"I was, but that was before I went to the baths. They truly do perform miracles. You want me healthy for the Nationals, don't you?"

"Of course, but . . ."

"And we really haven't given Martin and Maria Lourdes a chance. We've been behaving like spoiled children . . . you know, the kind who don't want daddy to remarry. I can't quite put it into words, but I feel as if I've come home. Maria Lourdes, all the women . . . Rick, I've never been so accepted."

"I know that."

"So please, let's not argue. Not when I'm feeling so good." Terri lifted a foot onto the top of the dresser and stretched. "Now, tell me about your day in the city."

No way would he tell her about Irene's tape, nor his futile attempts to learn more about the *urubús* at the bookstores in Floripa Central, which had only picture books of birds, and at the University of Santa Catarina, which was closed for the winter break. He hoped she might have heard something about Flávio.

"I went to see the condo Flávio is constructing. He wasn't there."

"Gabriela told me that he had to drive south to Pôrto Alegre on business this morning. He's not expected back until the end of the week."

Rick wondered why Flávio did not tell him his change of plans yesterday at the *churrasco* or his secretary mention it when he called today. Maybe she hadn't understood his Portuguese.

"Did you have a nice lunch?"

After Rick finished describing the urchins at *Macarronada*, she snapped her fingers. "You see? You *are* having a good time here."

"Sure, as I've said before the scenery is fantastic, but to tell the truth, I'm bored. A few days on the beach has been enough. We can do the same thing in Jupiter. And every day and night we see the same people."

"I thought you liked them."

"What gives you the idea I don't? But remember, we wanted to check out all those samba schools and dance clubs in São Paulo, Rio, and Bahia. We've been in Brazil almost a week, and we haven't really seen the country. I'd like some variety on our vacation. And I'll admit it. I'm still not satisfied with their explanations of how Irene died. Let's fly to São Paulo on Thursday as we originally planned."

I want to see the photographs Irene took

Terri pouted. "And I'd rather spend all our time here. Martin wants us to stay too. We owe him at least that. Everyone says the same things about São Paulo and Rio that our travel agent and students told us back in Jupiter. They're soaked in pollution and totally crime-ridden."

"It's almost as bad here." While she half-listened and alternated stretching each leg, Rick went on to describe part of what he'd heard listening to Irene's diary without naming the source. *Do not confide in Terri* continued to resonate through his mind. "With all those burglaries, assaults, and murders, it's still possible that Irene's death wasn't a swimming accident."

"Zé would be the first to hunt down the murderer, if one existed. He's Martin's best friend here. If he says the case is closed, the case *is* closed."

"Zé doesn't look as if he's working all that hard."

"That's because there's no crime to speak of here. Like everyone tells us." She hugged him. "Please, Rick, let's not fight."

"I'm not fighting."

"Then stop being a grumpy old grouch."

He held Terri in his arms and kissed her. "How about lovable young grouch?"

"Rick, I am serious about staying longer. I need more time at the baths. They can do more than strengthen my back. Everyone says they'll help my immune system too."

He reluctantly placed his own instincts and the warnings from Irene and Flávio on back burners. He would go along with just about anything that guaranteed an improvement in Terri's health. "Okay, I'll phone Nelson first thing tomorrow and change our getaway date."

"I knew you'd understand. Now stay here. Don't move. I bought something special, a surprise for you."

She carried a small package into the bathroom and came out moments later in a black *fio-dental* bathing suit and heels. She posed provocatively. Her eyes glowing like fiery coals.

Rick quickly shed his clothes. "I'd better put on the room heater."

"Don't bother. We'll generate our own fire." Terri flew into his arms, slithered against him in an improvised dance more erotic than any tango or bolero, and transformed her husband into a mindless gland.

CHAPTER 27.
ANOTHER DAY IN PARADISE

e rests his head on her lap at the far end of the long sofa. She bends, and they kiss on the mouth. He strokes her cheek and plays with her hair, twisting strands into curls. Then he buries his face deeply in the folds of her woolen garments between her heavy, capacious bosom.

"Everything is all right? You approve?"

She closes her eyes. "Yes, this time you have selected well and wisely, my beautiful boy."

"Mãezinha! Mommy!"

The following morning dawned clear, warm, and uncomfortably humid. At breakfast, Martin apologized for Maria Lourdes' absence. He said she had to leave early for the mainland on personal matters, and he had to go over documents and contracts in Floripa Central. He promised they'd be back in time for dinner at one of the local restaurants with the Batardis, Zimmermanns, de Andrades, and Silveiras.

Because Lico would be chauffeuring Martin and the domestics had been given the afternoon off, Rick intended to take advantage of their absence and make a discreet search throughout the house for anything Irene might have hidden relating to what she had discovered in the grotto. Except, how could he explain his snooping to Terri? More importantly, could he justify not letting her hear Irene's taped diary to her?

At the same time, he looked forward to being alone with Terri. Her stamina had never been so strong. Last night and again this morning, they were more emotionally and physically connected than ever before.

I'll have to light candles to Our Lady of the Thermal Baths.

After they showered and put on their bathing suits, Terri raced down the stairs ahead of him. Rick followed her into the living room and watched in surprise as she pushed furniture to the side and kicked the oriental rugs into the walls.

"What are you doing?"

"I can't remember when I've felt this good. Those thermal baths have already made me a new woman."

"Don't I know it, but why do you have to waste your energy and risk injury moving furniture?"

"Because we really haven't practiced since we arrived. Last Friday night doesn't count because my back conked-out."

"And you don't think it will this morning?"

She pulled the leather sofa out of the way. "I keep telling you . . . it's those thermal baths. The baths. I must go back to the baths. Maria Lourdes, Sônia, all the women . . . they're planning to leave early on Thursday, spend the night there, and all day Friday too. I hope you won't mind being left alone with the men."

Rick worried about Terri being away for so long in a strange country, especially among those mysterious clone-like women he mistrusted. Yet her absence might give him an opportunity to learn more about Irene and the grotto. "If it's good for your health, it's okay with me."

"I told them you'd give me the green light."

"That reminds me. Nelson will have to change our tickets. We should be able to leave next week sometime and limit ourselves to one city, São Paulo or Rio."

"Rick, I told you! I want to stay here our entire vacation."

Why am I not surprised?

She found a samba CD and inserted it into the player. "Come, listen to the percussions. Those musicians, they're real Brazilians."

"Go easy, Terri. Your back might not hold up, especially on a tile floor."

"No problem, you'll see."

They fell into the beat and danced a samba across the living room, onto the veranda, and back. Then a cha-cha-cha. Terri turned, twisted, and extended her body. She breathed easily. Her back, which had gone out on her more than a half dozen times in the past week, gave her no pain or muscle spasms. After the first piece, she replied to his unspoken question. "Like I've said repeatedly. It's the baths."

"I don't care what it is. If it works, don't fix it."

They selected specific CDs that fit their routines and spent the remainder of the morning rehearsing and improvising. They danced comfortably with finely sculpted top lines and moved as one in open position. Their hip-lines and rise-and-fall fit perfectly when they were in closed position. She danced feather-light with hair-trigger responses to his lead.

In the middle of a rumba, Rick considered changing their choreography and carrying Terri upstairs to their bedroom, but the *empregada* entered and tinkled a bell to let them know *almoço* was being served. They had worked up a hearty appetite, and he was sweating from the unexpected workout. He polished off a beer before settling into a warm lunch of rice, black beans, freshly baked rolls, and seafood cakes. This time Terri ate more of Sônia's delicacies than he did.

After *almoço*, they settled in a pair of lounges on Martin's patio. Terri fell asleep immediately. It was too early for him to search the house. The *empregada* and cook were still working downstairs. While Rick gazed out to sea, he had a delayed nostalgic reaction to several of Irene's old CDs, which they'd used for their dancing this morning. He reminisced about the past and remembered the most significant event of their senior year. Irene had invited them to a party at the dance studio where she and Martin had begun taking introductory lessons. That was when Terri had suddenly revealed herself to be a naturally gifted dancer, whose shyness disappeared the moment the music began. Show her a step once, and she mastered it. That same night, she decided to become a professional ballroom dancer, and Irene paid for her first lessons.

After graduating, Terri became a dance instructor at a studio, while he attended UCLA and worked in a bookstore. During his free time, she taught him all the steps and routines she'd learned. Over the next three years, Rick had restlessly changed majors while becoming progressively disenchanted with the academic world. He'd been appalled by the petty backbiting, jealousies, and vicious infighting among the professors. He'd also refused to tolerate deliberate slights and sarcastic comments directed towards Terri by campus intellectual snobs who'd perceived her as a working-class illiterate because she hadn't read this Great Work or knew who'd composed that alphabet plus-or-minus concerto. Her innate qualities were far more important to him than scholarly achievements. Besides, Terri was fluent in several languages and had superior business sense. She ran the studio and did the bookkeeping.

By the end of his junior year at UCLA, Rick had decided that he did not want to become a doctor, lawyer,

CPA, college professor, scientist, or obtain an MBA and qualify for some giant corporation that dealt in goods or services that had never interested him. What he'd wanted most was to dance professionally with Terri, nothing else, and he dropped out of school to work full time with her.

They had married that summer, with Irene and Martin as their only witnesses. Because Terri had resented being salaried when she could earn the full student fee on her own, they decided to rent studio space, advertise, teach and compete. They soon established a reputation as honest, committed teachers while winning assorted Rising Star championships. Five years ago after they competed at *The Breakers Hotel* in Florida, they'd fallen in love with the nearby water-surrounded community of Jupiter and moved there to open their studio, financed in part by the Kraais.

All that because of Irene.

He vowed to discover the true cause of her death before he and Terri returned to Florida.

CHAPTER 28.
SEARCH AND DISCOVERY

ick swam a couple of hundred yards eastward along the shoreline while Terri was asleep on the sands in front of Martin's house. He stopped and dog paddled to shore when he reached a familiar part of the beach where the old man still peered out to sea. The *pescadores* had just returned with a bountiful catch and were dividing the fish. A quartet of vultures stood nearby. The largest he had yet seen. They were at least three feet in height with sleek shiny blue-black feathers, matte gray faces and long, perforated narrow beaks. The *urubús* turned to look at him when he came out of the water. Again he asked himself which were male and female? Or were they the same sex? They looked identical too, like the dark, sharp featured women of the Island.

Rick shouted a *bom dia* to the fishermen, then realized he ought to have said *boa tarde* because it was past noon. They did not respond in either case. He chose not to greet the *urubús*. The quartet of vultures stood their ground and sustained eye contact with him at the water's edge. Had he imagined it? Did their dark brown eyes express recognition?

A much larger *urubú* soared above and momentarily blocked the sun. The quartet took off after it and joined more vultures from other parts of the beach and Ilha Mata-Fome. They flew away in perfect squadron formation towards the southwest. Directly to Sambaquí, as the vulture flies. Sônia's home. Near the grotto Irene had discovered.

Rick walked back to Terri who slept on her back with a beatific expression. Their lovemaking and dancing must have worn her out. Not even the shouting of small children playing nearby could awaken her. He went into the silent house. The cook and *empregada* had left for the afternoon. The temperature inside was comfortable, and the tile felt cool under his feet in the living room. He opened the jacaranda doors of the first bookcase. It held several hundred hard cover and paperback books arranged in precise order by subject. None were about vultures. And there were five more bookcases. He would have to go through over a thousand volumes with no guarantee Irene had hidden anything in so obvious a place. Hidden what? More photos? A detailed description of her findings? A clue where she put them? Maybe Martin and Maria Lourdes had already discovered it or them. At the very least, they would have meticulously gone through each volume. No, not in any book. Then where? Irene had never lived here. If she left anything for them to find, she might have concealed it among her personal things.

He went upstairs to Martin's office and adjacent bedroom. Both rooms had sliding glass doors opening to a spacious patio and an unobstructed view of the entire beach. Although the desk, drawers, and cabinets in the office had nothing he could use, their contents surprised him. Martin, it seemed, was heavily involved in real estate.

Next, he went through the master suite. Its walk-in closet filled with built-in rosewood drawers and cabinets was essentially another large room. None of Irene's possessions in there. Frustrated, he searched the emerald green and gold tiled luxurious master bath, complete with a round six-foot diameter hydro-massage tub, separate stall mist shower, commode and bidet, twin marble sinks, and sauna with tiered benches for four. After finding no evidence of Irene in the master suite, Rick figured that the guest suite might be a more likely place for Irene to have hidden something, if Martin or Maria Lourdes had not made changes.

He studied the three Araújo graphics and the Roni Brandão oil on the walls. Irene had purchased them during her earlier trips to Brazil. Had she placed anything behind them?

Rick gingerly removed each work of art. Except for hooks, the walls were bare. He hesitated, however, before hanging the Brandão again, and lifted it to catch the light. The more he studied the whimsical, surreal piece, the more he liked it.

The dominant male figure sat at a table filled with food and drink. Structurally, it might have been a Hals or Van Dyke, a typical painting of a seventeenth-century soldier at rest next to a table filled with food. With notable exceptions: His armor seemed to be hollow; his white *tabula rasa* head was an oversized ping pong ball; and the matte, slate blue background created an illusion that the entire scene was under water. Rick smiled at specific memories. Irene had formed his taste in fine arts, and the Brandão was the only original work in the guest suite.

He went back downstairs and searched through the oversized kitchen and breakfast nook with its impressive red granite counters and every modern electronic device. Terri had told him that the cook and *empregada* were cousins of Maria Lourdes, and sisters. Only foolish *gringos* hired strangers who always robbed them.

Some paradise!

He found nothing in the kitchen and the walk-in pantry. The adjacent *lavanderia* was the size of a master bedroom, with a heavy-duty double sink, cabinets for cleaning equipment, and a washer and dryer. He found nothing of Irene's there, nor in the maids' quarters, nor in the bedroom above the garage where Lico sometimes slept.

Rick returned to the kitchen, opened a beer, and filled a plate with Sônia's delicious seafood cakes. Terri was still sleeping, and he sat beside her on the blanket. He saw no vultures anywhere on the beach or perching on the homes. Unusual for this time of day. They must have all gone off to dine on choicer carrion somewhere to the southwest.

CHAPTER 29.
CHANGE IN THE WEATHER

*K*ee-roo-poo-ree! *A loud hissing!*

A loud hissing becoming a high-pitched piping!

A high-pitched piping hiss: Kee-roo-poo-ree! Kee-roo-poo-ree!

Storm-black wings gliding over windswept, glacial wastes. Storm-black wings soaring over sullen crags and rocks. Bloody eye-sockets in the black sky. The sun a crimson laugh.

Kee-roo-poo-ree! The piping hiss repeated over and over.

Something ghastly. Abhorrent. Something blasphemously pre-human.

Formless, yet identifiable. A thing to be feared. A thing that should not be.

Body clammy with oppressive fear.

Swooping downward. Matte gray faces, grinning. Attenuated slate blue-gray beaks with rows of sharp teeth.

Paralysis. Unable to flee a Promethean fate. Talons digging into his arm. A soul-wrenching chill. A yellow flash.

Wearing jeans and her bulky yellow cable-knit sweater, Terri shook Rick awake on the veranda. The ocean was turbulent. Strong winds had come up. Her expression was as opaque as the darkening gray sky. Had he spoken

163

aloud during that horrifying dream? Had he equated her with vultures, or mentioned Irene's diary?

"What time is it?" he asked sleepily.

"Five-thirty, and there's bad news. Louisa and the boys are missing, and we're going over to Sambaquí to give the Batardis support. Maria Lourdes is already there." She frowned at the menacing sky. "You'd better go upstairs and change into something warmer."

Rick was still reacting to the repeated soul-searing piping hiss of his dream, *Kee-roo-poo-ree.* Where had he heard it before? Had those vultures flying towards Sambaquí earlier in the afternoon triggered his hallucination?

He went with Terri into the living room. "Maybe Louisa finally left Ivo."

Martin shook his head. "No, her car is at the Batardi compound. Zé already checked with the airport, car rentals, and bus lines. He's convinced that Louisa and the boys are still on the island."

Rick remembered the young salesgirl at Ivo's lingerie store. Why shouldn't Louisa have a lover too? "A friend might have driven her to . . ."

"She has no other friends here" Martin had interrupted with absolute certainty, as if ordering him to stop speaking nonsense.

A half hour later, Rick stood bone-chilled in Ivo's dilapidated house even though he had on two pair of socks, woolen black pants, gray flannel shirt, and a white sweater with the same cable-knit design as Terri's. He wished he'd brought thermal underwear for this trip to the south of Brazil. Despite the violent winds coming from the Antarctic and Patagonia now raging across the Island, Ivo refused to close the windows. Rick suspected they would have leaked air anyway.

An unnatural atmosphere hung over the cluttered living room. Although Louisa and the boys were missing, it was no different from any other evening they had spent with Martin and his friends. Only Zé and Rosa were away, ostensibly leading the search for Louisa and the boys.

Sônia sat in the center of the largest couch in the living room and crocheted while her min-pin slept curled in her lap. She was cheerful tonight, not in the least disturbed about the disappearance of her daughter-in-law and grandchildren, perhaps welcoming it. Ivo's behavior intrigued Rick even more. Although his wife and sons had gone missing, he seemed to worry as little as his mother and enthusiastically discussed the upcoming Formula One races on Sunday with his friends. He was an absolute fanatic on the subject, and one wall in his living room was filled with video cassettes of races going back more than fifteen years.

Because he felt chilled, Rick asked Lico for a double brandy. He methodically scrutinized each aspect of the sienna titan: Unfathomable deep set eyes; stony features without expression. Something was different about the giant tonight. The *faxineiro* had a lively spring in his steps and moved more quickly, as if he, like Terri, had been rejuvenated at the baths.

Martin was on the phone again in Ivo's kitchen. Rick saw no point in going over to Terri. He could not fight the *gaucho* de facto segregation of the sexes at these social gatherings. There was man talk, and there was woman talk. He did not understand how Terri could be enjoying the fatuous chattering among Maria Lourdes, Fátima, Gabriela, and Valéria. Then he saw an unframed oil on the wall above the fireplace mantle and walked over to it for a closer look. Still wet, the painting was a beautifully rendered landscape of the wild cliffs above Sambaquí. He recognized the style and artist, but when he peered at the signature, he saw Batardi, not Whitby. He turned to look for Ivo and stepped back when he found himself facing Sônia, who was leaning on a cane and holding Bubi in the crook of her free arm.

"My son has taken up painting."

And I am not supposed to inquire how and when he learned to copy Whitby's style. "He's quite talented. Isn't he wasting his time working in a lingerie store?"

"That will change very soon."

Rick hoped to get more answers from her regarding Irene." I understand you were responsible for Irene and Martin moving here."

"I did what I could to help. Martin wanted to retire here. He made that clear to everyone each time he visited."

"And Irene?"

Bubi growled at Rick, and Sônia did not reply. She calmed her min-pin and returned to the couch where she resumed her crocheting.

Rick was on his third double brandy, not yet warm but at least getting mellow, when Zé and Rosa returned shivering in their wool-lined blue parkas. They looked as refrigerated as he felt. Their gestures and expressions let everyone know the news was bad.

Zé took a *Chivas Regal* neat from Lico and reported to Sônia in rapid sing-song Portiñol. Terri came over and translated for Rick. The worst had indeed happened. Louisa had taken her sons fishing earlier in the day when the bay was calm. The sudden appearance of winds and rough water must have capsized their fragile rowboat, and all three drowned. The two boys were found washed ashore near Jurerê. It was not necessary for Sônia or Ivo to identify them. They had little hope of finding Louisa.

Ivo nodded as if he understood and resumed his argument with the men over racing. Sônia became more animated, as if she had heard good news. She beckoned the women to form their usual semi-circle around her. Terri left Rick to join them as a young woman entered the living room. The women noisily welcomed the new arrival, Yeda Mello Gonçalves, yet another swart young woman, the pretty saleswoman who worked at Ivo's store.

*Curupuri is . . . something terrible,
something malevolent, something to
be avoided. None can describe its
shape or nature, but it is a word of
terror, a name for any kind of devil.*

—Sir Arthur Conan Doyle, The Lost World

SECOND WEEK
IN BRAZIL

CHAPTER 30.
A PERFECT SOLUTION

owerful gusts from the south almost blew Valéria into the water, and she dug her feet deeper into the sand. "You were right. She is the one."

Gabriela supported her. "Yes, an ideal choice."

Fátima also struggled to maintain her footing. "And she is so very beautiful."

Sônia faced south as if summoning more frigid blasts from the Antarctic to relieve the relentless fiery agony of her burns. "Yes, it will be Yeda."

Maria Lourdes moved closer to Sônia so she could be heard above wind and surf. "And Teresinha?"

"Although she is willing, she is unaware of the precise details as of yet. It is best we reveal them to her only at the last possible moment."

"Martin will be delighted with your decision."

"He should be. It was his idea in the first place." Sônia sighed. "At last. Two halves of a perfect solution."

Rick's mood was no less bleak and stormy than the violent north winds ripping the surf along Ingleses. Gray threatening clouds moved rapidly across the sky, with only evanescent openings of blue. Alone on the beach, except for a scattering of *urubús*, they wore shirts under their sweats, and Terri's face was barely visible. He was not pleased to see on her head and around her neck the bulky dull beige crocheted cap and matching scarf Sônia had given her last night. He put his arm around Terri to warm her, and she cuddled against him. This was more like it. Whenever they were alone, she was completely his, passionate and supportive. Among Martin and his friends, Terri became another person and shut him out, especially when she was with those damn undifferentiated women who seemed to have hatched from the same egg.

Rick's disorientation and disconnection intensified, and he held Terri tighter, as if clinging to some last shard of reality. Although he did not understand how the thermal baths worked, he would support any treatment that improved her health. Terri now had limitless energy, and her back had never been stronger. That was why he had agreed they should stay on the island for the duration of their vacation, but, would they ever be able to leave Florianópolis? Rick had come to believe the island had become a prison of pitiless weather, alien landscape, black vultures, and death, too much death.

Last night, Martin had at last revealed the *urubús* had gotten to Irene before she washed ashore. Rick did not believe his excuse for not telling them the truth sooner. Martin had said he wanted to spare him and Terri the image of what the vultures had done to her. Then why tell them at all? Maybe he was being too unfair. Over the years, Martin had been a father to them and had proven many times over to be their best possible friend. They owed him, owed him plenty—the old Martin!

Rick recalled everything he knew about the *old* Martin. Born in L.A., a graduate of UCLA, he served two uneventful years with the Army in Germany before things heated in Viet Nam, and after limited success selling stories to film and TV, he taught History at the high school level.

This *new* Martin, who lived in Ingleses married to Maria Lourdes, was a stranger, his subservience to Sônia unnatural. Rick worried Terri and he were being ensnared in a sticky web of intrigue spun by Sônia, definitely Sônia, and Rosa too, who dominated her husband the same as Maria Lourdes controlled Martin. The Zimmermanns had to be key players. As cops, they had the ability to cover-up anything and everything on the island.

What exactly were they covering-up? Was it something about the vultures? Flávio had said as much. Was it possible the *urubús* were not content to feed on carrion and also devoured the weak while they were still alive? Because tourism and real estate investment were the main sources of revenue on the island, the authorities would never reveal that the *urubús* feasted on living humans. They'd most likely create false autopsy reports. No funerals. Immediate cremation. As the old song went, *"Accentuate the positive and eliminate the negative."*

Rick's conjecturing brought him back to Louisa, the outsider who never had been accepted by Sônia and her exclusive clique. Although her body had yet to be found, she was presumed dead. Drowned, like her boys and Irene. Flávio also didn't belong. Rick hoped nothing horrible had happened to him, yet he feared the architect had already met a similar fate. He shivered, this time not from the cold. Like Flávio, he too was the quintessential *gringo*, blonde and fair, so unlike Terri who had adapted to the island while he accepted nothing, questioned everything.

Rick believed Sônia had all the answers. He reviewed everything that Irene had told him about her best friend over the years and filled in some of the gaps with what he'd learned during the past week. Sônia had been born in Sambaquí and moved with her mother to São Paulo when she was four. He had never heard any mention of her father, which must have been another good story to be told. During their teens and early twenties, Irene used to visit the island with Sônia. After she emigrated, their lives became unsynchronized. They rarely saw each other and communicated by letter no more than a few times each year until Sônia returned to live in Sambaquí. That did not matter. Irene believed they were friends for life.

The year after Irene emigrated to the United States, Sônia had married Dr. Vicente Morães Batardi, Professor of Ethnology at the University of São Paulo. Irene never had an opportunity to meet him. The Batardis went on digs together all over the world, and Sônia's husband died in 1977 during one of their expeditions to Tierra del Fuego.

How did Dr. Batardi die? Another mystery.

After her husband's death, Sônia had carried on with their work, traveling and raising Ivo and never remarrying. She retired in 1998 and returned to live permanently in Sambaquí. That was when Irene and Martin began to split their time visiting her family in São Paulo and Sônia here on the island.

"You're awfully quiet, Rick."

"I haven't been sleeping well." He told Terri about his recurring nightmares.

"And I haven't had any since we arrived in Floripa. You're probably upset over something more than Irene's drowning and what happened to Louisa and her boys, Cardinho. Martin thinks you should stop listening to Flávio."

"He does? What do you think, Terri?"

"Maria Lourdes says that Flávio hates it here and wants to move back to São Paulo."

"Why doesn't he?"

"Gabriela would never leave."

"And that's why I shouldn't talk to him? Terri, it doesn't make any sense."

"If you believe whatever Flávio has told you, it'll ruin your vacation. I know you haven't been yourself since we learned about Irene's death. I don't mean the shock. I'm not over it either. But you still suspect there's more to it than an accidental drowning. I blame Flávio for that."

"Isn't there more to it?"

"If there was, would knowing it give you any comfort?"

"No, but I'm still convinced that we haven't been given the full story about Irene. Or Louisa and the boys."

Her eyes filled with tears, and she kissed him. "Oh, Rick, you must stop imagining things. On the contrary, if you only knew."

He waited for her to continue. "If I only knew what?"

"How much I love you."

"And I love you."

Terri waited for the mournful wailing of the winds to subside. "You want my honest opinion?"

"Yes. Of course I do."

"I think a change of scene would be good for you. When you see Nelson at the agency this afternoon and change our flight back to the States to the last day of our trip, why don't you use your original ticket and visit São Paulo for the next two or three days while I'm at the thermal baths."

"You mean it?"

"Yes. We'd be separated anyway."

A trip to São Paulo would give him the opportunity to visit Irene's cousin, Sérgio Posner and see her photos of the grotto, but could he leave Terri alone for that many days with people he'd come to mistrust? Yes he could. He'd come to believe they meant her no harm. He held her while powerful gusts stirred the sand. The crashing of the surf and howling of the winds increased his strong sense of isolation, as if he were in another world, the forlorn desolate and haunted world of his nightmares. They'd been so disturbing that for the first time in his life he dreaded falling asleep.

He fixed his eyes on a quintet of black vultures no more than twenty feet away. Why were they so close? No carrion had washed upon the shore.

Damn, if they were not beginning to look more familiar. And not only as *urubús*. They seemed more than vulture, almost human in expression. Spying. Watching. His mouth went dry when he made a chilling connection. Maria Lourdes was usually away during weekdays. The same held true for all the other women: Valéria, Fátima, Rosa, and Gabriela. Vultures diurnal, women nocturnal. Odd coincidences, or unholy delusion? Could he actually differentiate among these vultures?

On impulse, Rick called out, "*Boa tarde*, Maria Lourdes, Gabriela, Fátima, Valéria, *e especialmente Doutora Sônia. Como vão vocês*, how are you?"

The vultures stared unblinking, and Terri pulled away from him. "That isn't funny, Rick. Not funny at all."

CHAPTER 31.
A GENEROUS OFFER

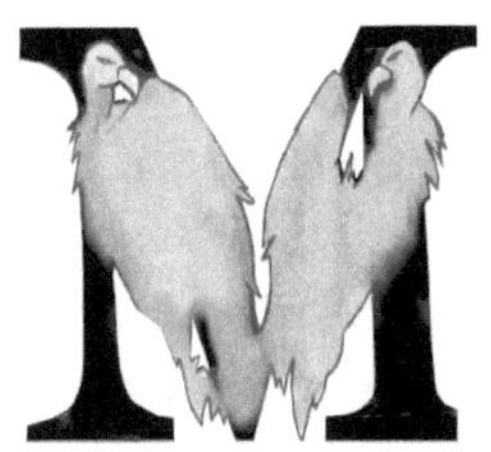artin intercepted Rick and Terri before they reached his front yard. "There you are. I hope you still feel like walking a bit. I want to show you kids something special" Turbulent gusts created brief sandstorms while they strolled along the beach to the west, past hotels and recently constructed condos. "These north winds are more violent than those coming from the south, and they tend to make people nervous. Irritable. Argumentative. Irene was impossible whenever they came."

"So is Rick."

"She thinks I'm a basket case because I want to see more of Brazil. You're an old hand here, Martin. It's our first time. To me, it seems a waste to travel to Brazil and not spend at least a day or two in Rio, Brasilia, Bahia, or even São Paulo."

"A mistake, Rick, and you know better too."

"Of course he does. That's why we left L.A. and moved to Jupiter. To avoid the pollution, traffic, and high crime rate."

"Rick, surely even this clean, natural violence of wind and surf is preferable to what you'll find in the big cities. Crime, vicious crime. Now that's real violence. Pollution too. Hordes of the great unwashed. And gridlock. Like Terri said, it's everything we all left behind in L.A.. And if you believe you're missing exotic places, let me remind you that *McDonald's*, *Burger King*, and *Colonel Sanders* came to São Paulo and Rio decades ago."

They had already walked half a mile past the point where the Estrada Geral turned onto the main road to Florianópolis Central. Martin pointed out a construction site on the sands between the shacks of two fisher families. Then he guided them away from the beach to a modular aluminum structure on a street named for a local breed of bird, Rua das Gaivotas. A sign on the roof and another at the front advertised in huge blue letters *Sôzémar Imoveis*, Sôzémar Real Estate, and below it were the names of the construction company, financing bank, and Flávio Vysocki as architect and chief engineer.

Inside the office, Martin introduced them to Pedro, a leathery, gap-toothed unshaven security guard, and to Osvaldo, his runty, sullen Azorean salesman seated by an inadequate 600 BTU heater. "I'm the mar in Sôzémar and equal partners with Sônia and Zé."

"Really? I'm so happy for you and Maria Lourdes. Isn't it wonderful, Rick?"

"Yes. Congratulations."

Martin took them to a long table and laid out detailed construction plans for a condominium. "There'll be six units, two per floor, *mais ou menos*, more or less four hundred *metros quadrados* each. That's more than four thousand square feet of interior living space. And the best units will be facing the water. I know how much Terri loves it here, and I thought maybe I could tempt you kids into buying one of these units. They'll be very plush. Look at the master bathroom. It's complete with bidet and large hydro-massage tub, and the kitchen is completely computerized. We'll use the finest tile and woods, marble too. What do you think?"

Terri studied Flávio's idealized watercolors of the interiors. "They're smaller and more manageable than those gorgeous condos on the Baía Norte."

"Yes, they are better because they're directly on the beach. And cheaper. Only a hundred and twenty-five thousand dollars."

"Is that all?"

Rick also was surprised at the low price. "Are you serious?"

"It's the price we are offering *you,* and your unit will be complete and fully equipped. No *condominio fechado* for my dearest friends."

For only the purchase of our souls? "Thanks anyway, Martin, but we'd hardly use it. Terri and I would never live permanently in Brazil, and we really don't have the time to take long vacations."

"Although you've made us a generous offer, Martin, Rick is right."

"If there's a financial problem, I can lend you the money. I'm doing that well with my investments, and I know you're good for it. Terri, you might need to benefit regularly from our thermal baths. It wouldn't hurt to visit here for a month or two each year. In the meantime, you can always use the condo as an investment. The Argentines will pay at least five thousand a month rent during our summer season. That's dollars, not Brazilian funny-money, and at least fifteen grand a year. But you don't have to make a decision right away. The apartments won't be completed for about two to three years. Think it over."

"We will," Terri promised.

Rick watched for Martin's reaction. "Tell you what. Since Flávio is your architect, I'll have a chat with him when he returns and get his input."

"Of course. By all means speak to Flávio."

CHAPTER 32.
CALM AND TRANQUILITY

When they arrived at Ivo's home, Rick saw Yeda sitting among the women. "Terri, Ivo's mourning period is even briefer than Martin's was for Irene."

"There's no getting through to you. Can't you understand this is not the United States? People behave differently here. That doesn't make it right or wrong."

"I wonder what the *urubús* are doing now, if they're also entertaining guests."

"I think you should forget about them. They're just part of the environment."

Martin joined them.

Martin came up behind them. "The *urubús* are roosting."

"Where?"

"At the cliffs, where no humans will bother them."

Rick turned towards Sambaquí. "At the Indian burial grounds?"

Martin led them to Sônia. "Rick will be leaving us for a while. He's going to São Paulo."

Bubi growled when Sônia interrupted her crocheting. "Teresinha will stay here with us, of course."

"Of course."

Maria Lourdes shook her head. "Still, to visit a strange and very dangerous city alone . . . you would be wiser not to go."

Terri squeezed Rick's hand. "He won't rest until he's seen another part of Brazil. *Na minha opinião*, my opinion is that all big cities are alike . . ."

"And unmanageable," Martin finished for her. "Where will you be staying, Rick?"

"The Maksoud Plaza."

"On second thought I'm delighted you're going. The foulness of the air, the crime and traffic, the craziness will all make you appreciate what a true paradise we have here."

Maria Lourdes placed a sisterly arm around Terri and smiled at Rick. "Then go with much peace of mind."

Sounds more like a threat to me.

Sônia resumed her crocheting. "I promise, we shall take very good care of Teresinha."

The way you took care of Irene? Just what I needed to hear.

Convinced that these women exerted an unwholesome influence on Terri, Rick believed they were allowing him to leave the island because they wanted him out of the way. He considered canceling his trip. He was taking a risk leaving Terri here alone. God knew what he would find when he returned, but he could not baby-sit her twenty-four hours a day. She had shopped and gone to the thermal baths without him and had made it clear that her two-day excursion to the baths was for the women only. No, there was nothing to be gained by staying on the island while Terri was at the baths. He might as well fly to São Paulo as scheduled.

Dinner would not be served until Edmur and Valéria arrived. In the meantime, Martin, Nelson, and Zé got into another heated discussion about Formula One racing.

Sônia held court from the sofa with all the women seated around her. Yeda sat beside her as if she'd always belonged in the group. Ivo stood behind them

Rick saw what he thought to be an unnatural amount of touchy-feely and kissing going on among Sônia, Ivo, and Yeda and reflected on their physical similarities. Years ago, he had read a theory that geography, air, atmosphere, and climate, could alter physiognomy. Others postulated that speaking a specific language formed one's jaw and facial structure. Because of what he had observed on the island, he concluded that the language, facial expression, and gestures of a relatively isolated society could indeed create a specific look. Most of the indigenous population appeared to be descended from settlers who came from the Azores and Madeiras, *açorianos* and *madeirenses*; so was Terri's family, which could explain her resemblance to Maria Lourdes, Gabriela, and so many other young women. Yes, there definitely were common denominator *catarinense* features: Dark complexion; sharp nose; jaw narrow and chin pointed, which thrust the teeth forward.

Rick concentrated his attention on Rosa. Although more chunky in build than the other women, she had the same long, shiny blue-black hair, brown eyes, sharp nose, and pointed jaw as the others. Even with pockmarks and a noticeable mustache, which intensified Rosa's repulsive persona, her face was undifferentiated from the other women. The same problem he had with the vultures. That reminded him of the repeated half-jest that dog owners often came to resemble their pets. Was it possible that the inhabitants of this socially incestuous community took on the physical characteristics of the dominant non-human life form?

Specifically *urubús*? *Urubús* and vulturine *catarinenses*.

Rick could well imagine Terri passing as a native of Floripa. What was he thinking? She was more beautiful than anyone else in this clique, with softer features, flawless olive complexion, and perfect teeth. She was an individual, a separate entity, completely unlike these unsettling women of uniform features.

Ridiculous theory. Pure fantasy.

Then again, although Martin had lived here for only one year, he could pass as the brother of Zé, Edmur, and other natives; whereas, outsiders like Irene, Louisa, Flávio, and Roger Whitby had kept their original faces. And Lico. If the circumstances of Irene's death was *the* great mystery, the *faxineiro's* origins had become as intriguing to him.

Rick stepped outside onto the veranda. The north winds had diminished in power although some of the gusts still blew at more than forty miles an hour. The cloudless evening sky held a jeweler's display case of sparkling stars and a platinum doubloon of a full moon, no less bright than the lights along the Baía Norte and the mainland across the bay.

Calma e tranquilidade. Calm and tranquility. So deceptive.

CHAPTER 33.
THE BLACK VULTURE

During his ride from the airport, Rick saw much evidence of São Paulo's unique perils and serious crime rate. His taxi driver took him along the colorful Avenida Indianapolis where gorgeous, scantily dressed hookers lined the streets for several miles. They beckoned to the motorists and when rejected flashed or pulled down their panties to expose their male genitalia. The cabby told him these transvestites were among the most vicious criminals in the city. They preferred to rob and, if necessary, kill rather than turn tricks.

When the taxi passed through exclusive residential neighborhoods, Rick saw high walls and fences topped with broken glass and barbed wire. Many of the larger homes had video scanners and armed guards stationed at the front gates with automatic weapons slung over their shoulders. And on the sidewalks, women clutched bags and purses to their breasts to discourage muggers.

After settling into his room at the Maksoud Plaza on Avenida Paulista, the banking and financial center of São Paulo, Rick phoned Sérgio Posner, Irene's first cousin and Margarita Fonseca's brother. Posner remembered meeting him and Terri at one of Irene's dinners during a visit to L.A. several years ago. After he offered condolences and asked if they could meet to discuss Irene, Posner invited him to be at his office on Rua Augusta at five that afternoon.

That left Rick with several free hours to seek detailed information about vultures. It would have to be done among the bookstores; the facilities and professors at the University of São Paulo would not be available because of the winter vacation.

At noon the temperature registered twelve degrees Celsius; nevertheless, he felt comfortable in his black warm-ups. Although the sky was cloudless, a rusty blanket of smog, thicker than any he had experienced in the States, covered the city.

He waited for the light to change at the busy intersection of Rua Augusta and Avenida Lorena between the exclusive *bairros* of Jardim Paulista and Jardim America. He would be within walking distance of his hotel and everything he needed to see and do because São Paulo was a densely populated commercial and industrial center, with narrow streets cut like canyons between concrete and glass office buildings and modernistic condos. Autos and trucks without smog-control devices were gridlocked on the noisy fume-engulfed streets. He had barely enough room to maneuver along the narrow sidewalks. At least he was familiar with big city dangers, so unlike the surreal unpredictable world of Florianópolis.

He crossed the street, and in the middle of the next block he stopped in front of a bookstore. The window display had caught his eye because many of the books were in English. With luck, he might find some material on vultures.

Inside the dimly lit narrow store, the clerk looked at him expectantly, "*Senhor?*"

Rick asked in his best Portuguese, "Have you any books about vultures in English?"

"*Momentinho*, one moment."

The clerk went to the far end of the store, climbed a ladder, and returned with a worn volume. Rick thumbed through it. The book had generalized information on the biology and habits of vultures all over the world. A start, but he needed more specialized books. "Is this all you have?"

"The others are in Portuguese."

"I'd like to see them."

The clerk went to other shelves and brought back several volumes. Two had language too technical for him to read without a Portuguese-English dictionary and plenty of time alone. The third book nearly caused his eyes to pop out. He translated the title as *The Vulture in Myth and History*, its author none other than *Doutora* Sônia Zenaiíde Batardi, Professor of Anthropology and Ethnology at the University of São Paulo. He scanned the table of contents and the index, then turned to the appropriate pages of the oversized, illustrated work. Exactly what he needed. It even included myths of the Tupí Indians.

He purchased both the monograph on vultures and Sônia's book. He also bought the most comprehensive Portuguese-English dictionary available.

Rick had a couple of hours to kill before his meeting with Sérgio Posner and settled at the desk in his hotel room with two beers and a *mixto quente*, a sandwich of warm toast, ham, and cheese delivered by room service. He really craved a batch of Sônia's seafood cakes. Except for the beaches, it was the only other thing he liked about the island. Terri would have to get the recipe before they left for home.

He flipped through the pages of Sônia's book on vultures in myth and history. From what he saw of the illustrations, it seemed to have answers to most if not all of his questions. Unfortunately, much of the vocabulary was technical and the syntax pedantic. Even with his Portuguese-English dictionary, he had difficulty translating. He collected his thoughts before tackling the other book. He drank his first beer, ate half a sandwich, and reviewed what he already knew about vultures.

Next to nothing.

They ate carrion, and they ranged everywhere over the island. They were not afraid of humans and seemed to have a higher intelligence than one expected from a bird. Or, was he being absurd, overdoing it and attributing to them human qualities? He wished now that he had paid more attention to the turkey buzzards in Florida. He checked the time and settled in a chair for some serious reading.

In the beginning, birds and dinosaurs both evolved from the archaeopterex, literally old wing,, the winged lizard of the Triassic Era more than 230,000,000 years ago, and pterodactyl, winged lizard, was the name given to flying dinosaurs. Rick moved ahead to a section on the black vulture. Its scientific name was *Coragyps* of the Cathartid family. It ranged over much of the Western Hemisphere from the southeastern United States, Mexico and Central America to the northern parts of Chile and Argentina. It had been sighted as far south as Tierra del Fuego and on rarer occasions Antarctica. At this time of year in the middle of the southern hemispheric winter, vultures left Chile and Argentina for warmer climes.

He next read that the black vulture had a stocky bone structure and a short square tail, with a wingspan about 1.5 meters, and a height of .60 meters. He converted the statistics to a height of about two feet and wingspan of about sixty inches. *That can't be right!* On the island he had seen many *urubús* significantly larger, over three feet tall with a wingspan of nine to ten feet. Larger than a condor. He turned the page. The black vulture's corporal feathers were glossy black. Its head, neck, and feet bare, a matte slate gray. The beak also was also gray, exceptionally long and slender, no surprise there. So, the black vulture could be from .60 to 1.25 meters in height, with a wingspan of 1.5 to 3 meters, all glossy black and slate gray except for dark brown eyes and light patches on its primary feathers.

Hold it again. The larger urubús *of Florianópolis have no light patches.*

Rick reread the descriptive passages and saw no mention of completely *black* black vultures. He wished he had some photos to compare the vultures on the island with the illustrations in this book, but they had forgotten to bring a camera with them.

The book confirmed that vultures were diurnal migrants and roosted at night. They had exceptional health and could live well beyond fifty years if they had the good fortune to avoid man or mishaps. Disease was unlikely because they were generally antiseptic. Rick found that surprising. He had assumed that vultures transmitted foul plague and loathsome disease the way rats did.

He read further. Vultures nested in a variety of places: hollow stumps, trees, limestone bluffs, and even on the ground. That described the terrain between Sônia's house in Sambaquí and the far end of Jurerê. Social and gregarious, vultures nested, fed, and roosted in large groups, sometimes as many as a hundred. He did not look forward to the possibility of encountering so many *urubús* at once on the island.

A typical day for vultures began when they left their roosts at dawn in a relentless search for carrion. Empirical observation on the island had confirmed they had no shortage of dead animals. Penguins and fish regularly washed ashore. Plenty of land animals were also available as road kill because of the way Brazilians drove.

When Rick turned to the next section dealing with their feeding and killing habits, his theory of a cover-up became more plausible. Vultures did attack the living on occasion. They dropped rocks to crack open turtle shells or to kill their prey, and they had been seen clutching small animals in their talons and throwing them against boulders. The author must have been a military flyer. He had written: *If falcons, hawks, and eagles have been equated with fighter planes, then the vulture can equally represent the bomber.*

The book also explained why he had seen only turkey buzzards around Jupiter. Black vultures were nearly extinct in Florida. Ranchers shot them whenever they appeared because they preyed on newborn calves and cows weakened from giving birth.

Rick thought of Irene, Louisa and her children, and Roger Whitby. Vultures, especially the super-size creatures of the island, might very well attack living adult humans provided their victims were weak and defenseless.

He didn't want to be late for his meeting with Irene's cousin, and checked his watch again. He still had enough time to scan through the rest of this book.

The largest, strongest, and most aggressive vultures naturally dominated, their pecking order based on size and sharpness of beak. Threatening behavior towards rivals included an aggressive stance, with biting, grunting, and hissing. Otherwise, vultures made no sound. Rick remembered hearing, when he walked along the beach at Ingleses, something that sounded like a huge intake of breath, a sucking. The book stated that, to the contrary, black vultures blew air, mostly when they were feeding or fighting.

Another interesting fact: *Urubú* nestlings could sound exactly like a rattlesnake when they felt threatened, and they were imitative. Their long necks made it possible for them to assume bizarre, protean shapes, which explained why at times they seemed to take on almost human form, most commonly suggesting old women hunching in black shawls, exactly like those he saw among the pews in the church at Ingleses. On the sand, they often mimicked the walk of penguins.

Rick had seen them feasting on carrion. Now he would learn how they fed. The black vulture used its feet to secure the carcass and its beak to tear and pull at its flesh. If necessary, it stood on top of larger prey while dining. No matter the size or genus, Old World or New, the vulture first plucked out the eyeballs, flayed the skin to lay bare the muscles underneath, and then ate the meat, bone marrow, and viscera of the carcass. The *urubú's* large rasp-like tongue enabled it to probe with astonishing depth, to pull flesh, innards, and marrow into the mouth and down its gullet.

Rick no longer had any appetite and left his partially eaten sandwich on the plate. He thought about the dead. No funeral for Irene. The same with Louisa's boys. As for Louisa, her body had not been found. So they had said. What was he to make of that? *More substantiation for my theory of a big cover-up.* If predatory vultures mutilated dead animals and also attacked injured humans, Zé and his gang most definitely would make false autopsy reports and cremate the bodies within hours after they were discovered. Yes, a rational cover-up made sense.

He stopped reading. Translating technical Portuguese had left his mind fogged. He refreshed himself and left his hotel still an hour early for his appointment with Posner. He stopped at the *Museo Nacional* on the Avenida Paulista, which was on his way. He spent most of his time in front of a triptych by Hieronymus Bosch, the first original Bosch he had ever seen. The demonic creatures, monstrous hybrids, and tormented humans brought to mind his vivid and horrifying nightmares, and the *urubús*.

CHAPTER 34.
"THE THING TO BE FEARED"

ick almost retched when he entered the *Edifício Posner*, a six-story building above a garage and arcade in the middle of Rua Augusta. The lobby reeked of urine; so did the elevator, which chugged fitfully to the top floor.

"Of course, the dancer." Sérgio Posner greeted Rick in clear accented English when a secretary brought him into a plush rosewood paneled office. "I am delighted to see you again, *senhor* Rick."

Posner, a successful investment banker and real estate speculator, was a tall and sleek graying man in his forties, whose double-breasted Italian-cut taupe silk jacket had been carelessly thrown across a burnt gold leather couch at the far wall. He wore a starched white dress shirt with gold French cuff-links, taupe and teal green silk tie and matching suspenders, and expensive Italian lizard-skin shoes. His blue eyes reminded Rick of Irene.

Posner seated him opposite his curved dark rosewood desk, on which he'd displayed photos of his wife, a chubby, agreeable honey blonde in a green dress, and his two strawberry blonde daughters aged five and three. Rick found another family photo on the desk to be of more interest. It included the Fonsecas.

He had not made the connection in Florianópolis. Now he saw that although Margarita Fonseca was blonde and not of Azorean or even Iberian origin, she looked a lot like Rosa. Her husband could have been Nelson de Andrade's twin. Their twenty-two year old son, Rodrigo, taller and more muscular with thinning hair bore a striking resemblance to Zé, and, unless his eyes deceived him, more closely to Martin. The new Martin. Rick had many questions for Posner, but could he be trusted to tell the truth?

A jet black *empregada* entered the office wearing colonial style dress, apron, bandana, and white gloves. While she served *cafezinho*, Posner asked Rick about his impressions of Brazil and the business climate in the United States. He remembered Terri and expressed regrets that Rick's lovely wife had not come with him. As with most of the Paulistas engaged in commerce, Posner was comfortable with the English language.

Rick waited to steer the conversation to Irene until the *empregada* left. "I appreciate your taking the time to see me, especially because it concerns tragic family matters."

"In this world, one receives nothing unless one gives. There are questions I wish to put to you as well. But please, you speak first."

"I know that your sister and her husband stole a hundred thousand dollars of Irene and Martin's money."

Posner pursed his lips. "It was all Mauricio Fonseca's doing. He frequently used their son, my nephew Rodrigo, to do his dirty work. My late father . . . may he rest in peace . . . he never approved of their marriage. But Margarita had a way of getting everything she wanted. She did not always select wisely. Mauricio was what you *Norte Americanos* call a loser. My father purchased him a partnership in a furniture factory, one of the larges in Brazil. Within the first year, the partner bought out my brother-in-law because he was a drag on the business. Mauricio took that money and failed miserably in countless ventures. You might call him a master chemist. He can turn gold into mud."

"But why would they steal from Irene? They were millionaires."

"My sister, not Mauricio. She inherited half of our parents' estate. Everything was in her name, although and against my advice, she did give Mauricio and her children signatory rights to her accounts in New York. And Europe."

"Did you offer to help Irene and Martin get their money back?"

"There were too many problems. Irene could produce no legal papers describing why she had deposited the money in their account. For all anyone knew, she had paid back a loan. Besides, Margarita was my sister. We were married to each other financially because of property and accounts we inherited together. My sister and her husband refused to discuss the matter with me. In the end, there was nothing I could do."

Probably didn't try all that hard either. "Then the Kraais were unable to take action against them here in Brazil."

His face clouded. "Nothing I can prove."

"What exactly are you saying?"

Posner leaned forward. "You know how my sister and her family died?"

"An auto accident."

"An accident? All I know is their car missed a turn on one of our notorious roads, fell below to the rocks, and exploded in flames. They were incinerated almost beyond identification." Posner stretched his suspenders with his thumbs. "Tell me. Your friend Martin . . . he is doing well in real estate now?"

"Yes."

"Would you know how he managed to obtain the capital after losing a hundred thousand dollars?"

"They had more money in CDs, I believe. Only last summer we paid them back the fifty thousand they loaned us to help finance our dance studio in Jupiter."

"Really?" That fact surprised Posner. "Even so, let me tell you. I have suspicions. Impossible to prove."

"What are they?"

"My sister's car . . . their bodies . . . before they were discovered, someone impersonated Margarita and cleaned out her Swiss and German accounts. Someone else impersonated Mauricio and did the same in the United States. I have seen the signatures. They are perfect copies."

Rick understood what Posner was suggesting, but even if Martin had planned some kind of violent revenge, to be able to loot accounts simultaneously and successfully in two continents in so short a time was impossible. "Surely, you're not accusing Irene . . ."

"No, not Irene. In spite of everything, she came to the funeral to give me and my mother her emotional support. Martin did not. That is why I believe him capable of hiring people to kill my sister without telling Irene. She said things implying as much. Nothing definite. I must tell you that I have never believed the official story about the circumstances of Irene's death. *Meu Deus*, my God! She represented Brazil in the Olympics. Impossible she should have drowned. And how could Martin have married again so suddenly?"

"That bothered Terri and me too."

"Good. You came here for information. We make a trade. What do you know about her drowning?"

Rick told Posner everything he'd learned of Irene's death and that of Louisa Batardi and the boys. "And here's her taped diary."

Posner shook his head sympathetically while he listened to the end. "Poor Irene. She was a very sad and disturbed woman. You say all deaths are listed as accidental drownings?"

"Or climbing accidents. And I don't trust that police chief."

"Why?"

"Because I sense he's covering up something. I don't know if Irene told you he is Martin's business partner."

"Indeed." Posner's eyes narrowed. She never mentioned it."

Rick described Maria Lourdes, the Zimmermanns, and everyone else in that tight clique. He voiced his opinion that Sônia Batardi was their leader and that Martin was not independent. He told Posner his theory of a cover-up to protect real estate investments and the tourist industry. "Martin told us that the vultures got to Irene's body before the police found her."

Posner shuddered. "The *urubús* of Florianópolis. Yes, I understand what is troubling you. The desecration of the dead."

"If she was dead."

"What are you saying?"

"I don't know a damn thing about vultures except that they're scavengers and aren't supposed to attack the living. But those bastards are everywhere. Big, beautiful, sleek and shiny mothers. Some more than a meter in height. Always watching. As if seriously considering whether or not to take a living meal. Have you ever been to Florianópolis?"

"Yes, the last time about eight years ago on business. I prefer the local beaches. They're about a two hour drive from here to the ocean, north of Santos . . . Guarujá, Pernambuco, Bertioga and beyond to São Sebastião."

"What were your impressions."

"There's a dark atmosphere on that island, the winds very disturbing. And the people, as one would expect, are extremely insular. Secretive."

"That's it—the people. The island itself has spectacular views and great beaches. Florianópolis is like a mini-San

Francisco, but not like the popular images of Brazil."

"Yes, after ones initial reaction to all that natural beauty dissipates, it becomes absolutely oppressive there. Many of us who visit Florianópolis have said *this is not Brazil.*"

Flávio's exact words. Irene's too.

"And, *senhor* Rick, I can understand your uneasiness about the *urubús*, although I've never heard of them attacking the living."

"It's possible they might have gotten to Irene while she was weakened."

Posner sat back in his chair again. "That would be a death most loathsome."

"I'll tell you what I think. The main industry on the island is tourism. The last thing they want known is that the *urubús* devour humans."

Posner did not seem surprised. "It is normal behavior for men to protect their investments." Posner tapped his manicured nails on the top of his desk. "What you have said about the *urubús* I find most interesting. There is something else about the death of my sister I did not tell you. One of the doctors, coroners, I believe you call them . . . well in any case, he thought it odd that among all four bodies there was no evidence of eyes, nor any of their organs."

"Burned to ashes?"

"So I was told. Although much of their flesh was left on the bones."

"Do you think the vultures . . .?"

"*Quem sabe,* who can say? I am more concerned about what caused the accident and the looting of my sister's accounts. This policeman, Zimmermann. He lives well?"

"Like a millionaire." Rick read his mind. "Just how much was taken from your sister's accounts?"

"More than ten million dollars American."

Rick experienced a surge of adrenaline identical to what happened to him immediately before a dance competition. Ten million would explain how the Zimmermanns, Silveiras, de Andrades, Batardis, and even Martin could afford such expensive property, but not how they were able to loot the Fonseca accounts. Posner did not know either.

He had postponed the most important reason for his meeting with Posner long enough. "I'd like to see those photos Irene left for me."

Posner handed him a large manila envelope. "I never opened it."

He pulled out a packet of photos covered by a written message from Irene: *Rick, these are merely samples of what I found along the walls of the grotto. There is so much more, but I dare not go deeper into the bowels of that labyrinth alone.*

The photos were not very clear, but as best he could make out, they were of glyphs and drawings of grotesque creatures that resembled demons and gargoyles from medieval church illustrations and horror films. Rick swallowed hard when he saw a rendering of a monstrous humanoid similar to that thing in Whitby's last paintings.

Rick had never before experienced such intense fear and revulsion. This was not the self portrait of a madman. Better if it had been.

The writing or glyphs appeared to be neither cuneiform nor hieroglyphic although he was admittedly ignorant about ancient scripts. Many of the marks were misshapen geometric forms, others absurdly curvilinear. Rick thought they might be primitive abstract decorations and not communication. He assumed they had been done by the Indians who inhabited the island before the white man. There might have been many layers of societies over the centuries. Archaeologists were always revising their estimates of emerging civilizations, as had recently occurred with the pre-Incas of the Andes.

What was it about these glyphs that had terrified Irene, and what in the hell did she expect me to do?

He showed the photos to Posner, who shook his head not knowing what to make of them. "*Senhor* Sergio, there's something else besides the vultures I find peculiar about Florianópolis. Your *empregada* reminded me of it. I've seen hardly any blacks there."

"There are naturally fewer of them in the south of Brazil, supposedly because of the colder climate, although I do know that in the State of Santa Catarina racism plays a significant role. In the town of Blumenau, for example, they refuse to let blacks in the hotels or restaurants. However, I have heard that they instinctively fear the island."

"Why?"

"It is said that no *candomble* nor *macumba* can combat what they fear."

"What do they fear?"

"No one will say. Perhaps actions will explain it better for you." Posner got his secretary on the intercom and told her to send in someone named Aparecida. Moments later, the black woman who had brought them *cafezinho* earlier entered the office. Posner interrogated her rapidly in a slangy Portuguese Rick did not understand. Overcome with terror, the woman babbled incoherently, then repeated one word over and over, and hurried out.

That familiar word, the sound of his nightmares: *Kee-roo-poo-ree.*

"What did you say to her?"

"I asked Aparecida what it is her people fear about Florianópolis, the island. You saw how terrified she became."

"Yes, but what did she say?"

"These analphabetics can be terribly superstitious, and Aparecida was quite ambiguous about something too horrible to describe. I can best translate it as The Thing To Be Feared. Something horrible whose nature and shape cannot be known. Absolute nonsense, is it not?"

Rick, to the contrary, was forming a clear image of where and what that Thing was.

CHAPTER 35.
SKY OBSCURER

One must be motivated to ask why a vulture first plucks out the eyes of prey already dead. What primal act is it imitating? The answer can be found in analogous human behavior.

When cannibals react to primordial stimuli of forgotten primate archetypes and feast on the organs and flesh of animals or men, they believe they take on their physical, mental, and spiritual characteristics. How far back do these stimuli go?

Researchers in the wild have witnessed chimpanzees dining on the brain of a freshly killed baboon. The headhunters of Borneo, like Paleolithic man, crack open skulls to eat brains, which they consider to be the source of wisdom.

But all human victims are dead when their hearts and brains are devoured during cannibal rituals. So, except for religious symbolism and some questionable nourishment, dead brains have to be biologically worthless. Returning to my question about the vultures instinct that impels them to pluck eyes . . .

Batardi, Sônia Z., Ph.D.
THE VULTURE IN MYTH AND HISTORY.
Editora Pinheiro Ltda., São Paulo, 1979. pp. 56-57.

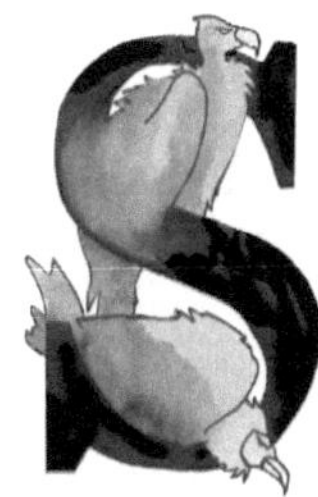hortly after noon, Rick carried his overnighter and his books past a pair of motionless *urubú* sentinels perched on the eastern wall of Martin's yard. He entered an empty house. Terri and Maria Lourdes would not be returning from the thermal baths until evening. Martin was away on business for the day. Lico must have driven him, or the *faxineiro* was with Sônia in Sambaquí. The cook and *empregada* also were gone. Odd, because Friday was not their day off. Well, he couldn't complain about that.

Privacy had its advantages. After Rick hid Irene's photos and tape among his clothes, he phoned Flávio's office. The secretary told him the architect still had not returned, no messages for *senhor* Rick, no answer at Flávio's home in Jurerê. Gabriela would be with Terri and the other women at the baths. Her *empregada* was probably on the beach with their son.

Rick put on his trunks and a T-shirt and took a bus to Jurerê, his least favorite beach community. It had one particular development of individually designed homes, which he thought to be bizarre, even otherworldly. They included massive two- and three-story nightmare fantasies in stone, brick, and tile with several styles in each construction, mostly an ill-fitting architectural mix of Portuguese Colonial, English Tudor, and Swiss Chalet.

Rick found Flávio's three-story, sharply angled house of brick, brown-tinted glass, and rust tile on the strand. After confirming no one was home, he stepped onto the sands. Jurerê was similar in shape to Ingleses, another crescent beach although smaller with tighter clusters of homes. The beach was crowded with humans and *urubús*. He ambled past them towards Ponta Grossa, the steep, rocky purplescent promontory at the western end. The sky was deep cerulean, the ocean transparent aqua under the hot afternoon sun, and the sand seared his feet through open thongs.

Rick almost tripped over a penguin carcass and nearly vomited when he took too close a look at it. Eyes gouged. Feathers and skin flayed back. Chunks of flesh missing. Viscera exposed in the relentless glare of the sun. A pair of dour *urubús* a few feet away waited for him to pass by so they could finish their meal in peace. Nearby, several children screamed and laughed as they escaped from waves rolling smoothly into the sands. He did not see Flávio's *empregada* and son anywhere on the beach among surfers and their groupies, penguin and fish carcasses, and vultures.

Timelessness and unlike objects. The entire scene was too uncomfortably surreal. The *urubús* had begun to remind him of the grotesque creatures in Irene's photos. If he was this obsessed with the vultures after a week in Brazil, how must they have affected Irene over a longer period of time? If only he could locate that grotto and see for himself.

High above dozens of *urubús* soared and circled before they disappeared beyond the promontory of the cliff. Something extraordinary had to be going on over there. He jogged toward the end of the beach and gingerly stepped over rocks and boulders along the base of the purple massif.

He removed his shirt and glasses, kicked off his shoes, and chanced a short swim around the bend. The surf refreshing, the tide gentle, he easily rounded the point. He saw about fifty yards away a small inlet with a narrow strip of clean sand, and on it a beached rowboat. Two tanned men in shorts and a chunky woman with a yellow parka over her bathing suit stood near an entrance to a cave or grotto. A body lay at their feet.

Rick dogpaddled between rocks without being

observed until he was close enough to figure out what was going on. Less than ten yards away from them, he hid behind a large boulder and squinted hard to flush stinging salt water from his eyes. A numbing fear chilled his blood when he recognized Ivo, Edmur, and Rosa.

Absolute nausea this time.

The body on the narrow strip of sand was in the same condition as the penguin he had just seen on the main beach. Bloody, pulpy eye sockets. Flesh stripped away. Internal organs devoured. Hair as blonde as Flávio's.

Rosa gestured impatiently. The men obediently carried the corpse to the boat, stuffed it into a body bag, and attached heavy weights at each end. They paused and lit cigars, Rosa a cigarette, as if it were part of the normal course of events.

Irene, Louisa and the boys, and now Flávio—all had died here on the island. How many others were there?

Rick moved around the rock as the men rowed Rosa and the body bag towards open water until a flash temporarily blinded him. His eyes were particularly sensitive to light, which was why he always wore heavily tinted glasses. He worried something threatening might have caused it until his vision returned. He saw nothing unusual, merely the glittering reflection of bright sun on the water.

Then Rick sensed a presence close by. He turned and was startled to see a black vulture watching him from another ocher boulder only a few yards away. No typical *urubú* of the island, it was far greater in size than any vulture or condor he had seen and read about. All black and matte gray like its smaller cousins, the hideous creature exhaled an asphyxiating odor of putrescence, the same he had experienced in Martin's car the day they arrived, the same as Terri's breath the first evening after she returned from the baths. Its expression was anthropomorphically intelligent, and, somehow, reminded him of Zé.

It stretched its neck to prehistoric saurian length, opened its night-black sky-blanketing wings to a span of more than ten feet, and obscured the sun. Was he imagining it, hallucinating, or was this grotesque creature, this ultimate monster of every childhood nightmare, actually real? Yes, a monster, how else to describe the demonic vulture whose open wings exposed sinewy arms folded across its squamous barrel-shaped torso? Or were they tentacles. Or both? He shuddered at the extended, reptilian neck, pitiless eyes, and great beak filled with sharp teeth, so similar to those beasts in Irene's photos.

Rick heard flapping behind him. Without looking back, he surrendered to his primitive instinct for survival and prudently dove as deeply as he could under the water. He swam beneath the surface back towards the main beach for as long as his breath held out. He prayed the creature was not amphibious and no equivalent sea monster lurked in these mysterious waters. When he broke the surface for air, the formidable monster had disappeared. So had the smaller black vultures. The promontory obscured his view of the rowboat.

Rick swam to the base of the cliff where he had left his things and warily watched the sky when he came out of the water. It was still empty of *urubús.* He came to a firm decision. He had to convince Terri that they must leave the island immediately. For the time being, he could only wait impatiently for her to return from the baths and imagine how Martin and his friends would fabricate Flávio's horrible death.

CHAPTER 36.
BLACK NIGHTWINGS

ick opened his third beer and wolfed several more delicious seafood cakes he'd found in the refrigerator. When he returned to the lounge on the veranda, the sun had already set. He zipped the jacket of his black warm-up suit and impatiently waited in the chilly darkness for Terri to return. He must have been more exhausted than he thought. The beer was making him sleepy. Probably had a higher alcohol content than the good old American brews. He caught himself drifting off several times. He had to stay awake. He needed to be fully alert when he dealt with whatever might happen tonight.

Tonight.
Night.
Pitch back night. Wings of night. Cold, melancholy night. He ought to turn on the lights. Better yet, go back inside.
Paralysis.
He was unable to move, imprisoned in the dark, not sure if he was awake or dreaming.
Black nightwings hovering above him.
Unwanted visions of forgotten childhood terrors buried deep in the recesses of his unconscious. Primordial engrams aroused. Adult memories of art, literature, and high-tech cinema special effects. Forbidden texts and primal legends.

Black nightwings transporting him beyond The Big Sleep. To Mythic Dream Time. Towards The Great All-At-Once.

Black nightwings lofting him away into an aberrant Boschian cosmos, towards the monstrous pre-human cities of Khatul, Goghu, and Uz-ulus, all populated by avatars of those abhorrent anti-gods on the grotto walls photographed by Irene Kraai.

Black nightwings carrying him beyond eldritch gloomy gothic forests of cathartine trees and gargoyle crags. Across sere glacial wastes and grim Ulalumic tarns. Over the limitless, desolate, evil tundra of Bab'yagh. Above fabled boreal Mount Yaanek.

Black nightwings carrying him to the Appalling Augustian Towers of Derleth and into The Mangled Maw of the Nameless Cylinder.

Down through the Bottomless Black Abyss. Inside the Windowless Solid with the Mega-dimensional Color Off The Prism.

And deeper into the drear deranged realm of Cthongh. There observed by The Fiery Eyes out of Darkness. Menaced by Lovecrafted Shoggoth un-shapes, repulsive humanoid megalonyx, demonic proto-pteroids, and more experiments of the Supreme Creator gone wrong.

Approached nearer and nearer by every foul joke and blasphemous mistake of The Venerable Archaics. Not for humans to see, not to be believed.

Seen and believed.

Black nightwings taking him past Eldmasters and Old Ones to the Great God Coz'thuli-Curupuri, The Eternal Self-Generator, taking him towards The Primal White Jelly. The birthing nest of the Ylem. The Primeval First Substance. To obliteration.

No, not obliteration. Not yet.

CHAPTER 37.
AN UNCONVINCING PERFORMANCE

Voices, familiar human voices, male and female. Lights coming on.

"Terri kissed his forehead, then recoiled worried. "Cardinho. Why, you're shaking, and soaked with sweat. And it's less than forty degrees out here."

"I had a nightmare."

"I'm not surprised." She frowned at the empty bottles of beer on the veranda tile. She helped him to his feet, threw her arms around his neck, and gave him a long, stimulating kiss, her breath scented from a strong minty mouthwash. "Did you enjoy São Paulo?"

"It was no fun traveling without you."

"And I missed you so."

Terri's response reassured him until he studied her in the patio light. She looked fit and well in her warm-ups and projected the same high-energy as the last time she returned from the baths. Was it his imagination, or had her features changed slightly during the short time they had been separated? It was something he sensed, not necessarily visual

"Everything go okay at the baths?

She pirouetted. "They were even better than the first time. And we're going again on Monday."

"I'll join you."

"Maybe later in the week." She kissed him again before they went back inside. "Tell me about São Paulo."

"Yes, how was life in the big city?" Martin poured himself a whiskey. Maria Lourdes brought out a spread of meat, cheeses, and assorted rolls.

The charade had begun, as if nothing had happened to Flávio. Rick shivered at his memories of the architect's mutilated corpse, the nameless monster, and his nightmare on the veranda. All of a piece. He struggled to sustain the pretense that he had not seen anything.

"São Paulo was exactly what you promised, Martin. Pollution, gridlock, incredibly noisy, plenty of crime, crowded sidewalks. My kind of town." He turned to Terri. "Are you still sure you don't want to see Rio or Bahia?"

"Absolutely. Martin and Maria Lourdes understand what I'm feeling. I can't find the right words to let you know how much I love it here. And the baths, Rick. I feel so much stronger than the last time I went. Like I could dance for days without stopping. Tomorrow night is Stefania's birthday party, and I promised Valéria we'd put on a show. I knew you wouldn't mind."

Leaving the island early seems to be a lost cause "I hope I'll be able to keep up with you." Rick managed a casual tone. "Anything interesting happen while I was away?"

Martin brushed his mustache. "No, and why should it? The rhythm is set here. Calm and tranquility. Did you accomplish everything you wanted in São Paulo?"

"Almost." *You sly bastard.* Martin was not going to mention Flávio. Why? Out of fear? Or had he become the coldest of fish?

"How were the *escolas da samba*, Cardinho?"

"I wasn't motivated to go without you."

Terri hugged him. "That's my man."

Zé and Rosa arrived. The two detectives had on drab woolen trousers and padded windbreakers of grays and blues as if they had been outside searching for their friend. Rick prepared himself for their announcement of Flávio's death, their usual con for his benefit. He put an arm around Terri, not for support but to gauge her physical reaction. The Zimmermanns glared at him like Vegas pit bosses when he was on a winning streak. *Giving heat*, they called it, a technique of intimidation. Classic cop behavior. Had Rosa seen him hiding behind the rocks?

Impossible. Only the monster-size vulture.

Zé accepted a whiskey from Martin. "We have some very bad news. Our good friend Flávio is dead. An auto accident, on his way back from Pôrto Alegre, just outside Laguna."

Rick felt no physical reaction from Terri.

"It's about a hundred kilometers to the south on the mainland," Martin said for Rick's benefit. "There are many very bad ungraded curves down there."

Zé drank his whiskey neat in one gulp. "Our Flávio lost control. He was burned, barely recognizable."

Like the Fonsecas.

Rick no longer believed . . . he *knew* that Martin, Maria Lourdes and the Zimmermanns were putting on this show for his benefit. He looked at his wife unable to read her expression.

Rosa glared at Rick. "We phoned Gabriela from Laguna, and she went to Sônia. We're going there now to comfort her."

Terri headed for the stairs. I'll get Rick's coat."

When Martin moved to confer with Maria Lourdes and Zé, Rosa reached out with long fingernails sharp as talons and dug them into Rick's arm. Her dark brown eyes burned with a malignant fire as she hissed, "Never again swim beyond Ponta Grossa at Jurerê. It is dangerous out there. We have had many fatal drownings."

CHAPTER 38.
MISTRESS OF LIFE,
DEATH, AND REGENERATION

t Sônia's sinister house against the cliffs at Sambaquí, Rick saw more wet unframed landscapes identical to Roger Whitby's canvases, but signed by Ivo. He whispered to Terri, "Suddenly, Ivo is a remarkably prolific painter."

She ignored his sarcasm. "Yes, he's closing his lingerie store and opening an art gallery in the arcade at the *Hotel Diplomata*. He's awfully good, isn't he?"

Frustrated by his wife's lack of curiosity, He took in the living room. Same ol', same ol', it was another typical social evening on the island. Gabriela gossiped with the women. Flávio's young widow had been content to accept the auto accident as an explanation and her husband's death. The men discussed money exchange rates and sports by the great ocher rock wall.

Although Rick was not surprised to see Yeda among the women, it was where and how that caused him to take a second look. The attractive salesgirl had on a low cut burgundy V-neck sweater, gray jeans, and black boots. She sat beside Ivo in Sônia's place at the center of the sofa and crocheted with Bubi curled in her lap, as if she, and not Sônia, were holding court. Ivo repeatedly fondled and kissed her.

Instead of reacting jealously, Sônia beamed at the couple. Tonight she had shed her layers of wool and wore a loose navy blue linen caftan that almost touched the floor. The baths must have worked miracles on her. Unusually mobile and vivacious, she moved vigorously throughout the room serving canapés and seafood cakes from a large silver tray. Sônia's benign friendliness was encouraging, and Rick intended to risk speaking with her later about her book on myths and legends of the vultures.

Lico handed Rick a beer before he asked for one and gave Terri a glass of mineral water. The *faxineiro's* smooth sienna-stone face and long brown hair, which fell to the shoulders of his black shirt, triggered sudden recall. Rick's memory flashed back to a photograph he had seen in Sônia's book. Impossible, incredible if true, the precise details eluded him. He would have to check it out later tonight.

Ivo came over to Rick. "I say, old man, did you find São Paulo as unpleasant as we all remember it?"

"You spoke English!"

"When it suits me, dear boy."

This was as inexplicable as Ivo's ability to paint in the style of Roger Whitby and Maria Lourdes' use of Americanese English at the *Diplomata* last week. What was the connection?

"Now then, be a good chap and tell us your impressions of São Paulo."

Rick refused to give Ivo the satisfaction of another remark about his mastery of Brit-speak. "As you all told me, it's another polluted, gridlocked, crime-ridden city. But it does have some great museums and art galleries."

Ivo preened in front of an oil. "I shall have the best *galeria* in all of Brazil. And quite soon."

Rick baited him. "I'd like to see your studio."

"Wish you could. Bit of a mess, and all that. Perhaps

next time you visit us."

"Perhaps." Rick watched Sônia come out of the kitchen with another full tray. "Your mother is looking exceptionally fit."

"The thermal baths, you know."

When Ivo went to his mother, Rick took Terri aside. "Sônia has come to life tonight."

"The baths."

"That's what Ivo said."

"Like I've been saying, Cardinho, they're fantastic, and they've done more than heal my back and increase my stamina. They've got the most recuperative qualities. That's why we have to stay here for the rest of our vacation. You want a healthy wife, don't you, so we can compete without worries at the Nationals in September?"

He could not go against that argument, and her mentioning the Nationals gave him cause for optimism. "Did you know that Ivo speaks perfect British-English?"

"Yes. I forgot to tell you. Sônia said she made sure he learned it, French too, when they lived in São Paulo. But he's such a Brazilian chauvinist, he hates to speak any foreign tongue."

You forgot to tell me about Louisa being a physician too. What else haven't you told me?

Terri joined the other women, and the wake for Flávio, Rick couldn't think of a more appropriate word, degenerated into another typically dull evening. He was sick of the whole thing. He didn't want to hear another word about Formula One racing, soccer, and assorted investments in any language. He took another beer from Lico and snooped in each of the bedrooms. They had not been altered since he had seen them last, except the photo of Whitby was missing, and so were his nightmarish canvases.

Sônia's den had been left open, and he went inside. Academic volumes and publications in the fields of Anthropology, Ethnology, and Epigraphology crammed her bookcases, many of them ancient books and manuscripts with titles in Greek, Latin, gothic German, Arabic, and several alphabets unrecognizable to him. Her scratched, ebony desk held more books and loose sheets of paper with exotic glyphs, runes, and drawings identical to but more delineated than the photos Irene had taken in the grotto. Beside them, Sônia had left her book on the vulture in myth and history. A worn geometric flat-weave rug hanging on the wall behind a high-back ebony chair caught his eye. Reds and blues dominated, with some ivory, black, burnt orange, and green.

Then the flat-weave rug's pattern shifted before his eyes from rectilinear abstractions of what he at first thought to be flowers to a clear depiction of a female human form holding a vulture by the neck in each hand—black vultures.

He turned when he heard a voice behind him. "That is a typical Anatolian kilim with a common motif. The Great Goddess, Mistress of Life, Death and Regeneration, holding two vultures."

CHAPTER 39.
SUPREME EXCARNATOR
AND REGENERATOR

ônia sat on the high-back ebony chair at her desk and adjusted her bulk until she was comfortable. She was an entirely different person without her usual layers of wool and Bubi on her lap. For the first time since they had arrived on the island, Rick saw something of the vibrant, intelligent woman with whom Irene could have been best friends. How and when did her good looks and slim figure deteriorate into bristly obesity? Surely, it had to have been caused by more than her severe burn.

"I believe you have become fascinated by our *urubús*."

"I used to think vultures were ugly, repulsive beasts, but the *urubús* here on the island are sleek and beautiful. Yes, I'd like to know more about them. That's why I picked up a copy of your book in São Paulo. I hope you'll autograph it for me when you come over for Martin's *feijoada* on Sunday."

"You were able to read it?"

"Not as well I'd have liked although the illustrations and photos helped. The Portuguese you used is too specialized for me, but I also found a helpful book in English."

Sônia listened to him recite its title and author. "How resourceful of you. Then you already have some understanding of the biology and habits of the black vulture."

"Very little, and absolutely zilch, nada, nothing about the vulture in mythology and history."

Sônia opened her book, and Rick held his breath. Was she going to explain what he'd been unable to translate?

"Martin has informed me that you are reasonably educated. Of course you would have learned there is a collective memory common to all mankind. Although it reveals itself in folk traditions and myth, it varies because of several factors . . . geography, environment, and the laws of cultural evolution. Nevertheless, we find many common threads concerning the vulture in world myth, legend . . ." She paused and pointed to the hanging kilim. ". . . and art."

Rick had been exposed to Jung's theories on the collective unconscious and primal archetypes in a college freshman Psychology course. Although twelve years had passed since then, he recalled s general overview. Carl Jung believed human memory held more than the events experienced in one's own lifetime. No baby was born with a completely blank hard drive. From the instant of birth, great primordial images were already present in the racial memory of each human. The individual's unconscious was the result of personal experience and manifested itself in dreams and neuroses. The collective unconscious was biological and instinctive, which explained how and why identical myths, even fantasies of the insane, appeared in every culture throughout the world. Given the proper stimuli, one might remember or dream as far back to the absolute First Instant.

My nightmares. They may not have been a mix of my experiences or fantasies and, instead, fragments of primitive memory.

"I'm surprised there's enough material on the vulture in history and myth to fill so large a book."

"Humans became obsessed with the vulture long before written history, as with other great animals like the bear, jaguar, and lion. From at least the Paleolithic to early historic times, it has been worshiped, revered, and feared as a god, sometimes even as The Creator."

Rick stood beside Sônia and looked at illustrations of wall paintings from Çatal Hüyük, a site she described as significant Neolithic settlement on the Konya Plain in Central Anatolia during the seventh millennium. One panel portrayed vultures hovering over human figures and skulls placed on towers, antedating Zoroastrian beliefs and practices. Another showed a female goddess in an arched niche holding two black vultures by the neck.

"Your rug is a copy of the wall painting."

"Copy, you say? That is open to debate. These wall paintings were not discovered until 1961. They date from about 7000 to 6000 B.C. My kilim is mid-nineteenth century. Although the weaver could not have possibly seen those wall paintings, his imagery may very well have been a product of a genuine collective unconscious. Assuming that is true, we might well ask what memory from the Paleolithic, or some earlier, remote era inspired Neolithic artists to draw these goddesses and vultures with such sophisticated iconography?"

One of the late Stone Age panels showed vultures carrying away bodies of the dead. In the next panel, they were reborn through the goddess. Another portrayed the same female goddess herself giving birth to a vulture.

"What do these illustrations symbolize?"

"The cycle of The Great Mother Goddess, Mistress of All Life." Sônia turned to a photograph of a majestic clay figure. The seated female had full pendulous breasts, elephantine legs, and an extended belly, as if about to give birth. Was the body Sônia hid under her loose-fitting clothes similar?

She summarized the text for him. "At the dawn of the Paleolithic era, the vulture had already appeared in man's collective unconscious and in religious symbolism that was further developed and refined during the Neolithic era and well into written history.

"Belief in the vulture as a supernatural medium of regeneration was not restricted to the cult of The Great Goddess of Çatal Hüyük. In the Hindu *Mahabarata*, the Great God of the Sky is the bird of life, destroyer of all, creator of all. The archetype for all mythical eagles and vultures. Through the millennia, from Tibet and India to the Nile valley, the vulture in manifold incarnations has been worshiped as the wind, the stars, the sun, or the storm."

One particular fact intrigued Rick. Because the vulture was associated with creation, death leading to rebirth, many of the ancients believed all vultures were female. A logical supposition. He'd read in some species the female was larger, stronger, and their roosts were run as a matriarchy.

A big-time connection.

The women of Florianópolis dominated the men despite their gaucho posturing. Lately, he had been no exception. Terri was having it all her way too.

Sônia turned to a gruesome scene depicted in the Sumerian Stele of the Vultures and translated the caption for him. "The people of Umma netted by the Patesi of Lagesh and devoured by vultures." She showed him more vultures among the inscriptions and reliefs of Sumeria, Assyria, Babylon, Hatti, and Egypt. "Look here how the Akkadians made an obvious copy of the Sumerian stele. It portrays their king, Sargon I, snaring enemies, and more vultures consuming the dead."

Sônia spoke not as a pedantic lecturer but used poetic English to create vivid images for Rick, who admitted ignorance of ancient history and religions. Until now, he had not known that in dynastic Egypt the *aleph* hieroglyph, the beginning glyph, represented the vulture and was associated with fertility. Two important Egyptian goddesses, Nekhebt and Mut, were portrayed as vultures. Vulture-goddess Nekhebt appeared on a wall in Queen Hatshepsut's temple near Thebes, *circa* 1500 B.C. More significantly, Nekhebt was the goddess of childbirth, the guardian deity of Upper Egypt in the pre-dynastic period; her image formed the crown of that region and part of the headdress of the mother goddess Isis, whose influence spread throughout Greece and Rome. Subsequently, and not surprisingly, according to Greek mythology, before creation there was Ancient Night, a bird with black wings.

The vulture again.

Its image commonly appeared on charms used by Greek and Roman midwives. At roughly the same time, the Zoroastrians did not burn or bury their dead for fear of defiling the sacred elements. Instead, they cast them into Towers of Silence for the vultures to devour.

Rick turned to the vulture-kilim. "Then the Zoroastrians had the same beliefs as the Neolithic inhabitants of Anatolia . . ."

"Who were, most probably, their racial antecedents."

"And the first inhabitants of Sambaquí also believed . . .?" Rick prompted.

Sônia did not confirm or deny. "Many mythologies describe the vulture as a god or messenger of the gods. The Amerinds used its feathers in the belief they could make their arrows fly accurately. They drank the juice of its talons for body strength. They worshiped it as Thunderbird, creator of thunder and lightning. Creator of the world."

"I'd always thought the Thunderbird represented the eagle."

"A common misconception." Sônia explained how legends of vultures and eagles, hawks and kites, all overlapped. The Old Testament had contributed to the problem. The Hebrew word *nesher*, which was sometimes translated as eagle or kite, more often referred to the Griffon Vulture, the most numerous among birds of prey in Biblical lands. Unlike their neighbors, the Hebrews had regarded the vulture as unclean.

Rick remembered the putrescent odor that had emanated from the monster at Jurerê and how vile Terri's breath had been after her first visit to the baths. Identical? He wasn't quite ready to make that connection, yet. If vultures had no noticeable scent, then that stink would have been from their prey, from whatever they had most recently consumed.

From unfortunate Flávio, and, God only knows, how many others.

Sônia pointed out a book for him to bring from the shelves. She opened the oversized volume of Meso-American art and laid it beside her own book on the desk. "The Mayan Codices described the vulture as the messenger of Hurakan, tempest god of thunder and lightning, which gave speakers of English the word hurricane from *huricano*. The Incas worshiped a Thunderer demigod in human form with hooked beak and wings. During the great solar festivals at Cuzco, the priests would chant to a vulture-fetish idol: *Oh, creator and sun and thunderer, be forever young! Do not grow old!* Of course, after the Conquistadors came, they replaced the old gods with Christianity." Sônia projected a short, forced laugh. "Still, as a result of the collective unconscious, the vulture appears on the coats-of-arms of Peru, Colombia, Bolivia, Chile, and Ecuador."

The phrase *be forever young* haunted Rick. Sônia had just explained the vulture's traditional connection with immortality, and last night in São Paulo, he'd read that at the very least it had an exceptionally long and healthy life.

This was getting spooky. Martin Kraai looked and acted twenty years younger, and he had spoken often of being rejuvenated. More than just a feeling of well-being? Rick had been wondering about the real ages of Maria Lourdes and all the other women in their circle of friends and how healthy everyone was, except Sônia, and even she had exceptional vigor tonight.

She showed him more illustrations of New World vulture-gods, which again reminded him of Irene's drawings. "Only two birds were represented among the day signs of the Aztec calendar. The eagle and *Cozcaquauhthli*, the vulture."

Cozcaquauhthli.

The dread-inspiring name resounded off the walls. "Let me see that book."

All the horrors of his dream-journey on the veranda returned. Glaring from the page, as if making eye-contact with him, was the malignant Coz'thuli-Curupuri of his nightmares. While Sônia continued to speak in detail about Meso-American deities, Rick came to understand why Irene had been in such awe of this woman and all the men groveled in her presence. This woman was brilliant, articulate, with extensive knowledge in far ranging fields. A forceful personality. A leader. Their leader.

Top of the pecking order.

He had already observed Sônia's cruelty towards Louisa, hateful behavior towards her grandsons, and autocratic manner when she ordered everyone about. Tonight for whatever reason she oozed charm. With the exception of relating her experiences in Mato Grosso at the *feijoada*, she had uttered no more than a few sentences to him. Now she was affable, generously answering his questions, and literally speaking volumes.

Why? For what purpose?

He did not delude himself. All his self-defense systems had gone on full alert. Sônia was revealing only what she wanted him to know.

"Consider this possibility, Rick. These may not be fanciful representations of some imagined god or demon, but realistic renderings of what Jung might have labeled as arch-vultures. Actually, I prefer proto-pteroid as a more user-friendly term. An entity similar to, but as superior in intelligence to those flying saurians, the pterodactyls, as we are to our primate cousins."

"I thought pterodactyls were extinct long before man came on the scene."

"Physically, yes they probably were, but it is possible that a few or a creature similar to them survived long enough to be indelibly etched into our primal memory. For the moment, let us refer to these particular illustrations of New World gods as proto-pteroids and not pagan deities or mythological. Think of the vulture's long neck and its ability to hiss, even to mimic the sound of the rattlesnake. In pre-Colombian Mexico, the Aztecs worshiped Quetzalcoatl, the feathered serpent. Feathered serpent, avian and reptilian."

"Are you saying the Aztecs worshiped an archaeopteryx, the winged serpent progenitor of birds and reptiles, but more fancifully drawn for religious symbolism?"

Sônia flashed a rare smile. "No, not fancifully drawn at all. Quetzalcoatl must have been a proto-pteroid indelibly etched in the Meso-American collective unconscious. And consider *this*, Rick. They may not be fanciful images of mythic gods or demons, but realistic portrayals of certain proto-pteroids, entities that predated even archaeopterex and the pterodactyls. Entities that somehow survived through the eons. "In my opinion, the gods worshiped by Mayans, Incas, and Aztecs . . . deities like Quetzalcoatl . . . they definitely existed."

Rick shuddered as his memory flashed back to the monster he saw at Jurerê. "You're saying we should take the myths literally."

"Yes. Primal memories of those intelligent pre-humans have appeared in religious and secular art over millennia. As fantastic creatures. Demons. Satan himself. Fire-breathing dragons. Feathered serpent gods like Quetzalcoatl. In any case, by the Neolithic age, our ancestors would have expressed their human psychic unity by worshiping assorted vulture deities all over the world."

Rick described his recurring dreams of black nightwings and journeys over aberrant, deranged landscapes to destinations filled with nameless horrors. He also described two Val Lewton films that had given him nightmares when he was a boy after he had seen them on a cable channel, *Cat People* and *Jaguar Man*. "And I was a sci-fi and horror buff in high school. I guess my individual unconscious has been putting on a retrospective of all the films I've seen and stories I've read by Poe, Lovecraft, Derleth, Campbell, and other writers of the supernatural."

"Not necessarily. Your own primal memory may be leaping farther back beyond your personal recall. I believe there are no such things as imagination or creativity. The writer or artist simply reacts to images and events derived from the individual or collective unconscious. Your dreams are nothing more than that."

Rick still had a long list of questions. "What can you tell me about the inhabitants of the island before the coming of the white man?"

"Nothing much to tell. No great ancient civilization developed in this part of South America. The Tupí and other Indian tribes ranged from the south of Brazil to the isles of the Caribbean. Their beliefs were a result of contact with the Inca and meso-American civilizations that in turn were influenced by . . ."

Why is she hesitating? "By?"

"More of that later. The pre-Tupí inhabitants of the Ilha . we really should not call them Indians . . . they were of unknown origins."

"Like the Sumerians?"

"Yes, and no. The Sumerians were decidedly human. We have their written history, their images. No, the pre-Tupí inhabitants had to have been those proto-pteroid entities that existed epochs before the appearance of the first primate, even before that seminal micro-organism which evolved into an arch-primate."

"You're telling me they're the ones who drew and wrote on the grotto walls?"

"Yes."

"And you're telling me they were proto-pteroids?"

"Yes." Sônia began to fade, her voice growing weaker. "They are of unknown origins, coming perhaps from another galaxy or another dimension hundreds of millions of years ago, then vanished except for a few that survived in remote places and climes later inaccessible to humans."

"But, as you've said, seen by our prehistoric fathers."

"And our primate mothers before them. The vultures you see everywhere on the island, anywhere in the world, condors too . . . they are devolved variants of the proto-pteroids."

Rick wasn't yet ready to ask about the terrifying creature he'd seen at Jurerê. "Getting back to what you said about vulture worship, was there, is there a cult of the vulture on this island?"

Sônia closed the book. "I am fatigued, Rick, but I we shall continue this discussion in the very near future. You should rejoin my other guests. Teresinha will worry about your absence."

He needed time and solitude to assimilate what Sônia had told him and to figure out why she had been so agreeable tonight. He also wanted to know why Sônia had avoided referring to one specific chapter of her book.

"Is Lico descended from the Tupí?"

"That is another long, and interesting story, which you shall hear when you are ready."

CHAPTER 40.
THE SHAMAN THING

"*. . . and so, when the time came, the elders made the dangerous journey across the vast angry sea of rocks to the frozen white land of the extreme south.*

And they trekked over and beyond the jagged pillars,

And they descended into the bottomless cavern of the mysterious light.

And they approached the Great God, Coz'thuli-Curupuri.

And She of the Numberless Eons listened to their prayers and assented.

And the elders selected one who was the most wise, the most perfect of health.

And Great God Coz'thuli-Curupuri was pleased and accepted the gift from the elders.

Oö, regeneration!

Oö, Supreme Creator of Prolonged Life!

Oö, Great God Coz'thuli-Curupuri!"

Ohm-Yorgh, last Ynu of Tierra del Fuego.

Interviewed by Dr. Sônia Z. Batardi, University of São Paulo, for her book, THE VULTURE IN MYTH AND HISTORY

nergetic and innovative, Terri more than compensated for the days and nights they had been apart. Rick's body was spent, drained of all fluids. His mouth ached. Even his eyelids hurt from her feral kisses and biting.

He caught his breath while Terri lay content against his chest. "I'd better go with you to the baths on Monday if I'm ever going to keep up with you."

"No, not until the end of next week." She turned over and fell asleep.

Rick lay wide awake beside her. His body might have been reduced to jelly by her love-making, but his imagination leaped from crag to crags of possibilities. At Jurerê, Flávio had been naked, no clothes nearby, no evidence he had been swimming. Rick thought it unlikely the architect could have fallen from the top of the cliff and impossible he would have been hiking in the nude, especially when he supposedly had been driving back from Pôrto Alegre.

Rick believed Flávio had been murdered, but murder for what purpose? He had another thought: What if cultists imitated the *urubús* and had mutilated Flávio as a sacrifice to their vulture deity? With the Zimmermanns in charge of police investigations and disposal of bodies, it would be impossible to challenge any official report.

Satisfied that Terri was deep in sleep, he slipped out of bed and dressed in his warmest clothes. He went downstairs with his Portuguese-English dictionary and Sônia's book on the vulture in myth and history, turned on a lamp in the living room, and settled in an armchair. He turned to the one specific chapter Sônia had not discussed, the Batardi expedition to Tierra del Fuego.

He studied a photo of the Batardi family. They had even brought six year old Ivo to the rugged inhospitable land. Sônia had been a striking beauty then, with a trim figure. Her resemblance to Terri, Maria Lourdes, and even Yeda was uncanny. Her husband, Dr. Batardi had been a tall, handsome man, blond and fair-skinned, and in the prime of life.

Sônia had interspersed her text of primitive creation myths with old photos of an extinct mountain people, the Ona, and the shorter, also extinct, sea-faring Yaghan. Portable fireplaces, which the Yaghan carried on their boats, had given name to their moonscaped land, Tierra del Fuego, Land of Fire.

Although Sônia's academic Portuguese created difficulties for him, her summary earlier tonight seemed to have cleared away some of his mental cobwebs. As best as he could make out, she claimed to have found and interviewed the sole surviving descendent of the mysterious Ynu, another mountain tribe completely unconnected to the other peoples of Tierra del Fuego and whose origins had been lost in remote time.

Rick turned the page and stared at a photo of the last Ynu. Standing on a moraine by a glacial lake, with only a wild llama fur cloak over his naked body, Ohm-Yorgh was excaeptionally tall. His gray hair was long, his eyes deep-set, his horribly wrinkled acromegalic features familiar, too familiar. Grizzled, leathery Ohm-Yorgh and smooth-skinned Lico were one and the same.

According to Sônia's text, Ohm-Yorgh, the last Ynu, had been 105 years old in 1976. If he was correct, Lico would be around one hundred and thirty-six-years old.

Be forever young.

A tidal wave of recent events flooded Rick's memory. The shock of hearing Irene's voice on her taped diary. Louisa's disappearance and the official report that the boys had drowned. His trip to São Paulo. Irene's photos. Posner's revelations. The creature at Jurerê and Flávio's ghastly death. Sônia's discourse. Terri's changed behavior, new health, and insatiable lovemaking.

The hour was late, his brain muscle-bound, but he had to press on. Rick selected a mix of books from Martin's shelves on anthropology, history, and some classics to refresh his memory. Joseph Campbell's *Hero with a Thousand Faces*. Frazier's *Golden Bough*. Homer Smith's *Man and His Gods*. He checked indexes and scanned through thousands of pages for related information.

Too much for him to assimilate here and now, he returned to Sônia's book and made some progress in her chapter on shamans and witch doctors. Throughout all world cultures, they went into trances in order to become one with the animals. Shamans believed that the Supreme Masters had originally spoken to man through beasts. Sônia cited many examples. Her illustrations helped. Rick was surprised to see representations of were-jaguars. In New World myths, the shaman-as-jaguar traveled through time and space. Would it also have been done as a vulture?

Sure enough, he read a few pages later that the Nigerians believed a witch's heart soared through the skies in vulture form while she was in a trance. When the vulture was killed, she died too. The same was true here in the New World, among the Condor Cult of Peru, and, Shamans commonly used hallucinogens for their out-of-body experiences. Did that explain his disturbing dreams where he also seemed to be out-of-body? Had he unwittingly taken hallucinogens?

Rick reviewed his diet. He'd overdone beer and cognac on occasion, and he eaten the same food as everyone else, often late ât night. He glanced towards the kitchen and pictured himself with a bright light bulb over his head when he thought of Sônia's delicious and addictive seafood cakes. Were the ingredients extracted from some local plant or mold? That raised more questions. How had those cakes affected Terri? What had she dreamed? Only once had he seen her eat them in large quantities. That was last Tuesday, before she fell asleep on the beach. And the children were forbidden to touch them.

Why had he been subtly encouraged to eat as much as he wanted? Were they trying to recruit him? Take away his will? Maybe those seafood cakes contained a hallucinogen strong enough to take him on those nightwing journeys. Like the shamans, did he become one with an *urubú* during those dreams? And where had those black nightwings taken him? Was it to some specific, fantastic place that never existed, or on a trip into the abyss of primal memory?

For the first time, he understood what one of his professors had taught many years ago. Like the individual unconscious, the collective unconscious also had a censor. That censor blocked out terrifying primordial images to maintain one's sanity. Those original LSD experiments and other uses of hallucinogens had been the keys for opening forbidden doors, doors best left shut, which was why madness had often followed their use.

He now had a hypothesis that made sense. A vulture cult existed on the island. He believed they used a hallucinogen in an attempt to become one with the *urubús*, and they ritualistically mutilated their victims as sacrificial offerings to their vulture gods.

Where did Lico fit into all this? To believe what he read and saw in Sônia's book, the *faxineiro* was more than one hundred-and-thirty-six-years old and generations younger in appearance than his photo taken in 1976.

Rick's eyes watered. Words on the pages blurred. Numbers merged. Threes and fives became eights. Too fatigued to think clearly, he rubbed his eyes and massaged his temples. Impossible to continue. Almost dawn. The *empregada* and cook would be awakening soon. He struggled to his feet and returned Martin's books to the shelves. Time for him to go back upstairs to Terri.

Terri.

He now believed his wife was becoming one of *them* and asked himself what she would want from a cult. He knew damn well what she wanted. Perfect health and a rapid ascent to the top of ballroom DanceSport. Terri repeatedly told Martin and Sônia she would do anything to achieve those goals.

Anything at what price?

And what could he do to stop her?

The activities planned for the weekend ahead seemed harmless on the surface: Stefania's fifteenth birthday party and debut Saturday night, and another *feijoada* on Sunday. Plenty of food and drink. But no seafood cakes. Rick intended to be clear-headed. He expected he'd get plenty of opposition when he announced his firm intention to go with Terri to the baths on Monday. He'd also keep her at his side until they left the island.

He squinted at a sudden glare and looked out the front windows towards the ocean reflecting a vivid pink and orange sunrise. High above, dozens of *urubús* glided in a widening circle.

CHAPTER 41.
THE CHOREOGRAPHER

Rick suffered through more days and nights with the same crowd, the same conversations and behavior, relentlessly watched by one or more of them and the *urubús*. He made it clear to everyone that nothing was going to prevent him from accompanying Terri to the baths on Monday. Because he ate none of Sônia's seafood cakes, he slept free from nightmares.

Accustomed to their behavior, he was not surprised when there was no ceremony and no mourning for Flávio. No one went to church to pray for him. Gabriela shed no tears and instead gossiped with her friends as if he never existed. He was disappointed that Lico did not make an appearance during the entire weekend. He wanted to verify that the *faxineiro* was indeed Ohm-Yorgh, the one hundred and thirty-six-year old last Ynu.

Sônia appeared only for Stefania's birthday celebration on Saturday night. She was failing rapidly and needed a wheelchair. Without missing a beat, Yeda took Sônia's place in the center of the clique. Everyone treated her as royalty, as the heiress to a throne. If Ivo's behavior was any indication, Yeda would soon become his wife.

The party at the Silveiras' country club was the only bright spot of the weekend when he and Terri fulfilled their promise to put on a ten-dance show. How could they not? Maria Lourdes and Fátima had surprised them with gifts of two matching outfits, which they had created: A daring crimson ballroom gown for Terri, a form hugging one-piece tuxedo for Rick; and a pair of Latin costumes in black and vermilion, all sparkle and glitter, and outrageously sexy.

Martin had a surprise for them. He had brought with him as a guest of honor the great Argentine choreographer, Felipe Gotelli, tan, sleek, and impeccably groomed The maestro's handshake with Rick was perfunctory, and he did not smile when he took Terri's hand.

When Martin began introducing Gotelli to the other guests, Rick shook his head. "I don't think he wants to be here. I wonder what kind of pressure Martin put on him?"

"It doesn't matter, Cardinho. We'll do our best, and just maybe we can get him to choreograph some dances for us."

"If we can afford him."

That night, in two minute bursts of music from a live band, they performed the fox-trot, waltz, Viennese waltz, tango, and an elegant quickstep, which had brought everyone to their feet. After they changed into their new Latin costumes, it was as if the design and material lifted them to a higher level. The Silveiras and their guests sustained loud cheering and applause while they flamed through the cha-cha-cha, samba, pasodoble, rumba, and jive. Stefania and Antônia were so awed and intimidated by their partnership, they stopped flirting with him.

Terri's back held up, and so did her stamina. Rick agreed with her assessment that no couple in the world could have beaten them that night. Not even the DeMarcos.

"Cardinho. Listen to their applause. We should give them an encore."

"Are you sure about your back, *passarinha*, my little bird?"

"Absolutely. Do you think we've impressed Gotelli?"

"Hard to say. He's got a great poker face. I'll give him that."

"Then let's see if we can crack it."

Rick inserted a new CD, which quieted their audience. The music was in three quarter time, a waltz unfamiliar to most, which began slowly and romantically. As the tempo increased, they separated to the far ends of the floor. Then Terri took a running leap towards Rick who caught her with one hand and lifted her high as she extended her limbs. While everyone cheered, he threw her into the air. She twisted until he caught her. They separated and repeated their *adagio* twice again, ending with another spectacular lift.

Martin brought them over to Gotelli. "What did you think of their performance, Maestro?"

"Adequate, although their choreography is very much dated."

Rick looked at Terri who nodded her encouragement. "*Senhor* Gotelli, we are well aware that we need better choreography, and we would like to engage your services."

"I doubt if you can afford me, and in any case, I am booked for the next three years. In fact, I have created some routines for a couple you have competed against, the DeMarcos, for their upcoming challenges."

Martin led them away from Gotelli. "Sorry about that. Perhaps we may yet change his mind."

"Like making him an offer he can't refuse?"

"No, Rick, nothing like that."

Terri kissed Martin's cheek. "Well, thank you for trying anyway."

"I promise you. We are not through with Gotelli."

CHAPTER 42.
ILL WIND

Once all lush green under golden sun and clear blue sky, by Monday morning, the island had become ghostly gray beneath a low mean scud with strong south winds and powerful gusts reaching hurricane-one strength. Malignant and wailing outside, the winds whistled and piped ominously through the shuttered windows of the guest suite in Martin's house. The wintry Antarctic blasts knifed through Rick's blankets and cotton T-shirt and shorts. Alone in bed, he awakened chilled to the bone in the frigid gloom. The small room heater was off. He reached out to jiggle the switch. No power.

His head felt heavy, as if he had imbibed too much the night before. Somehow they must have drugged him. And he'd been so damn careful too. He called out for Terri. No reply. Had she already left for the baths? Fearing for her safety, he imagined Martin and Zé blaming her death on the weather with their usual lies. An unfortunate auto accident. A tragic drowning.

He forced himself out of bed and got into his heaviest shirt and sweater, thickest socks, and black warm-ups. He would not be doing any exercises this morning, only the briefest of ablutions in the glacially cold bathroom.

On top of the toilet seat, he found a long note Terri had written for him. She'd gone with all the women for the thermal baths at eight this morning and didn't know when she would be back. Martin had already left for Floripa Central on business. The *empregadas* and the cook had another day off, so he was alone in the house.

In Martin's suite, Rick tried the phone. It was dead. The storm must have taken out the lines. He found another unsettling surprise on top of Martin's desk in the study unrolled and held open by paperweights. He looked down at professionally drawn detailed plans for a fourteen-story condo building on the Baía Norte. He took it to the window for more light. The design looked pure Flávio, but it had been signed by José Correa Zimmermann.

He needed hot coffee. Downstairs in Martin's dark unheated kitchen, every pilot-light was out. No propane left in the cylinders.

Incessant whistling and howling assaulted his ears. More frigid drafts sustained his chill. A mug of leftover cold coffee failed to clear his head. Despite Martin's attempt to construct a house with American creature comforts, air leaked through every window and door as it did through Sônia and Ivo's deranged homes in Sambaquí.

He went to the garage. It was empty, and he couldn't call for a taxi, any transportation to follow Terri. He returned to the living room and looked through the front window. Along the beach, everything was bleak gray with no horizon between foaming surf and morbid sky. He'd been told these funereal winds were supposed to last for two to three days. How did the *catarinenses* maintain their sanity?

He had a sudden dizzy spell and almost lost his balance, which convinced him that his food or beer definitely had been laced at the Zimmermann's *feijoada* in Trindade yesterday. He couldn't remember anything that happened after the meal. They must have drugged him to make sure he would sleep well into the next day and not make a nuisance of himself when Terri left for the thermal baths. After reviewing everything Sônia had told him and all he'd read, he believed his wife was in great danger.

Rick went to the bar and poured a stiff *Bisquit VSOP* to warm his innards. The winds leaking through the house now sounded like a monody sung by the Screech Owl Tabernacle Choir. He brooded over the strange occurrences and peculiar behavior he had been witnessing and reasoned algebraically: Irene is to Maria Lourdes, as Roger Whitby is to Ivo. Flávio is to Zé, as Louisa is to whom? Yeda? Ivo's mistress seemed to the most likely candidate. Then where did that leave Terri? No more speculating, he had to find his wife.

First, he needed transportation. He burst out of the house and stopped for a moment when he saw a pair of *urubús* perched on the east wall impervious to the gusts. He ran past them along the Estrada Geral for half a mile to the small local *farmácia* where he was told power and telephones had gone out all over the island. After some extensive haggling, the pharmacist's wife agreed to loan him her venerable Brazilian-made rusty green VW Beetle for a hundred U.S. dollars. Typical *catarinense exploitado*, but on this day he would have paid much more for transportation.

She gave him more bad news after he handed over a hundred-dollar bill. The bridges to the mainland had been damaged by the winds last night and were closed indefinitely. There was no way to drive off the island. No boats could possibly go out in this weather. The island had been cut off from the mainland before Terri could have gone to the baths this morning. Then where had she gone? His gut instincts advised him to hurry over to Sambaquí. If they were still on the island, Sônia's house was the most likely gathering place.

Thunder shook the island. Lightning split the

darkening sky as if a mad scientist had turned on his lab machines. And the rains came. Solid sheets. The Beetle's slow-moving wipers were ineffective with visibility barely beyond the nose of the car as Rick drove cautiously towards Sambaquí. Misty gloom shrouded the hills to the west when he veered off the main highway to Florianópolis Central and took the narrow two-lane road along the rocky littoral of Sambaquí. Here, the full fury of the south winds assaulted storm-battered dwellings and sullen cliffs. He saw no living thing on the muddy road, no sign of human life inside the frail shacks, no spectacular view across the bay to the mainland and condos of the Baía Norte. A gray horizonless veil hung over Sambaquí and obscured everything.

A piece of tile flew towards him from a cliffside home and grazed the Beetle. Rick swerved on reflex. He skidded, turned, and braked for a quarter of a mile along the muddy road. After he barely avoided slipping off the edge and falling to the rocky shoreline, he regained control of the car and drove slowly past Ivo's dark and uninhabited house until he reached the dead-end of Sônia's gated property.

The sky changed from murky gray to opaque charcoal black even though it was afternoon. When Rick got out of the car, the solid downpour soaked him. He hung onto the door handle as a powerful gust nearly took him off his feet. Flashes of lightning hurt his sensitive eyes. Thunder echoed overhead, shook the ground, and rattled his eardrums. Trees around him twisted in permanent agony. Rocks appeared to him as misshapen monsters and gargoyles struggling to break free from their petrified prisons. Was this the real world of a typical sub-tropical storm, or had he entered a grim mythic realm? He was coming to believe they existed co-equally on the island in overlapping dimensions.

The surf was too high and treacherous for Rick to risk the slippery trail to the rugged rocks below and approach the house along its water side. Instead, he climbed the slick ten foot high iron gate and prayed he would not impale himself on the sharp spikes at the top. He dropped to the muddy ocher sludge of the driveway and slid for several feet. He saw no cars at the bottom, no lights on in the house. That did not guarantee it was uninhabited, power being out all over the island.

The driving rain poured off rocks and roof with the roar of a waterfall. Branches and debris flew all around him. Shuttered windows rattled. Roof tiles crashed and shattered on the veranda. Chimes danced crazily to the sustained gusts howling like a hundred auto alarms going off at once.

The veranda door was unlocked, and he stepped inside. The living room fireplace roared full blast. Dressed in her usual layers of beige and gray wool, Sônia crocheted in the center of her couch without acknowledging his presence. Bubi looked up, growled, then snuggled in her lap. On the table in front of her was a *cafezinho* service and plate piled with seafood cakes.

CHAPTER 43.
"THERE IS NO VULTURE CULT."

ônia's flabby flaccid cheeks and jowls obscured her neck. Her mustache and bristly chin hairs also disgusted him. Her greasy unwashed graying hair radiated from her face as if she were indeed the dreaded Medusa. He really didn't know what kind of body she hid under those layers of wool, didn't want to know. Her repulsive appearance did momentarily turn him to stone as the wind wailed, piped and whistled a dismal dirge through each crack in every door, window, and ceiling beam.

Water dripped from Rick's clothes to the tile floor. As he moved towards the fireplace, he saw that the walls were filled with more recently painted landscapes in the style of Roger Whitby, all signed by Ivo.

He still felt the effects of the drug he'd been given last night, mind fogged, limbs heavy. He turned his back to the fireplace and tried to focus on the woman. "Where is Terri?"

"You will see her presently. And whatever terrible things you are imagining, forget them."

"Why should I believe you?"

"I . . . we all want the very best for Teresinha, and for you too." She stroked her min-pin. "However, your untimely arrival complicates matters. Fortunately, I was alerted."

"How? By whom?"

'Do you think our *urubús* go out in this weather for pleasure?"

"So that's why they were out in the storm." He was not yet convinced, but he had to say it. "You must be doing the shaman thing, having out-of-body experiences with the vultures."

"In general terms, yes." Sônia mocked him in a high-pitched witchy voice, "Would you like some seafood cakes, dearie?"

"A hallucinogen?"

"Yes, an essential ingredient of my recipe. There is a lichen unique to the island."

"Which explains my dreams."

Sônia bared yellow teeth in an unnatural smile. "In part. The Tupí, who inhabited this island before the Europeans arrived, and later a few *açoriano* immigrant families, mine among them, used that particular lichen hallucinogen, which enabled them to fuse with vultures."

The other night, Sônia had described her research into vulture myths and history. Moments ago, she'd admitted to out-of-body experiences. Sônia must have been revealing to him in stages what Terri already knew, and she wanted him to join their cult, or whatever it was. He had to keep her talking until he could devise a viable plan of action to rescue Terri.

"The significance of *Kee-roo-poo-ree* . . . is it really The Thing to Be Feared? The Thing That Shouldn't Be?"

"Excellent, Rick. An adequately enough pro-nunciation. You have investigated very well. I am sure Irene's tape and photos helped."He stared at her dismayed. "You've known about them?"

"From the moment she began to explore the grotto, photograph and record. It was not Flávio who hired that urchin to give you the tape."

Of course not. He was probably already dead.

"What is the meaning of all those drawings and glyphs in the grotto?"

Sônia put her skein of wool aside. "There are more grottoes, caves, and other remote places like it all over the world. The week before Teresinha's father butchered them, my mother and sisters visited me at a particularly significant site I had discovered in the mountains of Georgia north of what you call the Florida Panhandle." Rick stared at her in shock, and Sônia anticipated his questions. "I did not think it necessary for Irene to know that I am Teresinha's aunt. After they moved here and when the moment was right, I did tell Martin. Thanks to Irene's letters and our conversations about my niece over the years, I knew she was well taken care of. I expected she would visit Floripa soon after Irene and Martin moved here. I made sure he pressured you to come after Irene met her unfortunate end."

"And does Terri know you're her aunt?"

"Yes, of course."

"When did she know?"

"Within a few days of your arrival. She wanted to tell you, but we thought it best for you to learn our relationship at a more favorable time. In any case, the grotto Irene discovered has been known to my family for almost two hundred years. When I was a child, my mother moved to São Paulo where I could be educated in languages, symbols, and mythology. My family wanted me to acquire the skills and intellect necessary to translate the glyphs and understand the wall paintings. You already know that I was in Mato Grosso many years ago. There, I encountered more than primitive tribes or unusual flora and fauna. I entered a cave, a very deep cave with walls of an unknown substance. Man-made, I originally thought. I could not have been farther off the mark And it was covered with writing and drawings."

"Like those Irene found in the grotto?"

"Similar. As you may have read in my book, my husband and I were in Tierra del Fuego where the extinct Ona, Ynu, and Yaghan once lived. Previous expeditions had already recorded their legends, which were identical to those of the tribes in Mato Grosso. We explored many more caves where the Andes end at the tip of our continent, with very significant findings."

Sônia related how she and her husband had left Tierra del Fuego with Ohm-Yorgh as their guide on a secret expedition to the Antarctic, and there they found proof for the theories she had first formulated and confirmed as fact in Mato Grosso and other places throughout the world.

"I discovered the existence of a mysterious Thing whose nature could not be known. Primal, primordial. Described in distorted legend and myth by peoples all over the world. Surviving to this day in remote locations. Breeding more actively again because of global warming and holes in the ozone layer directly over Tierra del Fuego and the deepest recesses of Antarctica.

Although Sônia's narration had answered some of his questions, it created many more. How exactly and where did she first encounter Ohm-Yorgh? How could he survive to be an active and strong one hundred-and-thirty-six-year old? What secrets had he revealed to her.

"Then your husband was still alive when you went to the Antarctic. Is that where he died?"

"That is all you need to know about him, for now. In any case, after my travels all over the world, I returned to the island of my birth and in the grotto Irene accidentally discovered, I translated the glyphs and interpreted the drawings. I learned how one could attain greater knowledge, perfect health, and approach immortality. Rick, you have no idea how old the women are. Maria Lourdes, Rosa, Gabriela, Fátima, and Valéria. And some of the men."

"Like Ohm-Yorgh aka Lico?"

"Yes."

"And Martin?"

"He knows everything and has accepted it. You have seen for yourself how he has peeled away the years."

"What about your health?"

Sônia sighed. "Even the longest lived creatures can have their time on earth cut short by unexpected events. Cosmic catastrophe or viruses. In my case, it was carelessness. An unexpected gas explosion. It altered the pattern of my metabolism and created metastasizing cancers, as so many accidents do. True, I can postpone the inevitable, live at least another six months, perhaps a year. Exist is a better word. I can exist in a medicated stupor, or function in unbearable pain and discomfort."

"And you're still telling me that Terri will be all right?"

"Better than all right."

"Why should I believe you when Irene, your best friend . . ."

"She did not need to die. I did not want her to die. When Irene's cousins stole from her, I wanted to help her take the sweetest revenge. I loved Irene. She was the best friend of my youth. But she would not listen. Not to me, not to Martin. If only she had not found the grotto, seen the drawings on the walls. When Irene threatened to expose everything, we could not let her destroy us."

"I never really believed she drowned."

"Please, Rick, listen to me. Martin and I want you to understand. Teresinha did your first night here."

He moved away from the fireplace and stood over her. "Terri understood what?"

"The truth. Her destiny. I am her aunt." She gestured to take in the entire room. "*This* is the house where Teresinha's mother was born. Her father could not kill us all. Maria Lourdes, all the women, we are her blood. Teresinha has come home to family."

Rick felt sick to his stomach that he had missed the obvious. "I should have seen that. Tell me, what really caused Terri's father to go berserk?"

"João Alves was a *gringo* from Pôrto Alegre who came to Floripa on holiday. He and Yara, Teresinha's mother, fell in love, and despite our advice and pleas, she married him. Several years after Teresinha was born, he found out what we are."

"*What* are you?"

Sônia ignored his question. "He took his family away from us and emigrated to the United States. Eventually, he could not face the reality about us and took to drink. He became an abusive drunk. Yara wanted to leave him and return to us with her children, but she lacked the resources to do it. We decided to help. My mother and sisters flew to Los Angeles where, as you know, they, Yara, and her daughters except for Teresinha, were hacked to death by that madman."

"Where were you when it happened?"

"I stayed behind in Georgia. If I had gone with them, I might have prevented the slaughter . . . or died with them."

"Why didn't you raise Terri when she was orphaned? Those awful foster homes . . ."

"She was in shock and too young to understand. By the time I was ready to claim Teresinha, she had become Irene's surrogate daughter, which made it easier for us to watch and wait. After Martin and I encouraged Irene to move here, I knew that Teresinha would visit them and come home to us. And, we have been allowing you discover the truth bit by bit, especially during your hallucinatory sleeps. Understand this. I, Terri and Martin . . . we do not want you to meet the same fate as Irene and Flávio, or go mad like João Alves."

"And that's why you've been trying to get Terri to join your vulture cult."

"There is no vulture cult."

Rick sensed someone behind him and turned around. Lico stood in the doorway covered only by a cloak of animal skins.

CHAPTER 44.
SECRETS OF THE GROTTO

t is time for you to go. Lico will take you to Terri," Sônia handed Rick a halogen lamp sitting by the fireplace.

"To *Caldas de Imperatriz* on the mainland? How? All the bridges are out."

"Teresinha is here on the island. I promise you this, Rick. You will never have to worry about her health again."

Before he could ask Sônia what she meant, the woman stretched out on the couch and closed her eyes. Lico removed several large stones from the boulder wall to the right of the fireplace and motioned for Rick to crawl through the opening ahead of him.

Concern for Terri overrode any dread of the unknown. He got on his hands and knees and entered the orifice where high-pitched winds echoed in counterpoint to the basso-profundo roar of agitated surf. After covering no more than ten yards, he stood on a ledge only a foot above surging water. Some wiser person in the past had constructed the house against a land-side opening into the grotto that Irene discovered.

Lico grunted and pointed for him to move out to their right. As they trudged along the flat, slippery surface above the water, Rick's legs were less than steady, his head heavy, but the damp cold air helped sharpen his wits. How could Lico tolerate the near freezing temperature in that loose cloak of llama skins?

He guessed that the path went all the way to the isolated strip of beach in Jurerê where he had seen Flávio's mutilated corpse. He figured it would be about fifteen linear miles away to the north, and ten times that through this diabolically laid out maze of honeycombed interconnecting passageways, tunnels, and dead-end caves. He never would have been able to find Terri on his own. Just as well that the sienna colossus was guiding him. Lico, however, was a poor spelunking companion. He would neither answer any of his questions about Terri nor react when Rick addressed him as Ohm-Yorgh and asked half in jest how things used to be in Atlantis, or Mu, or Cthongh.

After many confusing turns, the grotto ended in a murky, subterranean bay. The footpath widened and snaked in and out of serrated tunnels. Rick often came close to retching. The atmosphere was humid and foul, as if he were walking through a limitless reeking exhale. He stopped abruptly when the bright light of his halogen lamp caught an albino misshapen form the size of a child, repulsive and blob-like. As it slithered away, he also saw chalky spiders, efts, slimy worms, and blind mutated ghostly-white penguins.

From the darkness to his left, a dull, scraping noise became louder. Something large was approaching from a converging tunnel. Rick turned his lamp to the sound and stepped back against Lico. A beast crawled towards them slowly and purposefully. Covered with fine damp silky fur, it was albino like all life in the grotto. Its long sinewy arms and egs had three fingers and three toes with long curved nails that made the scraping noise on the grotto floor. Although the creature's oversized round head definitely was not primate, it was eerily humanoid.

Familiar.

The tormented creature in Whitby's paintings.

This disgusting albino thing, which he could not name, was only a few feet away when it rose to its knees, its blind eyes level with his. It reached out with extended fingers and curved nails to embrace him. Rick swung his lamp and hit its shoulder. The creature opened its mouth and cried out in high-pitched pain, *"Ai, ai, aiiii!"* It rolled away from the light and disappeared in the darkness with a slow, measured scraping sound. And unbearable human whimpering.

Shivering with revulsion and fear, he rested his free hand against the wall and vomited. After he recovered, he said, "What the hell was that? It was so human."

"Yes, that's the worst thing about them," Lico said in perfect English. "It is a mutation of the megalonyx, a giant ground sloth. It has survived from the Pleistocene Era, like so many of the living things down here. They are harmless but can be a disagreeable nuisance."

Rick knew he ought to have been surprised that Lico understood and spoke educated English. What Sônia had told him, a specific photograph he remembered, and his reasoning and speculation had coalesced to prepare him for this moment. He believed the unbelievable and that this hundred-and-thirty-six-year old forbidding man would have had several identities.

"Ohm-Yorgh, you must be more than the last Ynu of Tierra del Fuego. You are Sônia's husband, Dr. Batardi. But how?"

"I am Lico." He gripped Rick's shoulder and pushed him ahead. "We must continue."

He felt Lico's deep-set eyes fixed on the back of his neck like two laser beams when they entered a huge opening filled with stalactites and stalagmites. He wanted to ask more questions and learn everything about his massive, ageless dour guide, but his concern for Terri overrode everything.

Was he having another realistic bad dream? Or was he being taken into the bowels of an antipodal, infernal Shangri-la? He took in his surroundings. No, he was not dreaming. He was walking through The Mangled Maw of his nightmare, the same journey he had taken on black nightwings.

They emerged from the fanged conduit and descended into a spacious vestibule. Rick froze when Lico took the lamp from him and illuminated the walls of a worse than nightmarish gallery. He stared in horror at realistically rendered drawings and paintings of the same non-human shapes he had seen in Irene's manuscript. Here they were in every possible monstrous variation and combination. They were beaked, winged, tentacled, and taloned. Saurian and insect. Vegetal and plantal. Bloated microbial blob shapes. All of them more terrifying than all the demons, dragons, gargoyles, and bug-eyed monsters of religious, artistic, and literary fantasies. In most panels, the creatures feasted on domesticated quasi-human slothoids, wild saurians, and pre-primate mammals.

Several paintings were of pteroidic beasts. He guessed they were from five to ten feet in height with black, scaly, ridged barrel-chested torsos, muscular arms, two pair of sinewy tentacles, and membranous wings spanning twice their height. Attached to the torsos, their extended saurian necks supported vulturine heads of slate gray with long beaks. Keen intelligence emanated from their pitiless eyes. Gray tarsi and feet with five talons completed the ghastly portraits of things that most definitely should never have been.

But they existed, definitely existed, and not only on this wall. Also in his primal memory at the very least. And in reality, if he had not been hallucinating the other day when he saw Flávio's corpse on the beach at Jurerê and the monster on the ocher rock.

Rick was not hallucinating now but wished he was when Lico illuminated a series of panels that graphically portrayed in sequence the disgusting feeding habits of the proto-pteroids. If the *urubús* ever forgot why they plucked out the eyes, these wall paintings were here to remind them. Somehow, these same bloody images had been indelibly etched in the human collective unconscious as well. How else to explain that photograph of Mayan basaltic rock sculpture in Sônia's book: A sinister, reptilian black vulture perched on a human head; the *urubú's* perforated beak piercing the center forehead of its prey; the victim's eyes already plucked.

On another series of panels, other-worldly yet relatively benign entities waged war against ghastly pteroidic creatures that were more evolved and complex than even the proto-pteroids.

"Who are they, Lico?" What are they?"

"They have had countless names, as many as there have been deities and demons. Although I am a scientist, I prefer the names given them resulting from the primal memories and collective unconscious of the virtuosos of horror tales, Lovecraft, Derleth, and others . . . probably a rough equivalent of these entities' true names. Elder Gods or Eldmasters, and Great Old Ones or Ancient Ones."

Rick remembered what Sônia had told him. "You're saying if we think of or create such monster in our minds, they actually existed."

"Do not confine yourself to past tense." Lico lectured as if he were Dr. Batardi back in college speaking before his students. "Long before that first one-celled mother of us all appeared in the ylem, the primordial ooze, hundreds of millions, perhaps a billion years ago, these non-human Eldmasters and vulturine Old Ones struggled for control of the Universe. They fought great wars with hordes of avatars created in their images out of intergalactic slime."

"Were there any good guys among them?"

"The Eldmasters fought for light and order, while the Old Ones supported darkness and chaos."

Rick could not avoid thinking of his favorite sci-fi TV series, *Babylon Five*, in which the Vorlons fought for order against the Shadows who sought to create chaos and war. Had it been the product of creativity or the collective unconscious?

He looked again at the panels. "It seems that the Eldmasters won."

"Yes, they were victorious and banished the Old Ones to our hellish young planet, which became the cosmic equivalent of a penal colony . . . and war zone." Lico took him over to more panels. "Look here. Over eons, the vulturine avatars of the Old Ones were contemporary with other malformed primal monsters also banished to Earth by the Eldmasters, against whom they warred for control of our planet."

"And the Eldmasters never interfered with what they were doing on Earth?"

"Not for a very long period of time. The Old Ones were left to their own devices, and those beings, with intelligence far beyond human understanding and the secret of immortality because they were as gods, created their abhorrent civilizations and built mythic evil cities in which they carried on their unwholesome, unspeakable practices."

"If they were immortal, why did they disappear?"

"We do not know exactly, although we have narrowed it to two theories. Both may be correct. One is that when the Eldmasters saw the loathsome civilization the Old Ones had created, they decided to eradicate them. A second theory postulates that about 230,000,000 years ago . . . if you can conceptualize that much time . . . by the end of the Paleozoic era, in the Permian period, about ninety-five percent of all living species on earth had been rendered extinct. Again, about 65,000,000 years ago at the end of the Mesozoic era, in the Cretaceous period, still a very long time before the appearance of the first primates . . . the dinosaurs and about seventy-five percent of all other living creatures also became extinct."

"And the proto-pteroids?"

"Even they. If they were not destroyed by the Eldmasters, there would have been unexpected cosmic catastrophes, terrestrial disasters, radical climactic changes, and viruses that can attack all living things. But, as I said before, some survived in places unknown to us, evolved . . . or, I should say, devolved and adapted to our changing planet. The first primates would have been awed, at the very least, when they encountered surviving proto-pteroids, or their images. It is also likely that the first primates were the result of experiments by the Old Ones to create food, beasts of burden, and fiendish amusement."

Lico illuminated several panels portraying the obscene experiments of The Old Ones. Experiments gone wrong. False starts with tortured mammals, some evolving to became primates.

Rick turned away disgusted. "Although I haven't consistently practiced my faith, I prefer the Book of *Genesis* to be the true story of Creation if this is the alternative."

"Look again at these panels, these illustrations. Even if you still believe the Biblical myth of creation, is it not obvious that Lucifer-Satan was one of the Old Ones? That the serpent in the Garden of Eden had wings and feathers?"

All Rick's defense mechanisms went into play. He blocked out other revolting images. He refused to face the only logical conclusion to everything he was seeing in this hellish gallery. He thought only of Terri. He would not rest until he held her in his arms.

"Take me to my wife."

"Yes, it is almost time."

Lico shepherded Rick out of the vestibule, through an arched entry, and into a circular arena. Its diameter was the length of a football field, with more archways, and a peculiar rectangular stone monolith in the center, about fifteen feet long, six feet wide, and four feet high. illuminated directly from above by a bright light from some unknown source, or from within.

No, not rectangular.

Not of stone.

A protean, mega-dimensional form. No accident of nature. Not man-made. Perhaps not even of this planet.

Its shifting brilliant colors disturbed Rick's eyes and agitated his memory.

The Color Off the Prism.

CHAPTER 45.
INSIDE THE
WINDOWLESS CYLINDER

ick stood at the bottom of a massive metal cylinder hundreds of feet deep, its top obscured because of the lighting below. The smooth vertical walls emitted soft reflected light between dozens of arched niches shaped to hold, and Rick's blood froze, shaped to hold the average *urubú* indigenous to the island. A half-dozen more alcoves were large enough to accommodate the creature he had seen at Jurerê and those ten feet tall proto-pteroids depicted on the vestibule walls.

A loud unpleasant sound assaulted his ears when dozens of *urubús* flew out of the niches. They hissed, blew air, and exhaled an overwhelming fetid odor, mephitic, asphyxiating, musty. Several black vultures took turns to dive towards Rick. He raised his arms to defend himself. It was not necessary. The *urubús* pulled up at the last moment and flapped over him. They flew back to their niches and settled like old women in black shawls waiting for some priest to bless them. These vultures no longer looked beautiful to him.

And where was Terri? Which archway led to her?

Lico gestured to take in the entire area. "This is The Windowless Cylinder of Birth, Death, and Regeneration."

"I don't give a damn what you call it. I want to see Terri. Now!"

Lico held Rick's arm. "You must stay where you are, no matter what you see."

Rooted to the arena floor in surprise, he watched Martin, Zé, Ivo, Edmur, Nelson, Maria Lourdes, Rosa, Gabriela, Valéria, and Fátima file into the cylinder from another tunnel. More men and women emerged from the archways until there were as many humans along the walls as vultures peering from their niches. The *catarinenses* were dressed in their everyday clothes and conversed normally as if they were taking a *cafezinho* break in Floripa Central.

It was a *cafezinho* break. Surreal and incongruous in this other-worldly pit. Eva was among the *empregadas* serving demitasses of coffee, and he recognized other faces, including a short diffident man of Indian extraction, the Governor of Santa Catarina.

Only Terri, Yeda, and Sônia were missing. That did not bode well. "Where is my wife!"

"*Calma.* You shall see her soon enough."

After Zé, Ivo, Edmur, and Nelson conferred with their wives, they left through one of the archways. Sônia's son was rubber-legged and had to be supported. Martin started to move towards Rick but was held back by Maria Lourdes. She authoritatively moved him to a place along the cylinder wall below a niche. She then went with Rosa, Fátima, Gabriela, and Valéria to the gleaming, ever-shifting shape.

Rick felt a stone of disappointment sink to the pit of his stomach. Although Martin had no autonomy among these *catarinenses*, he obviously was a willing though minor participant in their disgusting practices.

The five women waited at the base of the luminous form. Rosa held a small bowl. The others sipped their *cafezinhos*. The circle of men and women murmured when Zé and Nelson returned through another archway dragging a sobbing, naked blonde woman between them.

Louisa.

Ivo's wife had not drowned after all. She had been selected and saved for their profane ritual.

Rosa and Maria Lourdes supervised Zé and Nelson while they placed Louisa face-up at one end of the mega-dimensional shape. Invisible bonds restrained her limbs and prevented her from writhing and turning her head. She screamed for help, begged for mercy, and called out familiar names while Gabriela, Valéria and Fátima taped open her watering, terrified blue eyes. The elusive configuration beneath Louisa stabilized to a rectangle similar to what Rick had just seen among the vestibule panels.

More than a sacrificial altar, it was a feeding trough.

The men returned to their places under the niches. The women remained at the altar. Rosa glared at Rick from afar, leaving no doubt she wanted to see him there with Louisa. A concerted hush was followed by a silence penetrated only by Louisa's cries for help and mercy. Edmur wheeled Sônia into the arena. Pale and trembling, Ivo shuffled alongside his mother's chair and held her hand.

When Edmur pushed Sônia towards the altar, Rick almost called out Terri's name, but it was Yeda who had came out of an archway. The pretty young woman wore a beige dress that Sônia had been crocheting for her. She walked to the wheelchair, dropped to her knees, and placed her head on the older woman's lap. Sônia stroked her forehead as if dispensing a benediction. Yeda stood again, went over to Rosa, and ate from the bowl. When her eyes glazed over, Maria Lourdes gently placed her on the floor at the far end of the shimmering alien mass. She was unconscious within seconds.

Edmur wheeled Sônia closer to Yeda, and Ivo helped her out of the chair. Mother and son exchanged a passionate kiss on the lips. Gabriela, Valéria, and Fátima disrobed Sônia, and Rick grimaced at the spectacle. No wonder she wore so many loose layers of wool. Her bloated body was covered with bristly hairs, scaly scar tissue, welty red blotches, and breast-sized pustules. She resembled a Great Mother Goddess about to give birth to a litter of mythical monsters.

Or vultures?

Had she really been burned? Was she metamorphosing? Or both?

Ivo and Edmur lifted Sônia onto the altar and laid her out opposite Louisa so that their feet almost touched and her head lay directly above Yeda's face. Gabriela, Valéria, and Fátima secured Sônia with the same invisible restraints and taped open her eyes. Edmur put an arm around Ivo and helped him walk to the wall.

Rick thrashed, all too aware of his inability to act. Lico still held him in a firm grip. He thought he could break free when the time came for action. Even if Terri appeared, he had no idea how they could make a successful escape.

If she wanted to escape. There was only one possible role left for Terri in this grotesque tragedy. Rick tried to close his mind to what it had to be.

CHAPTER 46.
"BE FOREVER YOUNG."

o not struggle. It is useless."

Lico restrained Rick from behind when Terri emerged from an archway dressed in her scarlet and black-trim warm-ups. She moved fully conscious and of her own free will looking fit and confident.

"Terri!"

She flashed a cheerful smile and approached him. Only Louisa's screams broke the silence in the windowless cylinder.

"Terri, if they've harmed you . . ."

She touched his lips with her forefinger. "Hush, *meu amado*, my love. Please understand. I'm doing this for you, for us."

"*What* are you doing, Terri? Why?"

Her eyes reflected the unbearably bright color off the prism. "Oh, Rick if only you'd stayed at the house and waited just one more day."

"I had to find you."

She stood on her toes and quieted him with a kiss. "Listen to me, my love. Listen to me carefully. I'll never be sick again. I'll never miss another competition. We'll be world champions, and . . ."

"No, Terri, you listen to me. You can't go through with this. Nothing is that important."

"And I'll be able to discuss art, literature, music, even play the piano. Everything. I'll be perfect. I'll make it all up for letting you give up your academic dreams to …"

"I gave up nothing. I wanted to dance with you."

"Rick, please. Just stay where you are and do what they say. Don't fight them. It will spoil everything for me. For us."

"Terri …"

"If you really love me you'll listen to me, to Martin."

Terri went to the women. Rosa fed her from a fresh bowl. Maria Lourdes guided her to the floor at the end of the altar opposite Yeda and directly below Louisa. Terri did not react to Louisa's crying and guttural screams. Her eyes rolled back, then closed. Rick made a sudden move to rake Lico's shin with the side of his shoe, but the massive Ynu caught him in an unbreakable choke-hold.

Martin hurried over. "No, please, do not hurt him."

Lico slackened the pressure. Although Rick could barely speak, he recited every invective in his vocabulary, invented more, then finally rasped, "Martin, you bastard. What have you done?"

"Believe me. All this is for you. For you and Terri."

Powerless in Lico's grasp, Rick watched Terri sleep peacefully at the altar. Somehow, he had to break free and rescue her.

An *empregada* brought them *cafezinho*. Martin handed Rick a demitasse. "We wanted you to learn about us gradually, so that the sudden shock of discovering everything at once wouldn't make you hostile, as it did Irene, hysterical like Flávio, or insanely murderous like Terri's father."

Rick was not aware he was drinking his *cafezinho* until he had trouble swallowing. "How could you?"

Martin winced. "Forgive me, Rick, but think back. Think back over the past fifteen years. You know I've always regarded Terri as my daughter and you as my son.

I want the best for you. Everyone adored Terri from the moment you arrived. That first night, after you fell asleep from eating the seafood cakes, we explained everything. We promised her perfect physical health. Terri loves you, Rick. She's doing everything for you."

"Doing what?"

"You'll see. You don't have to join us. Just accept what we are, what Terri will become. Don't fight us the way Irene and Flávio did, the way you're now struggling to be free of Lico."

The Ynu said, "Martin speaks the truth. Everyone has gathered here to help Teresinha and you."

A half dozen selected men and women ingested the hallucinogen and stretched out below the vultures' niches. An equal number of *urubús* became restive. As the noxious odor of decay and death increased, Rick heard a powerful beating of wings echoing first high above, then throughout the windowless cylinder. A pair of formidable creatures descended with arms and tentacles clasped against their scaly ridged torsos. They opened their beaks to expose sharp, serrated teeth and hissed through nasal perforations their unearthly sound: *Kee-roo-poo-ree! Kee-roo-poo-ree!* The proto-pteroids glided around the cylinder before settling in the oversized niches where they folded their massive wings and waited.

In spite of Martin's assurances, Rick feared for Terri. She lay too vulnerable and exposed on the floor. What if they had lied to him? What could he do anyway? Unable to interrupt the sacrificial ritual, he prayed there was a benign reason for Terri not to be on the altar with Sônia and Louisa.

"What hell did they come from?"

"Not hell," Lico said. "Specifically, from somewhere around Tierra del Fuego and the Antarctic . . . and before that, who can say for certain?"

Rick saw a change in the monsters. Their pteroidic faces became less avian, less reptilian, almost, but not quite human. One suggested Yeda. The other . . .No, not Terri. God help them If he were to believe everything he'd recently read, seen on the grotto walls, and had been told, the hallucinogen would cause Terri to become one with that fiendish aberration of nature.

Fresh sanguinary images from the vestibule gallery overwhelmed Rick's memory. The eyes of the victims in those panels had been open. They had been alive, like Louisa and Sônia.

All defense mechanisms evaporated. In a flash he had absolute understanding.

Rick turned away from the demonic beasts above and suffered through crimson visions of the most horrible death imaginable. He tried but could not shut out images of a Maria Lourdes *urubú* consuming Irene's living brain, as Ivo must have done to the artist, Roger Whitby. As Zé had dined on Flávio. And Ohm-Yorgh, aka Lico, must also have eaten the brain of Sônia's husband, Dr. Vicente Morães Batardi.

He stared anew at Martin, so physically fit and looking a good twenty years younger than his chronological age, and remembered the Fonseca family photograph in Sérgio Posner's office. Young Rodrigo had stolen the Kraais' hundred thousand dollars. What a perfect, perfectly horrible revenge: Martin, through a proto-pteroid, must have eaten his living brain: Zé had done the same with Mauricio's; and Rosa had consumed Margarita's and Janine's brains. All that explained how the Fonseca accounts could have been looted.

And Sônia's grandsons, Tinho and Jairzinho. They were so young. They could not possibly have been a threat. He looked again at Lico/Ohm-Yorgh, the hundred and thirtyish-year old man. Weak one day, fit the next. The boys: Here one day, gone the next.

Goya, the great Spanish artist, had illustrated another primal tragedy: Saturn-Kronos devouring his young. Sônia must have given her husband to the last Ynu during their trip to the Antarctic wastes; and only a few days ago, Ohm-Yorgh/Dr. Batardi/Lico/*et al.*, an eternal being from some remote civilization, devoured his grandchildren to reverse the aging process.

Rick turned towards Sônia, who lay calm and composed on the eye-blinding shapeless luminescence. The terminally ill woman expected to be reborn. To die in body, and be regenerated to live *forever young* through Yeda. The perfect solution to an incestuous relationship.

And what about Terri, lying there beneath Louisa? She had told him she was going to have perfect health, yet he could not face that one final, most appalling image of all. He looked away from his wife. "Lico, how is it possible, that by eating a living brain you can live forever?"

"Not forever, but for an exceptionally prolonged and healthy time. We do not know how and why the transference works from proto-pteroid to human. But it does. I believe it is partly psychic. Their powers are so awesome, they can morph their physical appearances. Watch."

The great proto-vulture that resembled Terri took wing from its alcove and glided in sweeping circles towards Louisa. *"Kee-roo-poo-ree,"* echoed throughout the great ocher cylinder.

Louisa struggled to move on the altar. Her watering, taped-open eyes expressed knowledgeable horror of what was about to happen. Her screams were drowned out by a chant led by Lico and echoed by Martin and all the men and women in the cylinder:

"Oö! Oö! Coz'thuli-Curupuri!"

The monster landed on Louisa's creamy white stomach. Its sharp talons settled deeply into soft flesh, from which poured rivulets of crimson blood. Sinewy tentacles and muscular arms embraced her body on the altar not an altar.

Rick watched the megaform change from a sterile geometric rectangle into something resembling a pulsating nest, a nest of non-prismatic color, the primal nest, the primordial nest of birthing and life—the Nest of Ylem.

All the hair on Rick's head and neck bristled at the sound of Louisa's sustained shrieking and his knowledge of her beyond-loathsome fate. The proto-pteroid thrust its open beak into her right socket, plucked out and swallowed a bloody eyeball, and just as ruthlessly consumed her left eye. Louisa's cries intensified when the monster again plunged its beak into one of her pulpy eye-pits to her thalamus and cerebral cortex. Louisa continued her agonal screaming until she was drowned out by a powerful high-pitched sucking sound as the demon vacuumed her brains and cortical neurons through its nasal perforations and ingurgitated them.

After her final death-gargle, silence prevailed in the cylinder. Blood dripped and flesh hung from the satanic beast's beak as it spread open its massive wings and soared back to its alcove. Terri continued to sleep, her face flushed, her smile beatific.

The second black pteroidic horror took off, and hissed, *"Kee-roo-poo-ree!"*

"Maezinha!" Ivo fainted before the creature landed on Sônia. It plucked her eyes, sucked out her brains, and returned to its alcove.

Next, a half-dozen *urubús* descended upon the bloody nest. They took turns flaying, extracting marrow and liquid flesh, and eviscerating the corpses of Sônia and Louisa.

After the *urubús* finished, Zé and Nelson placed the remains in body bags, and the women carried Terri and Yeda to one of the walls. Then Rick saw Edmur and Martin dragging a struggling screaming man into the cylinder. They secured choreographer Felipe Gotelli on the megaform and taped open his eyes.

Martin came over to Rick. "I told you we'd do everything possible to help you and Terri win your championships.

Your decision now, Rick. Make the right one. I beg you. Make the right decision."

Lico released him. Rosa brought over a bowl and licked her lips in anticipation of his refusal. Martin again urged him to take the hallucinogen.

Rick turned towards Terri. From the instant that first proto-pteroid landed on Louisa, he knew what he must do, what he wanted to do.

*There shall the vultures also be
gathered, every one with her mate."*

—ISAIAH 34:15

EPILOGUE

CHAPTER 47.
SEPTEMBER IN JUPITER

fter a long, satisfying shower, Rick put on a pair of black shorts and carried a bottle of beer to the screened patio of their third floor condo overlooking the swimming pool and mangrove-lined Intracoastal. He sat on one of the adjustable lounge chairs, placed his legs on an ottoman, and began his two-beer process of relaxing after six hours of grueling rehearsals and training for the Nationals. He listened to Terri playing a soothing Chopin etude on the piano they had purchased after their return from Brazil.

In four days, they would be driving to Orlando for the United States Ballroom DanceSport Championships. Because Terri now had perfect health with limitless stamina, their dancing had taken a quantum leap in quality and energy, and Rick had been inspired to create new routines with imaginative choreography.

Their coach had told them they should take second place in Latin at the Nationals and do as well in Modern. Tatiana believed, however, they would still need a miracle to beat the DeMarcos, who were the judges' favorites. She also had told Rick how pleased she was that he was at last following advice given by one of the judges and darkening his blond hair and eyebrows. He did not tell her it was a natural phenomenon. He'd used no hair dye. He agreed with Terri that they did not need a coach anymore and would dismiss Tatiana after the Nationals.

Rick glanced at his watch. If on time, the Kraais would have already landed in Miami with the Zimmermanns, de Andrades, Silveiras, and Batardis. They were making the trip to watch him and Terri dance. He expected their friends to arrive in Jupiter within a few hours so they could spend a few days together before the competitions began. He thought fondly of the Silveiras' lovely blonde daughters, Antônia and Stefania, who died in an auto accident, according to Zé's official report. Typical teen confusion at the wheel, everyone said.

Terri brought out a plate filled with seafood cakes and sat beside him. She smelled fresh and looked gorgeous, trim, and deeply tanned in her sleeveless white cotton dress. Amazing how her nose seemed to be less sharp even though she had not gone to a cosmetic surgeon. Her hair had unusual light streaks. She had used no artificial coloring. It was a recent natural occurrence.

She selected a seafood cake and mused aloud, "I wonder where the DeMarcos are at this moment?"

"Everyone knows that Cal and Svetlana avoid flying whenever they can. They even travel overseas by boat and rail for the international competitions. From Houston to Orlando? I'd guess that they're on I-10, somewhere between Pensacola and Tallahassee."

"Yes, I think that is exactly where they'd be." She nibbled on a seafood cake. "Cardinho, I believe our coach is wrong. We shall win it all in Orlando."

Rick searched the sky. "It's guaranteed."

"And after that, we'll go to L.A."

"Definitely. For the first time I'm actually looking forward to seeing my family again."

"And we'll be sure to introduce them to Martin and our friends."

"Absolutely. It's at the top of our agenda."

Terri fed him another seafood cake. "And while we're in L.A., we should lay the groundwork for appearing in a movie, or better yet, getting our own TV series."

"You've read my mind. I've already surfed the Internet and found the people who can green light and sponsor us."

"And those who might create obstacles?"

"Oh, yes, those too."

"Then we'll go into training for the Ohio Star Ball and the World Championships."

Rick drank his beer, ate Terri's delicacies, and watched assorted boats and yachts moving along the Intracoastal. A pair of ospreys swept by the condo towards the orange and pink beginnings of a florid sunset. Pelicans and blue herons dove into the green water for fish. Last night a family of raccoons had taken their usual drink from the swimming pool, and this morning the shrill barking of tree squirrels had awakened him and Terri. Add small colorful birds, manatees, green and brown anoles, and the entire condominium complex was a lively zoo. "Such is life in the tropics," to quote Martin Kraai.

They sat quietly, each lost in thought. Rick played out in his mind several scenarios for his long-awaited final encounter with his stepmother and brothers. He looked forward to having Jack's knowledge of the law and William's skill in real estate investments. He'd almost dozed off when he saw something unusual. It was the first day in September, too early for the turkey buzzards that annually arrived in mid-October. Yet, beyond the mangroves, black wings glided and circled against the Navaho-blanket sky of orange-pink-lavender above the Intracoastal and Loxahatchee River.

He watched a pair much larger than the buzzards alight on the apex of the sloping roof of the clubhouse adjacent to the swimming pool. They folded their wings over tentacles and squamous torsos and flashed a look of recognition at him and Terri with intelligent brown eyes. Then the creatures extended their necks and soared into the bright orange and vermilion sunset reflecting off their broad shiny black wings to join other pairs circling high above the mangroves.

Terri took Rick's hand as time and space coalesced for her. She believed nothing could be more wonderful than to be weightless, out-of-body, while gliding with her husband in ever widening circles into the purpling sky high above the Intracoastal. Never before had she experienced so much liberation and power. When she turned to communicate her euphoria to Rick, no human sound came from her throat. Instead, it blew out through her nasal perforations. A powerful, unearthly piping hiss:
"*Kee-roo-poo-ree.*"
"*Kee-roo-poo-ree.*" Rick echoed.
And they flew north-by-northwest with their friends towards Tallahassee.

THE VULTURE ALPHABET

The entire alphabet, A-Z, was developed for this book, but 8 letters didn't make it in the book as illuminated letters at the beginning of each chapter. So just in case you were wondering what the others looked like, the missing letters are provided below.

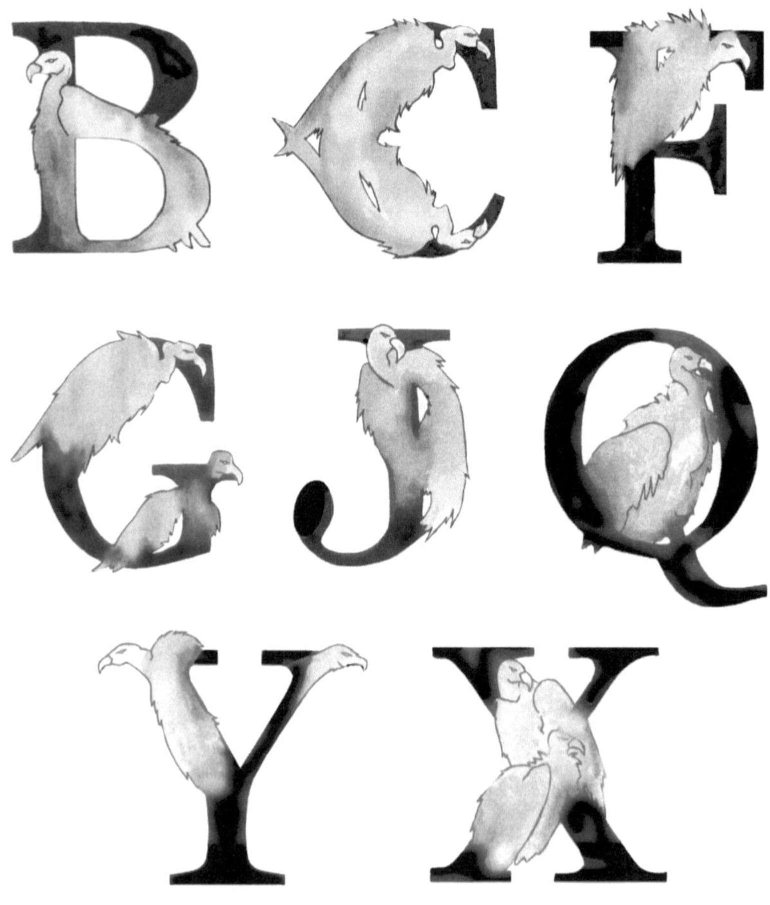

ACKNOWLEDGEMENTS

I want to thank my friend, Pam Marin-Kingsley, , for her wonderful cover, for designing my web site and page on myspace, and for her lively collegiality and sense of humor.

I thank Hilda Weisburg for her final editing and the ease of working with her.

I thank Peter Szmer for taking my idea of a vulturized alphabet and executing it to perfection. His work can be seen at www.peterszmer.com.

ABOUT THE AUTHOR
DONALD MICHAEL PLATT

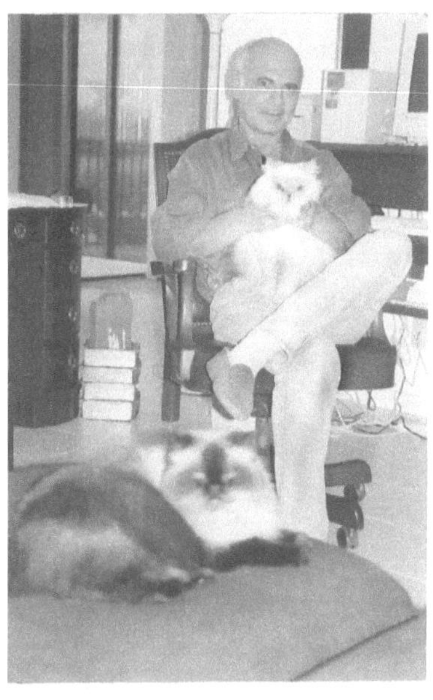

Photo courtesy of:
Gwen Saska-Brown
Saska Star Photos
New York/Florida—(212) 724-6462

The experiences Donald and his wife Ellen had while living in Florianópolis, Brazil, and their adventures in ballroom dancing inspired him to write *A Gathering of Vultures.*

In Hollywood, Donald sold his writing to the TV series, *Mr. Novak,* and worked for and with diverse producers. After moving to Jupiter, Florida, Donald co-wrote *Vitamin Enriched,* 1999, for Carl DeSantis, founder of Rexall Sundown Vitamins; and *The Couple's Disease,* 2002, for Lawrence S. Hakim, MD, FACS, Head of Sexual Dysfunction Unit at the Cleveland Clinic.

Born and raised in San Francisco and a graduate of Lowell High school and U.C. Berkeley, Donald also has taught History, English, and Creative Writing and has been an Adjunct Professor of Writing at Polk Community College. He currently resides in Winter Haven, Florida with his wife, Ellen.

9 781942 756347